LETTING GO

SARAH BOURNE

BLOODHOUND BOOKS

Copyright © 2025 Sarah Bourne

The right of Sarah Bourne to be identified as the Author of the Work has been asserted by them in accordance with the Copyright, Designs and Patents Act 1988.

First published in 2025 by Bloodhound Books.

Apart from any use permitted under UK copyright law, this publication may only be reproduced, stored, or transmitted, in any form, or by any means, with prior permission in writing of the publisher or, in the case of reprographic production, in accordance with the terms of licences issued by the Copyright Licensing Agency.
All characters in this publication are fictitious and any resemblance to real persons, living or dead, is purely coincidental.

www.bloodhoundbooks.com

Print ISBN: 978-1-917449-8-92

For Neil

WALTER

I heard the first words the doctor said: pancreatic cancer. Stage 4. Secondaries. Blah blah blah. He went on and on. I watched his mouth move, saw the earnest look on his face but no more went in.

Until: six months max, more realistically, three.

So, there it was. Three to six months. The sentence for a minor misdemeanour: a bungled mugging or possession of a small amount of dope with the intention of selling a bit to friends. Or allowing cancer to infiltrate the body and eat away at it. Hardly a minor misdemeanour. A big fuck up, really.

I heard it, that pronouncement, but it sat outside of me at first like a heavy dark mass. No pun intended. Formless. A shapeshifter. One minute curling round my head and beating at my skull, hammering to be let in, the next, clutching at my innards, squeezing them so tight I couldn't breathe.

But at least I had a name for what I'd been going through. Here was my future laid out before me. My much-abbreviated future. I wanted to vomit. I wanted to scream. I wanted to cry. I fixed my gaze on the man who had delivered this cruel news.

He seemed genuinely apologetic. Another life he couldn't

save. I almost felt sorry for him – poor sod, having to give people The News. But it was me receiving the shock. My body that was full of cancer. I didn't grace him with my thanks.

I shook his hand, though. Out of habit, I suppose. He'd given me my death sentence, but I shook his hand like we'd just played a round of golf. He'd won but I was a good loser. Drinks are on me in the clubhouse. Good old Walter, he's such a stoic.

Physically, I was exactly the same walking out of the appointment as I had been when I walked in. It wasn't as if the cancer had suddenly grown in the space of fifteen minutes. But the weight of the diagnosis bore down on me so I could hardly stand, couldn't walk with my normal stride. I was bent by it. I must have looked like an old man, leaning on my wife. She was crying, holding a tissue to her eyes and dabbing them repeatedly, so I had to steer but she was the brace, rudder and ballast. That was us in that moment.

I was dry-eyed. Annoyed. Not even properly angry. Not yet.

Annoyed. Pissed off. Disappointed.

Disappointed. Yes, more than anything else, disappointed. Let down by this body, counting off all the things I'd miss out on, all the things I wouldn't be able to do.

Fuck.

For the record, my wife is a saint. She cried a lot at first but then straightened her spine, rolled up her sleeves and got on with the job of living with a husband in 'end stage care'. She bought a book about death and dying. I caught her reading one afternoon and saw it before she could hide it behind her back. So, we read it together. Five stages of grief. Denial, anger, bargaining, depression, acceptance. We joked about making a chart so we could tick them off as we progressed through each one.

Actually, Jeanette did them in the wrong order, which is

strange for her; she's usually one to follow the rules. She did the depression and the bargaining and then got off the death bus at denial.

I, on the other hand, surprised myself by trotting through each stage like a good boy.

Denial: This can't really be happening, not to me. There'll be a new drug out soon that'll cure me. Everything's going to be all right. Let's book a holiday, take the girls to Greece or Thailand.

Anger: FFFUUUCCCKKK. Why me, you rotten bastard God (I don't even believe in you, you old parasite). I smashed things. I drank a lot. Drove fast. Shouted at people. (Sorry, darling – you took the brunt of it.)

Bargaining: I'll donate all my money to charity if I can live long enough to see my girls married and happily settled down. Just another five years, maybe ten. Jeanette needs me – I'll hand the business over to Sebastian if I have to. Just give me more time.

Depression: Bleak. Black. Dense. Heavy. Empty. Nothing.

Acceptance: Knowing you're dying and accepting it are two totally different things. Knowledge is something you can grasp hold of, turn the information this way and that, ease it into a position where it can reside without too much attention. Acceptance? Ha! The guts twist with fear and torment, hot acid churning and scorching its way to a throat crying, NO! I'm too young to die. I'm not ready to go.

But then, what to do with this death sentence? There is no escaping it, I know it now. I don't want to die, don't want to leave this life and my wife and girls. But I am so tired, so very, very tired. Maybe acceptance is just exhaustion, the lack of will or energy to fight.

I've survived the three months but won't make it to the six, so the doc was right. Well done him. These days I spend a lot of my time staring out the window, not a thought in my head. When I feel up to it, I reflect on my life. I used to love the film, *The Good, the Bad and the Ugly*. It would be a good title for the story of my life, except they're in the wrong order. Mine would be the Ugly, the Bad and the Good. Not as catchy but more accurate. And probably not as clear cut. There were some good bits in the beginning and ugly bits in the bad. Probably bad bits in the good. Jeanette would be the judge of that. I hope I've been a good husband to her – I've done my best, but was it good enough? Or was I so entrenched in my old self that my good was another person's bad? I do love her with all my heart, but I also know my heart is a small shrunken old thing pumping not only blood but also venom through my veins. Love, but also other things that make love weak: anger, aggression, resentment, fear, pain.

I don't want anyone feeling sorry for me – I do enough of that myself. I want – what do I want?

Life.

That's what I want.

Fuck acceptance.

ONE

Not everyone can admit they're dying. Many people deny it right to the end, demanding treatment after painful treatment, desperate to cheat death.

Walter Armstrong was not one of those people. He knew he only had a short time left and wanted to live it as well as he could, or so he said.

That's why he called me, Hester Rose, to help him navigate the end of his life.

Mrs Jenkins, the daily help, showed me in and then disappeared with her duster. Mr Armstrong got straight to the point.

'I've stopped all active treatment. There's nothing more to be done but I want to die peacefully, no pain.'

'You've got the palliative care team for that,' I said. 'I'll work with them, but I can't prescribe medication.'

He grunted and adjusted his position in the hospital-issue bed. I moved towards him, but he waved me away with an emaciated arm. A stubborn man. A proud man. I stored the impressions away.

'Are you a believer?' he asked.

That was always a hard question. I was but I'm not now. I can talk the talk, quote chunks of the Bible, belt out hymns with the best of them but I don't believe in God, not any more.

'Are you?' I asked.

'No. And if you think you're going to convert me on my death bed, you can bugger off right now.'

'Nothing could be further from my mind,' I said.

'And I don't want any of this New Age mumbo-jumbo – waving crystals around and talking about my guardian angel.'

'Noted.'

He looked at me. 'Do you go in for that sort of stuff?'

'No. I'm a bit more practical.'

'Thank Christ. What can you do for me then?'

'I can be with you. Listen, talk, make you comfortable, support your family.'

'Ha! Bunch of piranhas they are, apart from my current wife and daughters. The others can't wait to see the back of me.'

He coughed, his face contorting into a grimace of pain. I poured some water and held his head as he drank. As he sank back against the pillows, he said, 'Thank you, Hester Rose. You'll do.'

I've met a lot of people and been at a lot of deaths, but that was the strangest interview I've had. I'm usually asked by family members to assist in the final days of a relative's life. They often don't even know what they want when they hire me but I'm good at fitting in, seeing what they need before they know it themselves. A meal cooked, shopping done, a bath filled, a hand held. I listen, watch, advise. Sometimes for a few hours, sometimes days. I live in or just visit for certain hours during the day or night. I've heard confessions, though as I have said, I'm not a religious person. I wash bodies, comfort the bereaved, help arrange funerals. I know I can be a bit schoolmarmy at times, I don't mean to be, but sometimes it's the quickest way to get to the point when family members and loved ones are trying to avoid it. When someone's dying, there isn't a lot of time for avoidance and obfuscation. Really, if someone's dying, I'm your woman.

'Fine,' I said. 'I can start right now if you want.'

He nodded, looked at me. 'Once you've seen me off, what then?'

'I'm not sure what you mean.'

'I have a complicated family. Not easy. Do you types stay after the patient has died?'

'There are no rules, really.'

'Good. I want you to stay for at least two weeks after I'm dead. Longer if need be. You'll be paid well. I want you to help my wife with all the mess that comes after.'

'Are you anticipating anything in particular?'

He grunted. 'In this family, things are always messy. Will you do it?'

I thought about it. Financially it would work well. I was only casual at my other job, so it was easily arranged.

'All right,' I said.

If I'd known then what I was letting myself in for, I might have refused.

'Good. Let my wife know. She'll show you your room, Hester Rose. You'll find her in the kitchen – across the hall, second door on the right. I hope you'll be comfortable.' Then he turned towards the French windows and closed his eyes.

I looked at the view of the fields and the tall church spire in the distance and thought, there are worse places to die.

'Mrs Armstrong? I'm Hester,' I said as I entered the kitchen.

'Baxter. Jeanette Baxter. My stand for feminism – I kept my name. And I told Walter if we had boys, they could have his surname but if we had girls, they'd take mine.' She paused, giggled self-consciously. 'Sorry. Too much information.'

I smiled, both at her stand for feminism and at her need to tell me.

She was a tall woman, a little older than me, maybe nudging fifty, so quite a lot younger than her husband who was in his early seventies. She had soft grey eyes with laughter lines fanning out from them. Her fair hair was caught up in a clip, but several strands had fallen out. She was up to her elbows in flour and had a smudge of it on her cheek where she'd wiped her face.

'He must like you to have sent you to me,' she said in clipped Home Counties English, a stark contrast to his northern accent.

'He says I'll do.'

'High praise indeed. Do you have whatever you need with you, or will you come back later?'

I looked over my shoulder towards the front door. 'I brought my things, just in case. They're in the car.'

'Well then, give me a mo and I'll show you to your room. And since you're going to be here for a while, call me Jeanette.'

I went out to get my case and looked at the house I was about to call home for however long I was needed. It was huge. A manor house if ever I saw one, built in sandstone with large windows and a portico. Walter Armstrong was a wealthy man. Or his wife was. I knew nothing about the family.

The bedroom Jeanette showed me to before returning to her baking was bigger than my entire flat. It overlooked the same fields and church spire as Walter's, although from this height I could also see the roofs of the houses in the village nestled amongst the trees. The carpet was powder blue, the wallpaper featured delicate flowers on a butter yellow background. Not my taste at all but the bold primary colours of my flat would have been out of place here. I would probably spend very little time in the room, so it didn't matter whether I liked it or not.

I unpacked my toiletries, put them in the en suite and tidied my unruly hair. It's never done what it's supposed to. It's thick and wilful, always falling over my rather angular face. I tend to avoid looking in mirrors. I returned to the bedroom, took a moment to take in the view out the window and settle myself.

I'm always aware that going into other people's homes at a time when they are feeling scared and vulnerable is a tall order. Although they ask me to be there, often the families don't really want strangers around at this most intimate of times. At its best, it's a time when they gather to say their farewells and address issues that need to be resolved. A time when all other demands drop away, and they can focus on the dying and what comes next. At worst, families bicker and snipe, old enmities are resurrected, daggers drawn. As I gazed at the rural idyll before me, I wondered what I would find here.

I haven't always been an end-of-life doula, although I suppose it was a natural choice for me; I almost died when I was five. I awoke one night to my father praying over me, asking the Lord to take me into his arms and receive me into Heaven. I saw a white light and felt peaceful. Since then, death has not scared me.

It was measles of all things. While most children in England were vaccinated, my parents, missionaries in Sierra Leone, trusted God to keep us safe. Even at such a young age, with a fever burning me up and God ready for me to join Him, I remember thinking I had more to do on this earth before joining the Lord and His angels in Paradise. Dawa, Jusu, Brima and I had more exploring to do, more harmonies to sing. We sat together in school every day under the great spreading trees and vied to be the loudest, most tuneful singer of all our favourite hymns. My father, the teacher-pastor, would smile at us and raise his hand in blessing. My heart used to expand then, under the glory of God and His representative on Earth. At least, in our tropical corner of the planet.

I survived to sing another day, to run and play with my friends in the village, to praise the Lord and help my mother with the chores. It was, in many ways, an idyllic childhood.

Gathering my thoughts and taking a last look at the very English view out over the Sussex countryside, I turned and made my way downstairs to see what was needed. In a room with light floral wallpaper, that had once perhaps been a study, French doors offering a view of the garden, Walter's hospital bed and equipment now dominated. He was breathing easily, eyes still closed. Leaving the door open so we could hear him if he called, I returned to the kitchen.

'Anything I can do?' I asked.

Jeanette was at the sink, shoulders hunched forward, head bowed. As I entered, she was wiping her eyes on a tea towel.

'I'm fine. Really. Just every so often... well, you know.' She sighed and leant against the kitchen counter.

'Do you want to talk?'

She shrugged. 'It won't change anything, will it. I mean, it won't stop him–' She bit her lip.

'Dying?' I said gently. I believe in naming things for what they are. I hate euphemisms. Kicking the bucket. Passing on. What do they really mean? They're just ways of denying reality. But I don't push hard. If the family really want to talk about their relative going over the rainbow, or meeting their maker, I'll go along with it. After all, denial can be a comfort.

Jeanette nodded, tears pooling in her eyes. 'I still can't believe it. He's always been larger than life: loud, boisterous, the life and soul of the party. All that and more. And now to see him confined to that awful hospital bed, shrinking every day, it's too much.' She lowered her gaze and shook her head.

'Tell me how you met,' I said. 'Did he sweep you off your feet?'

Some people need to talk about the good times first even, or perhaps especially, when they are facing death. It's important to remember the fun bits, the love, the life. Rapport building they called it in our training. Common sense, I say. There will still be time for talk of death, dying and funerals.

Jeanette smiled although tears still glistened on her cheeks.

'We were at a wedding. Such a cliché, isn't it? The daughter of one of his friends was getting married, and she'd been one of my friends at school.'

I nodded, sitting quietly so as not to interrupt her story.

'He was the most striking man in the room. Tall, upright, handsome. So sure of himself but not in an arrogant way – he was comfortable in his body, I suppose, in a way none of the younger men were.' She paused, her eyes focused on the past. A light blush crept up her neck and onto her cheeks. She closed her eyes for a moment and sighed.

'Love at first sight?' I asked.

'For me, yes,' she said. 'I'd been out with people before but no-one who had his bearing. I've never felt such an upsurge of joy and hope and wonder in the presence of anyone else.' She laughed. 'Oh, listen to me going on. You must think I'm some ditsy air-headed thing.'

'Not at all. It sounds romantic. It's important to remember the good times.'

A bell rang and Jeanette jumped up, her forehead knitting into anxiety. 'That's Walter.'

'Do you want me to go?' I asked.

'Would you? He probably needs the loo, or a drink. I'll

check the cake, and Grace will be home soon, so I'll get the kettle on. Cuppa for you?'

'Lovely. A dash of milk, no sugar, and as strong as you can make it.'

Crossing the hall to Walter's room I saw a teenager in school uniform cycling up the drive. I paused to watch, her red hair lifted by the wind and her speed. Then the bell rang again and I hurried in to see what it was Walter needed.

'Where's Jeanette?' he asked.

'Making tea and getting dinner ready. And Grace is just home.'

'Ah. Always busy. Too busy to see to me. They're all disgusted by me, you know. Are you?'

'Why would I be?'

'I'm turning yellow, and my body is rotting from the inside. *I'm* disgusted by me. Fucking disease. I'd rather have gone in a car accident, or with a massive heart attack. Bang. Dead. All over. This way is cruel. Can't even piss or shit on my own. And the doctor won't give me enough drugs to end it myself. I should have joined Exit years ago.' His voice grew weaker and he started coughing. 'See what I mean?' he wheezed.

He had a drink and a wee in a bottle and I left the room to deal with that. When I returned, Grace was with him, sitting on his bed. I waited by the door.

'How are you feeling today, Daddy?' she asked.

He took her smooth young hand in his wizened one and I saw her struggle not to pull away from his grasp. 'Better for seeing you, my angel,' he said and smiled. 'You're home early, aren't you? How was school?'

'I had frees all afternoon so I left after lunch. I thought I'd get more work done here. Anyway, I got a B for my French. Football training this morning was awful as usual. Oh, and Miss Wainright told us she's getting married in the hols.'

'Miss Wainright – the ugly old English-teaching harridan?'
'Exactly. Who'd want her?'

Walter laughed but it turned into a cough, and I went over and offered him another sip of his drink.

'Oh – sorry. I didn't know anyone was here,' said Grace.

'I'm Hester. The doula.'

She smiled and raised her eyebrows. 'The doula?'

'A helper. I'm here to help. In whatever way I can.'

'What about Mrs Jenkins?'

'Not that sort of help, Gracie. Hester Rose isn't a cleaning lady.' Walter turned to me. 'Mrs Jenkins is about five hundred years old and has been cleaning this house nearly every day for as long as I can remember.'

'I see,' I said.

'So you're here to help in other ways? I don't suppose you speak French, do you? I need to do better if I'm going to get into Oxford.' Grace laughed.

'As a matter of fact, I do. I lived in Gabon for a while as a child and if you pick up a language early, you never really forget it. Although I might be a bit rusty. Not up to A-level standard, I shouldn't think.'

'Full of surprises, Hester Rose,' said Walter.

'Where on earth is Gabon?' asked Grace.

'Good thing you don't want to read geography, my girl.' Walter laughed at his own joke.

'Central Africa. My parents were missionaries. We moved around a bit.'

'Wow. It sounds so exciting,' said Grace, her grey-green eyes bright.

'I loved it. It was hot and sunny all the time, there were fascinating insects and reptiles everywhere, no flushing toilets or plumbing of any sort and electricity only when the generator worked.'

'God, how awful! How did you cope?'

I smiled at her change of tune. 'We had to, there was no alternative.'

'I think I might be able to take a little soup if there's any on offer. Jeanette usually makes me some each day,' said Walter.

'Of course,' I said. 'I'll go and see what I can rustle up.'

Grace followed me out but picked up the schoolbag she'd left in the hall and went up the stairs.

Jeanette wasn't in the kitchen, so I lifted the lids of the saucepans on the Aga and discovered one of them contained a meaty broth. I ladled some into a sipper cup, leaving the lid off to let the soup cool enough for Walter to drink. Meanwhile I washed the dishes and put them away.

'Here you are,' I said as I returned carrying a tray with the soup, some thinly sliced bread and butter and a napkin.

But Walter had his eyes closed listening to a concert on the radio and he waved me away.

People who are dying can be like that: want something one minute, change their mind the next. I've sometimes wondered if it's the last way they can exert any control over their lives. Or if they simply forget they'd ever asked for anything. I didn't think there was anything wrong with Walter's memory.

I looked at him, lying in his bed. Walter was weak but I didn't get the impression he was going to die imminently.

I went outside to feel the afternoon sun on my skin. A childhood in Sierra Leone made living in the cold climate a challenge, even after all these years.

I heard someone call, 'Come here, Milly,' and a moment later a brown and white springer spaniel bounded round the corner of the house, ears flapping, and what looked like a pair of knickers in its mouth, followed by a puffing Jeanette who stopped short when she saw me.

'Sorry. Milly's been at the washing basket again. She likes to chew underwear.'

I laughed. 'Could be worse, I suppose. She could favour cashmere sweaters or silk scarves.'

'Oh Lord. Don't even suggest it, she'll hear you and think it's a good idea. She really is untrainable. And now she's on her way to Walter's room with her prize. She'll sit outside the French windows crying to be let in. It drives him mad.'

'Then let's go and get her before she ruins his day. He was listening to music just now. He seems quite peaceful.'

We walked along the back of the house together.

'He has his moments,' she said. 'Some days he's in a lot of pain and nothing's right, other times he's quieter. He hates this though. He's so used to being in charge of everything. He was still working – running the business – until a couple of months ago.'

'It must be hard seeing him like this,' I said.

'It's awful. He's stuck in bed most of the time, just waiting to go.' She paused, fiddling with her necklace. 'What's it like, you know, at the end?' Her breath caught and she wiped her eyes.

'Peaceful,' I said.

She nodded, her eyes on Milly who was sitting at the French doors, wagging her tail furiously. 'Will he want us all there?'

'Walter may have ideas about how he wants it to be.'

'We haven't – I mean, we don't – he won't talk about it.'

I put a hand on her arm. 'He might have spoken to the palliative care team about it. Or perhaps he'll talk to me about what he wants. Would that be okay with you?'

She took a deep breath, exhaled slowly.

'Would you? I mean, I don't really know what to ask.' She bit her lip. 'What do people want, usually?'

'Everyone's different. Might he want to go into a hospice, for example?'

'Oh no, definitely not. I know that much. It's why he wanted you.'

I had thought as much but it's good to be clear about these things. 'And you're okay with that?'

'Yes, whatever he wants. What other sort of things do... well, you know?'

'There's no right or wrong, no "normal". Some people want to be alone or just have their partner with them, others want the whole family or a priest. Music or silence, light or dim, candles. That sort of thing.'

'I see. I hadn't really thought about any of it.'

'That's probably why Walter wanted me here. So you don't have to worry about the details. You can get on with doing what you need to do, spending time with him, preparing yourself and your daughter.'

'Daughters. We have two. Ellen's at university. She'll be home tomorrow for the weekend.' She smiled at the thought but then her face clouded over again.

'Actually, it's a bit of a gathering of the clans. The whole family is coming on Saturday and if I know anything about this lot, it'll be a boozy affair and they'll all end up staying and ruining the whole weekend.'

'Sounds like a bit of an ordeal. What can I do?'

She shrugged. 'I doubt there's anything you can do with this mob, to be frank.'

'I'm a practised gatekeeper,' I said. 'Sometimes people will listen to a stranger when they are deaf to people they know. I could suggest when they get here that they'll need to leave at a certain time. Walter is our primary concern and he needs rest. And he certainly doesn't need conflict whirling around him.'

Jeanette raised her eyebrows, looking momentarily hopeful but then she sagged. 'You haven't met them yet. They're... forceful.'

I stopped, put my hands on my hips, drew myself up to my full five feet three and said, 'So am I.'

She laughed. 'Let's talk more before they get here. Now, Milly, give me those bloody knickers, you horrible dog!'

Milly, tail between her legs, dropped the underwear on the patio outside Walter's room and slunk away. Her shame didn't last long, however. In the middle of the lawn she spied a squirrel and sped after it with little chance of catching it as it raced up the great chestnut tree at the side of the house.

Later, Cassie, the nurse from the palliative care team, dropped in for her daily visit. Jeanette introduced us in the hall and then went off to do more gardening.

'I've worked with doulas before,' said Cassie. 'I'm glad you're here, although a little surprised at the timing.'

'Because Walter isn't knocking at death's door quite yet?'

She nodded.

'What do you make of it then?' I asked.

She looked towards his door, brow furrowed. 'It's a complex family. He's been married several times and there are adult children who visit and from the little I've seen, don't get on very well. Maybe he wanted someone to buffer him from all the negativity. Who knows?'

'Well, I know nothing, I only got here today but I must admit, I was also surprised to have been called in now. Usually I only work with families in the final days.'

'Have you been doing this long?'

'I've been an enrolled nurse for many years. Then I did my doula training four years ago. Still have to do casual shifts at the nursing home to make ends meet.'

'You'll have seen the full gamut of human nature then: the good, the bad and the bloody awful! At least you'll be familiar with pain management meds. I've talked it through with Jeanette a few times but she gets easily flustered so maybe you could step in if Walter needs top-ups for breakthrough pain. He has fentanyl patches which work well, but occasionally needs a bit of morphine elixir too.'

'No problem.'

'I'll be in daily and more towards the end if you need me, but do call in between times if you have any questions or if anything changes. With end stage cancer, you never know. It can take a sudden turn for the worse. He chose to stop active treatment so we're all he's got.'

We went in to see Walter. He'd been dozing but stirred and opened his eyes when she took his hand.

'You,' he said.

'Me,' said Cassie. 'How are you feeling today?'

'I've got myself a new carer,' he said, nodding towards me.

'So I see. Don't go giving her a hard time, will you?' She smiled.

'As if. You know me, a softie to the core of my being.'

Cassie laughed. 'Always the comedian.'

Walter grinned and winked at her.

Cassie went on. 'You should get up and sit in the garden, Walter. It's a beautiful afternoon.'

I'd seen a wheelchair in the corner of the room and brought it to his bedside.

'I'm dying. Why do you insist on making me get out of bed, you witch?'

'Because,' said Cassie, 'you don't need to lie there like a

prima donna waiting to take your last breath. Come on, you'll enjoy it, you know you will.'

He shook his head, but I saw the smile lift the corners of his mouth. I suspected this was not the first time he and Cassie had had this conversation, or others like it, and he loved the banter. I could see what Jeanette had meant about him being larger than life, even now.

'I seem to remember,' I added with a grin, 'although forgive me if I got it wrong – it was a couple of hours ago, after all – you told me you wanted to make the most of your last days. I'm not sure how lying in bed achieves your goal?'

'Ganging up on me now, and me a dying man.' He shook his head, but the smile was still there.

Cassie helped Walter into his wheelchair and then left, promising to come and bother him again the next day. I pushed him out into the garden and found a spot under the trees in the dappled late afternoon light. He sighed and looked up towards the sun.

'I'll miss this,' he said quietly. I wasn't sure if he'd said it to me or to himself, so didn't respond.

'My wife's scared, you know. Can you talk to her? I've tried to tell her I'm not afraid of dying but she doesn't believe me. And she's frightened of being alone.'

'I can talk to her, of course, but maybe you should try again. I could be there too, if it would help?'

He closed his eyes and took a deep breath. 'You talk to her then, maybe we'll be able to talk to each other, her and me. I miss her, you know. She hasn't been the same since my diagnosis. Spends more time with that stupid mutt of hers than with me.'

I wasn't surprised to hear that. It confirmed an inkling I'd already had.

'Off you go, Hester Rose, go and get some gardening gloves on; she'll find it easier to talk over the runner beans.'

'Anything you want before I go?'

'Ten more years would be nice.'

'If only I had a magic wand,' I said.

He waved me away with a thin smile.

Jeanette was in the middle of a vegetable bed in the walled garden, forking compost into the soil.

'I've made you a cup of tea,' I called, holding the mug up for her to see.

'Oh, heaven,' she said and sank the fork into the ground next to the wheelbarrow. She wiped her forearm across her forehead and made her way over. We sat on a stone bench against the wall.

'I love this time of year,' she said. 'The end of May – all of summer to look forward to and we get some beautiful days like this to remind us of what's to come.'

I've always been amazed by how the English can harp on about the weather. And their capacity to delude themselves as to its nature. It was like some sort of national psychosis. I once read that the average Brit spends four and a half months of their life talking about weather. Jeanette was eulogising about British summers when in all likelihood it would be wet and miserable for the most part. I've lived here for well over half my life and I can count on the fingers of one hand the number of warm, dry summers we've had.

'Are you actually from around these parts?' I asked.

She seemed surprised by my question. 'Surrey, originally,' she said, having missed the irony. 'How about you?'

'I was born in West Africa and spent my childhood out

there. We only had one setting: hot and wet. I love the unpredictability of English weather.'

Once again she ignored my weather jibe. 'That's your accent then. It's very slight, but I was wondering where it came from.'

'As a child I spoke Krio with my friends in Sierra Leone. I suppose there are traces of it still in the way I talk.'

'You've led an interesting life, by the sound of it.'

'Haven't we all in our own ways? Every one unique.'

She sighed and took a sip of her tea. 'Mine hasn't been as exciting as I thought it would be when I was leaving home and going off to university.' She paused, laughed. 'Don't get me wrong, I love Walter and I've been very happy, but I planned to travel, live overseas, perhaps marry a swarthy Greek or a passionate Italian.'

'Italian men are married to their mothers. That's what someone told me, anyway.'

She smiled. 'I saved myself from an overbearing mama then. I only met Walter's mother once – she wasn't exactly possessive.' Looking out over her vegetable garden, her face softened into sadness.

'Tending a garden is a constant reminder of change, isn't it?' I said.

'I'm not good at change. I want everything to stay the same. I want Walter to be well and the girls to still need me. I want there to be time to do the things we always said we'd do together.' Tears shone in her eyes. 'Sometimes I hate him for doing this to me. Does that make me a terrible person?'

'Not at all. But I suspect it's also making you lonely, keeping it all in. He wants to talk to you. He's missing you, too. We think of our own grief at losing the one we love but the dying grieve too. They have to let go of so much.'

She wiped her eyes. 'I'd never thought of it like that. He

used to be so alive. The room would light up when he walked in. Ask anyone.'

'He's still alive and inside he's the same man you fell in love with at your friend's wedding.'

'I'm so scared,' she said. 'I don't know how to be with him anymore, how to look after him.'

I took a breath, considered what to say. 'I know this isn't a terribly feminist comment, but it's in your bones. As a woman and a mother you've been looking after people most of your life, I suspect. So do what you know. Make soup, change the sheets, hold his hand. Do it when you're scared, when you're crying, when you're happy, when you're confused. It's okay to let him see how you're feeling. He knows anyway. Just be with him; that's both the easiest and the hardest thing you'll ever do.'

She looked at me and for a moment I thought she was going to throw herself into my arms and weep but then she pulled herself up taller, balled her fists and clenched her jaw.

'You make it sound so... doable.'

'But I also said it wasn't easy.'

When I went back into the house, Grace was in the kitchen ferreting through the pantry for something to eat. She'd changed into jeans and an old T-shirt and tied her beautiful red hair back into an untidy ponytail. And still she looked elegant in the way teenagers can when they're comfortable in their bodies.

'Oh, Hester, you gave me a fright,' she said, turning at my footsteps. 'I was looking for cake.'

'Your mother asked me to come and get dinner ready. She's in with your father.'

'Wow – that's–'

'Lovely. It's lovely.'

'I was going to say unusual, but lovely will do.'

I smiled. 'I'll get some pasta on and put together a sauce of some sort, shall I?'

'Great. Thanks.'

I was tempted to ask how she was doing but suspected I needed to get to know her a bit better before she wanted to talk to me about anything. The young are often slower to open up, in my experience. Sometimes it was a matter of pride, other times they just didn't know they needed to talk. Either way, I felt we needed to know each other better.

I smiled at her. 'Can you wait half an hour?'

She groaned, then laughed and went back to her homework.

I sautéed onions and browned some mince, chopped vegetables and threw them into the pan, and then went to see if Jeanette needed help getting Walter into bed again. They were sitting side by side, holding hands. It was a mild evening. The lowering sun cast long shadows across the lawn. I left them to it and returned to the kitchen.

WALTER

I think I chose well. Hester Rose has settled in already and has taken some of the pressure off Jeanette.

Why is Jeanette under pressure? Because she's afraid of death. Of my death, particularly. She hasn't lost anyone before; both her parents are still alive. They're about the same age as me. It was an issue when we first met. Not for Jeanette and certainly not for me. For them.

I worked on them. Dismantled their arguments one by one. A war of attrition. Not really a war. They didn't even really have arguments, just concerns. My age, her age. The twenty-three years between us. A whole generation, as they pointed out. Repeatedly.

'Love is love,' Jeanette would say.

'We have many years ahead of us and I'll leave her a wealthy woman,' I would say.

'But but but,' they would say.

In the end they gave their blessing. Not that we needed it. But they needed to give it. To feel they had agreed to our marriage and retained some control of the situation. We thanked them. Refused their offer to pay for the wedding, which

I'm sure came as a relief to Jeanette's father who is a parsimonious man. Presbyterian. May have had something to do with it. Who knows? Maybe he just grew up poor and didn't like giving away his hard-earned cash. I can understand that. But I didn't ask. Wasn't interested.

Hester Rose. She's a canny one, as my mother would have said. Haven't thought about her for years. Ma, I mean. She was a hard worker if ever there was one. Seven children in nine years and took in washing and mending to support us.

Da was a wastrel. Worked on the docks and drank his pay the minute he got it. Came home and fell asleep in front of the range. At least he was a soppy drunk. Didn't bash us like other dads. He was more of a crier than a fighter. When Ma shouted at him, he'd sob and cover his ears with his hands, apologise and agree he was a worthless worm of a man, just like his own father. Promise he'd change then go out the next day and do the same.

He died on the docks one day. Keeled over and that was it. Ma carried on as if nothing had changed. One thing had changed though – there were no more babies. No more mouths to feed. Which was a blessing.

Hester Rose. Bring my wife back to me, would you? Soothe her fears and her anxieties. It's only death.

God Almighty, listen to me. Talking about my death as if it means nothing.

Well, it's true in a way. The closer I get, the easier it becomes. Funny that. No kicking and screaming from me. Not today, anyway.

My death. Jeanette will continue on. That's what she's afraid of. All the lonely, sad days to come. I can't do anything about that. There's nothing I can do to prepare her.

Maybe it was selfish of me to have married her, after all. Perhaps I should have listened to the but but buts and left. But – my but – I didn't want to live without her. She was so vibrant, so youthful, so beautiful. And her love was honest and pure and full. I'd never felt anything like it before. It was like a force of nature; strong and inescapable. Her love made me feel buoyant. Cocky, if I'm honest. And lucky.

I've never known what I did to deserve her but I'm grateful.

We don't believe in God, or life after death. We don't have the comfort of a promised meeting in an afterlife where we'll never be parted again.

Even if there is a Heaven and a Hell, there's no guarantee we'll end up in the same place. She'll definitely go up, but chances are I'll be down below. I haven't lived a blameless life. Well, you don't, do you, when you grow up with nothing but the desperation to get out of your situation any way you can.

Hester Rose, look after my wife.

TWO

Walter assured me he didn't need attention during the night, so after I'd checked on him at eleven, I got a good night's sleep and woke early to the sound of birdsong. The sun thrust fingers of light into the sky, promising another warm day.

I got up, enjoyed the softness of the thick carpet under my feet, and did my stretches. It would be a push to call it yoga, although they were moves I had learnt from a yoga video years before when my son, Justin, was young and I had no time or money to do classes.

Then, a quick shower and clean clothes.

I knocked quietly on Walter's door in case he was still sleeping but he called me in.

'You're an early riser then,' he said.

I smiled. 'Always have been. How did you sleep? Any discomfort?'

'No. I drug myself up at night. Can't bear the idea of lying awake for hours thinking.'

'You can always call me. We could get a monitor so you can give me a yell if you need me.'

He ignored the idea. 'Thank you for yesterday.'

'How did it go?'

'We didn't talk, but at least she sat with me and didn't seem desperate to get away.'

'It's not easy for either of you.'

'I'd like some tea.'

Walter Armstrong was a champion of non-sequiturs.

'Consider it done,' I said.

As I waited for the kettle to boil, the back door opened, and an elderly lady charged in.

'Oh – he hired you then,' she said, taking off her coat and hanging it over the back of a chair.

'He did.'

She looked me up and down. 'I do for the family, and I don't like people getting in my way.' She narrowed her eyes at me, daring me to encroach on her turf.

'Understood. I'll just make Walter's tea.'

She nodded. 'I'd be grateful. There's lots to do and only so much time.'

Old she may be, but formidable with it. She bustled out of the kitchen, duster in hand. I felt sorry for any dirt that might have gathered where it shouldn't.

Alone again I thought about the days ahead. Of course, I'd be spending time with Walter even though at this point he seemed to need me less than Jeanette did. And then there was Grace. And Ellen coming home tonight. The family lunch tomorrow. I decided that for now the best thing would be for me to take over as many of the household tasks as possible, stay in the background, and observe the family to see what they needed of me.

I took the tea in to Walter and sat with him while he drank it. He was still able to do things for himself in spite of his rant the day before about being incapacitated.

'What day is it?' he asked.

'Friday. Ellen's coming home this evening.'

'And the vultures are gathering tomorrow. Keep your wits about you with them around, Hester Rose.'

'You're not fond of your family?'

'I would defend them to the death – ha! But I wouldn't trust them with my life.'

An interesting take on a family that didn't really answer my question, but it wasn't my job to pry. I would do as Walter had suggested; stay in the background and observe.

Grace flew down the stairs as I crossed the hall on my way back to the kitchen. 'Holy crap, I overslept,' she said. 'Any chance of a cup of tea? I haven't got time for breakfast.'

'Mais oui, bien sûr. Tu bois ton thé et je te fais un sandwich à emporter avec toi.'

She frowned at me. 'Merci beaucoup.' Then she smiled. 'Oh, I see – you're trying to help me with my French.'

I shrugged. 'Rumbled,' I said.

'It's okay. You don't have to, but thanks. Nutella would be great.'

'Surely ham or cheese would keep you going better?'

'Okay. Both, and some tomato, please.'

She was like a whirlwind, shoving books in her bag, pulling on socks she found in the clean laundry basket, rushing over to say goodbye to Walter, downing her tea, and finally running out the door, sandwich in her mouth, then pedalling furiously on her bike, hair flying in all directions. A gorgeous tornado.

She made me think of Justin at the same age. Always busy with friends, his part-time job at the local cinema, rushing in for food and clean clothes, a 'how are you, Mum?' and a kiss on the cheek. I used to spin, trying to keep up with him. And then he was gone, off to university up north and the flat was suddenly still. Not just quiet, the air actually felt different without him there to stir it up. I'd never lived alone before for any length of time and didn't know how to. What point was there to the day when there was no-one to make meals for, clean up after and wash clothes for? How did people measure time when there was no-one coming home at the end of the day, no conversation, music or sound of voices from another room?

Over the years we've forged a different relationship, my son and I. Born when I was only seventeen and thousands of miles from the only home I'd ever known, we'd muddled through his childhood, more friends than mother and son. And then he was grown up and we spoke on the phone, visited each other for weekends, tried to make it like it was before, but how could it be? He had another woman in his life, the lovely Georgia. She was the one who shared his secrets now, who ate with him and knew his friends and his habits.

Jeanette flopped onto a kitchen chair and yawned. 'Has Grace gone already?'

'Yes, a few minutes ago. Said to tell you she has a rehearsal after school, so she'll be late.'

'Oh, damn. On a Friday. This bloody play – they seem to rehearse all the time.' She looked out the window as if expecting to see her daughter there. 'I was hoping she'd be here when Ellen arrives. Oh well, can't be helped, I suppose. She loves her drama.'

After her breakfast, Jeanette went to see Walter and I cleaned up in the kitchen and looked through the fridge and pantry to see what I could get ready for lunch. I was glad Jeanette had chosen Walter over the mundane tasks this morning; it was, after all, what he wanted. But I'm not a great cook and even preparing a simple lunch for others makes me anxious. Not that anyone has ever complained. At a time like this, remembering to eat anything at all can be an achievement. So I chopped vegetables to make soup for Walter. Jeanette and I could have a sandwich.

LETTING GO

Milly scratched at the door to be let in. She had a sock in her mouth and was wagging her tail so hard her whole body wriggled. Laughing, I prised the sock out of her mouth, checked to see if she'd put any holes in it, then took it back to the laundry.

I've never owned a pet. In the village we lived in in Sierra Leone there were strays – mangy things we were warned to stay away from, and which would often disappear suddenly. We children were used to the dead and dying. Chickens were regularly beheaded in front of us, and wild pigs were paraded through the village, strapped by their legs to poles carried between two men, then slaughtered amid much squealing and bloodshed. It was hard to avoid seeing death. We accepted it as a natural part of life.

When Jeanette entered the kitchen to get some juice for Walter, Milly dashed out of the door and across the hall.

'Bugger!' said Jeanette. 'She'll jump straight up on Walter's bed and he'll get upset.'

'I'll go and get her,' I said and followed at a run.

The dog was indeed up on the bed, but Walter was laughing as she licked his face while he tried to turn away and push her off at the same time.

'Sorry about that. My fault. I shouldn't have let her into the kitchen, but I had to perform Operation Retrieve the Sock.'

'She's a mischievous one, that's for sure.'

She'd settled and was now lying next to him on the bed and with the blankets stretched over Walter by her weight, I noticed how distended his abdomen was in stark contrast to the thinness of his limbs.

'Would you like to sit up in the chair?' I asked. 'If we can dislodge Milly, of course.'

'Later. I'd like to have a chat if you have time. Perhaps after lunch? Jeanette mentioned going into town to do some shopping.'

'I'm at your disposal, Walter.' I had a pretty good idea what he wanted to talk about that he didn't want Jeanette hearing.

Later, I got Walter up to sit in his wheelchair under the tree again and I took a kitchen chair out to join him. Jeanette had told us she'd be out for a couple of hours, shopping for Saturday's lunch and 'popping to get a haircut'.

'More like three or four hours, I'd say,' said Walter. 'She spends ages at the hairdresser and comes out looking exactly the same.'

I laughed. 'Don't let her hear you saying such a scandalous thing. We ladies like to think we're transformed under the magical hands of a hair fairy.'

'She doesn't need transforming. She's fine as she is.' He cleared his throat, took a sip of his drink and looked at me. 'I've only known you a few hours, Hester Rose, but I need to ask you something.'

Here it comes, I thought, and met his gaze.

'What are your thoughts about assisting someone to end their life when the time comes?'

No surprise then. I'd had this conversation with patients and their family members dozens of times.

'It's against the law,' I said.

'That's not what I asked. I don't care what the law says, what do you think?'

I had turned my back on God many years ago, but I hadn't ever been able to let go of my belief in the sanctity of life.

'Yesterday when we first met, you told me you want to die peacefully, without pain. I can guarantee you that.'

'But you won't put a bullet in my head?'

I raised my eyebrows. No-one had ever asked me to shoot them before, even though I knew he didn't mean it literally. Or hoped he didn't.

'I'm an end-of-life doula, Walter. I'll help you to the end, but I won't bring it on.'

Walter closed his eyes and let his head drop forward. His hands curled into fists in his lap. 'I don't want to go on when I can't do anything for myself. You must have seen it before in your line of work – bags of bones having things done to them that don't help. We put dogs and horses down when there's no hope. Why not humans?' He opened his eyes and stared at me. 'Not literally a bullet, of course, but an extra dose or two of morphine slipped down the throat?'

'At the end you'll be sleeping a lot anyway because of the medication, and the disease will have sapped your energy. You won't feel anything, I promise.'

He pursed his lips. 'But you won't help me die at a time of my choosing.' It was a statement not a question and I thought he'd accepted my answer.

'Would you prefer me to leave?' I asked.

'No, Hester Rose. I want you to stay but I will ask again. I will try to make you change your mind.'

'That's your prerogative.' I was tired already at the prospect of endless conversations, both of us tucked firmly into our own corners.

'Needless to say, this stays between us,' he said. 'But just for the record, what do you think is the purpose of a long, slow death?'

'Purpose?'

'Yes. I mean, when it is possible to end a life at a time of one's own choosing, why carry on?'

'There's still work to be done, even in dying. Lessons to be learned.'

'Tosh! Like what – how to be treated like an imbecile who can't do anything for themselves?'

'Not that, no. I meant more about the process of stripping life down to its essentials – letting go of the ego, I suppose.'

'Oh, psychological mumbo-jumbo. Don't bore me with nonsense.'

I smiled. 'Okay.'

He grunted and crossed his arms over his chest.

'Perhaps the lessons are for the living too? Your wife, your daughters?' I suggested.

'What do you mean?'

'They can learn something from your courage in facing your own death.'

'Bloody bollocks. Is that what they teach you at doula school? Sanctimonious rubbish.' He turned away, biting his lip.

I waited. Part of me thought he was right.

Eventually he looked at me again. 'They won't learn anything from this. They'll still be shit scared when it's their time only by then euthanasia will be legal and they'll be able to go quickly. Lucky them.'

'You might be right. I'm just offering a different perspective.'

'And now,' he said, 'I wonder if you'd read the newspaper to me. I can't hold the bloody thing up these days. I can't think why they make the damn things so unwieldy.'

And so it went. Walter had moved on. At least he didn't hold a grudge.

I read out the latest exploits of our political leaders, but after a few minutes his chin fell to his chest, and he let out a little snore.

Looking over the garden and stretching my arms over my head to relieve my back and shoulders, I saw two cars following each other up the drive – one new BMW, the other an old Ford Focus weighed down by dirt.

Jeanette stepped out of the Beemer and waved. A young blonde woman unfurled herself from the other and looked in our direction. I mimed sleep and pointed at Walter then joined them to help unload the shopping from the boot of the car.

'This is my daughter, Ellen,' said Jeanette, gesturing towards her. And to Ellen, 'Hester is here to help us with Walter.'

'Pleased to meet you,' I said. 'You've driven down from London?'

'Yes. I'm at uni there.' She looked over at her father, in his chair under the tree. 'I'll just go and see Dad. It's okay, I won't wake him.'

Jeanette and I watched her go over and bend down to give Walter a kiss on the forehead.

As we took the shopping in and started putting it away, Jeanette said, 'They're very close. Always have been. She was devastated when he was diagnosed. We all were, of course, but Ellen took it particularly badly. She suggested giving up university and coming home but Walter convinced her to stay on. Funny, really, since he'd been so against her going in the first place. He didn't even finish school and can't understand why anyone needs tertiary education.'

'Gives you more choices in life, I suppose.'

'Yes, but Walter wanted to keep the family together. Sebastian, his son, works for him in acquisitions and Anna, his eldest daughter, did something in the accounts office until quite recently. Her husband, Jeff, is head of marketing. It really is a family business.'

Hearing voices from Walter's room, we went over and found Ellen had taken him back in and was settling him into bed. There were tears on her cheeks, but she was smiling and telling her father about some party she'd been to the night before.

'A week-night?' he asked, frowning.

'It was a bit of an impromptu thing. Halls is like that. A couple of people get together and suddenly everyone's there. Anyway, it wasn't a late one.'

'It's good to see you, darling. I'm glad you're having a good time.'

She brushed the tears from her cheeks.

Jeanette approached them, laying her hand on Ellen's shoulder and leaning down to give Walter a kiss. But then she retreated again, excusing herself to make dinner.

Walter's gaze followed her, his expression sad – no, longing. He longed for his wife even though she was still living with him.

'Anything I can get you?' I asked.

'Water, thank you, Hester Rose.'

I paused by the door and turned. 'Why do you always call me by my full name?'

'Doesn't everyone?'

'Rose is my surname. But I like you calling me Hester Rose.'

'Good, cos it's stuck in my head now. What kind of surname is Rose anyway?'

'French, originally, I think. A long time ago.' That was true. But it was also true it hadn't always been my name.

He smiled. 'Bloody frogs.'

When I got back with his drink, he and Ellen were chatting away, Ellen doing most of the talking but Walter chiming in from time to time. He was more alert than I'd seen him before, as if he had uncovered a desperate desire to force himself back to wellness. Strangely, it made him look closer to death.

Grace arrived just before dinner and filled the house with her bright energy. She swept into Walter's room as I was collecting the glasses and empty plates from Ellen's afternoon tea. She gave her father a quick peck on the cheek and hugged Ellen who had stood to greet her.

Dinner was eaten in Walter's room, but he ate very little and started yawning before we'd all finished.

'We'll have coffee in the drawing room,' said Jeanette, getting up to leave.

'No. Stay, please.' Walter smiled even though his eyes were closed. 'I'm listening.'

Jeanette hovered, looked towards the door as if planning her escape and then sat down again with a sigh. Ellen stared at her; eyes narrowed.

Grace laughed and said, 'Let's play a game. Charades!' She looked at her father. 'Remember how we used to play it when we were little, and you always pretended not to be able to guess what we were miming? Ell and I would get so frustrated.'

Walter raised his eyebrows, his eyes still closed. 'I never could guess. You always did books or films I'd never heard of.'

'I'll clear up,' I said, gathering the plates.

'No – stay. Please,' said Jeanette, her hand on my arm.

I put the plates down and nodded. This was more than Jeanette including me to be polite.

'I'll start,' said Grace. 'An easy one. Even you'll guess this one, Daddy.'

She stood in the middle of the room and held her hands in front of her like an open book.

'Book,' we all said.

She nodded and held up two fingers.

'Two words!'

Nodding again, she lifted one finger.

'First word,' said Ellen.

Grace made a T with her fingers.

'The,' said Jeanette.

Grace held up two fingers again. And then tapped one against her forearm.

'Second word, first syllable,' said Ellen.

Grace waved at us, turned and walked away.

'Wave,' said Jeanette.

'Hand,' said Ellen.

'Bye,' came Walter's weak voice. 'Bible.'

Grace laughed. 'Told you you'd get it,' she said and sat down.

'You take my turn, Ellen,' said Walter. He looked exhausted, forcing himself to stay awake. Ellen stood to take her turn.

She mimed *The Great Gatsby* which Jeanette guessed, and she did *The Lion King*, which Ellen got. After a few more rounds, Ellen said, 'I don't feel like any more charades.'

Walter looked relieved.

'Hallelujah!' said Jeanette.

'Do you remember the time in Cornwall when we stayed at that weird hotel on the edge of a cliff run by the creepy man we decided was probably a murderer?' said Ellen.

I left as their talk turned to reminiscences of past holidays and family times. Loading the dishwasher and tidying up the kitchen, I thought of Ellen, desperate to share old memories and squeeze in new ones before time ran out. And Jeanette, who seemed so reluctant to be around her husband.

We all deal with loss in different ways, and I was no role model in that department. My parents had cast me out at seventeen, just weeks before Sierra Leone erupted into a civil war that lasted eleven years and claimed hundreds of thousands of lives. The timing of my departure was a complete coincidence but a lucky one for me. In fact, I had no knowledge of the war for a long time. I was busy with other things when I first arrived in

England and even if I had read the newspapers, I doubt there was much coverage of a war in a faraway West African country.

After they sent me away, I'd sometimes let myself fantasise about a reconciliation. I wrote letters that were never answered and eventually, after more than a year, made contact with their Missionary Society headquarters in Sheffield. I received a reply some weeks later telling me my whole family was dead. My parents had stayed in Sierra Leone in spite of the Mission suggesting they leave. Father had entrusted his own wellbeing and that of my mother, brother and sister to God, but He had let them all down.

My father had always lacked any regard for safety – he didn't need to think about mundane things like keeping his family safe with the Lord to look after us all. And because of his stubborn self-righteousness my family was dead. He might as well have killed them himself.

I spent days feeling as though I was outside of myself watching as I carried on doing the things I had to do. But a disconnected part of me raged and screamed silently, and occasionally not so silently. It was his fault I had lost them. My brother. My sister.

I grieved for Rachael and Caleb. Days of hot tears and waking nights when I would remember how close we'd been as children, the odd ones out in an African village. I remembered the last time I'd seen them, tears streaking our faces as we said our hurried goodbyes. I tried to be sad for my parents; I tried to mourn their deaths but all I could find in those early days was anger and resentment.

And I would never get an apology now. There would be no reconciliation. My parents no doubt died believing they were in the right, that it had been okay to send a seventeen-year-old back to England to stay with grandparents she'd never met in a grey, windswept town on the north-east coast of England.

Grandparents who had done nothing to make me feel welcome in their austere home, in spite of being devout members of the church. As far as I could tell, these people talked about God's love and forgiveness with sanctimonious smiles on their faces but when it came to act, to show care and concern, that was a different thing entirely.

It wasn't until years later that I woke one night, my cheeks wet with tears, yearning for my mother's touch, my father's words of comfort. I got up and went to Justin's room across the hall, watched his eyes move behind his eyelids as he dreamed. Suddenly I was filled with gratitude that I had been spared for this moment and all the other moments of my life, hard though some of them had been. I was alive. I had my son. My parents had saved my life even if it hadn't been their intention.

I spent several months in a state of limbo, not knowing how to grieve for parents about whom I was so conflicted. In the end, I contacted their church again to find out more about how they'd died. I was told the whole village had been wiped out by rebel forces. By then I had read some accounts of the atrocities carried out by both sides in the conflict and my head was crammed with images of women being raped and men being dragged into the centre of villages, disembowelled, and left to die.

Why had I asked? Why had they told me? Couldn't they have lied and said they died quickly, a bullet to the head? Or that my parents had been killed shielding their children with their bodies? Such a noble deed might have allowed me to take pride in their deaths rather than become angrier with them and their total disdain for self-preservation.

I still had nightmares about their deaths, the jungle reclaiming their bodies. In these dreams, vines wound through their ribcages and fungi grew out of their mouths in grotesque blooms. Huge vulgar ferns shaded them, dripping raindrops like Chinese torture onto their bloated corpses after the noonday showers. The jungle, always an interloper, restored itself with no-one to keep it at bay, its fecundity an insolent contrast to the events it camouflaged.

My grief was complicated, unfinished. I had become adept at keeping it buried.

Jeanette had bought a baby monitor in town, and I went down later to install it before I went to bed.

'So this is what it's come to.' Walter clutched his sheets.

'You might want something in the night. Or someone. This way all you have to do is call and I'll be down.'

'Not Jeanette then?'

'She needs sleep. If you need her, I can get her though.'

'And you don't need to sleep? Are you a zombie, Hester Rose?'

I laughed. 'Not last time I looked, but I can rest during the day.'

He smiled and turned away, ending the conversation.

'Goodnight then, Walter.'

I checked the monitor when I got to my room, turning the sound up, listening to his breathing, slow and steady. There was something voyeuristic about it – trespassing on a private act – but it was necessary.

I was fast asleep when he called and for a moment, I thought it was part of my dream.

'Hester Rose,' he called again, and I shook my head to wake myself fully.

'Walter.' I was still tying my dressing gown as I entered his room.

There were tears on his face and his bedclothes were askew. His claw-like hands were scrabbling at the bedclothes.

'Let me get you comfortable.' I held him upright with one

arm as I carefully straightened the sheets, disturbing him as little as possible. He calmed down and let me tuck him in.

'Can I get you anything?'

'No, but would you stay awhile? Nights are the worst time. It's so quiet and there's nothing to do but think.'

I smiled. 'I thought you said you drugged yourself up.'

'Bravado, Hester Rose, pure bravado. I'm a bloody old fool who can't admit I'm scared shitless.'

'Do you want to tell me more about what your particular form of scared shitless is like?'

He sighed and let himself sink further into the pillows. I pulled a chair close and waited.

'I've been in control all my life. If I wanted something, I got it, whatever it was, because I planned, set goals. Now the only certainty is that in a short while, I'll be unable to do anything for myself and then I'll die. There will be no dignity in it, no choice, no plan.' He shrugged. 'Unless...?'

'I'm sorry, Walter. I won't change my mind, but you'll have your family around you, you'll be at home.'

'I can't do anything to make you change your mind?'

'No. Sorry.'

He nodded and closed his eyes for a moment. 'What do you think happens after?'

'Peace, I suppose,' I said. 'No pain.'

'Is that the best you can do?'

'It's the best anyone can do, isn't it? You're not a believer and neither am I.'

'I'm tired, Hester Rose.'

'I know. Being ill is exhausting.'

'Dying is exhausting. I need to sleep.'

'Shall I go?'

'No, stay. I don't want to be alone. Talk to me. Tell me about you. Why did you leave Sierra Leone?'

I turned the lamp off. The curtains were open and the moonlight shone across the carpet. I took his hand.

Where to begin?

'When I was seventeen, I fell in love with my best friend. I'd known him all my life, but suddenly our feelings for each other changed. It was as if one day we saw each other differently. As you know, my parents were missionaries and very conservative. But Jusu and I loved each other, and God was all about love. We didn't know what we were doing was wrong. I still don't believe it was wrong.'

'He was a local, your boyfriend?'

I nodded, took a deep breath and continued. 'One day my mother found us together. She went straight to my father who came and stood in the doorway shouting fire and brimstone and raining curses down on our heads. We held on to each other, covering our nakedness with our discarded clothes.'

'That's the trouble with religion – God's love is the only kind that's acceptable.'

'How true.'

'Sorry, I interrupted. Go on.'

'Are you sure you want to hear it?'

Walter nodded.

'Okay.' I closed my eyes, imagining the scene. 'My father's shouting brought others. Soon the whole village was gathered outside our house, craning their necks to see what was going on. And then my father got his staff – he used to walk about with it like Jesus in the desert – and started beating us.'

I paused. Why was I telling Walter this? I hadn't spoken about it for years.

He squeezed my hand. 'Bastard. Go on. What happened?'

'After a while my mother stopped him. We were bruised and bloody but neither Jusu nor I had made a sound. Several men came in and we tried to cover ourselves, but they ripped our clothes out of our hands and carried us outside. In the middle of the village, with everyone there to witness it, my father denounced us. We were no longer part of his church; I was no longer his daughter. No-one stood up for us, they just watched on in a silent circle. Some of the more pious members of my father's congregation spat on us.

'I wasn't allowed back into our house, so I slept against the wall. My sister brought me a blanket but didn't dare speak to me. I don't know where Jusu was taken. I never saw him again. I was frantic with worry – no-one would talk to me to tell me what had happened. I thought maybe he'd been killed. I tried to find out but after I left Africa there was no way of getting any information.' Again, I paused. There was a lump in my throat. I didn't often allow myself to think about Jusu.

Walter grunted. 'Still listening,' he said. 'Have you tried looking him up on the internet?'

I bit my lip. I had tried to find him, but all the records were destroyed in the war. A part of me was glad I didn't know what had happened to him – I was scared, I think, of discovering he had been punished, even murdered, because of what we'd done, and I didn't think I could bear the guilt or the rage I would feel if that was the case. As it was, I veered between believing he was still out there somewhere and the more likely outcome – he'd been killed in the civil war.

'I had no success,' I said.

Walter grunted again. 'What happened to you?'

My stomach had started churning and I lay a hand on it to calm myself. 'Within two days I had also left the village, my home, forever. My mother accompanied me to Freetown and put me on a plane to England. The last thing she said to me was that I was a whore and no-one would want me, especially after being with a native. That's what she said, a native. In our household, native meant uncouth, unsophisticated, backward.

I'd heard them talk with little respect of these natives, but I had thought they were talking about those who didn't come to believe the word of God as my father taught it – the heathens who continued to worship their own gods, or none at all. At that point I realised they included our neighbours and friends. My parents may have spent their lives bringing the word of God to Africa, but they were still as racist as it was possible to be.' There were tears running down my cheeks. I couldn't talk anymore.

Walter was asleep, his mouth open. He looked old and vulnerable. I closed the curtains so he wouldn't be woken by the sun when it came up and took myself back to bed, but I didn't sleep. Old wounds had been reopened and once the memories had seeped out, they wouldn't leave me alone. At dawn I was sitting in the garden with a coffee wishing I could talk to my friend Peggy, the only other person in the world who knew the whole story. I don't know what had made me tell Walter. Perhaps it was simply because he'd asked and no-one else ever did.

WALTER

I'm getting weaker. I can feel my body festering. I stink like rotting meat. I want to clean my teeth all the time and wash my groin and armpits.

My girls are around me. Grace, pretending all is well. Ellen being brave. Jeanette – not a girl, a woman, but a girl to me – still terrified. But at least not staying away. Hester Rose – whoever has a surname like Rose? – is a witch, I'm sure of it. A white witch, working her magic on the house and the people in it. She is worth her weight in gold. Or salt, depending on which century you're in. Maybe bitcoin. Although it's virtual, so weightless.

I lose my train of thought easily.

Hester Rose. Jeanette. Ellen. Grace. Milly the dog. My household. All female. How did that happen? Even the nurses coming in to see to me are women. Perhaps I should have insisted on a male dog, at least.

Who am I kidding? I didn't even want a dog. I was ganged up on. Didn't have a say on whether we had one, let alone breed or sex. The girls love that dog. Stupid mutt.

Family lunch. They're all coming to look at the freak. The

yellow, foetid freak. I know I've lost weight. My hands are like talons and I clutch the sheets like a baby eagle desperate not to fall out of the eyrie.

Monty Python did a marvellous sketch about it. Kicking the bucket. Going to meet your maker. Falling off the perch. Pushing up the daisies. Six foot under. All the other euphemisms about death and dying. I cried with laughter.

It's not funny anymore. It's real and close and I'm not ready. I don't want to go. I don't want to leave this life, this family. I want to plant daisies not push them up.

What will dying be like? Fighting for breath? Hester Rose promises peace, no pain. But she has refused to help me on my way. Maybe I can still persuade her.

My breath is getting short. I panic when I can't breathe properly.

I've never been good with pain. Mine or others'. Could hardly stand to be in the room when the children were born but I wouldn't have missed it for the world. True what they say, though: if men had to give birth, the human race would have died out by now. Women are more resilient. Hardier.

Hester Rose was thrown out of her family for loving someone. She survived. More than survived. Flourished. Uses her experience to help others.

Jeanette will manage.

I'm so scared. Of what comes before death, not after.

Maybe after, too.

If only I could have another year – see Grace finish school. Or a bit more – see her settled into university and Ellen finished. I always thought I'd walk my girls down the aisle and live to ninety, bounce my grandchildren on my knee. I'd give anything for more time. I'd give everything.

THREE

Jeanette was up early, getting out the good dinner service and wiping cutlery with a silver polishing cloth before holding it up to the light to make sure it's streak-free.

'Tell me what you need me to do,' I said, refilling my coffee cup. 'Want me to keep the family at bay?'

She smiled but shook her head. 'I think it would only make matters worse, to be honest. They'd see it as a challenge if you tried to deny them access to Walter.' She put down the fork she'd been polishing and wrung her hands. I realised how anxious she was about them coming.

'Walter is my patient. He hired me to look after him. If I think he's getting tired, it's my duty to ask them to leave.'

Jeanette bit her lip.

'I'll be very polite. I'm not looking to make trouble. But I will be firm.'

She nodded and let out a deep breath, relieved, I think, that I was taking this responsibility from her.

'Okay, that's understood then. Now, what do you want me to help with? Walter's still asleep, I just looked in on him.'

We'd had breakfast and had started preparing the vegetables

before the bell rang to tell us Walter was awake. Jeanette took him a glass of apple juice while I put the enormous joint of beef in the oven.

When Cassie came, we managed to get Walter into the shower and he insisted on wearing a suit and tie for his family coming. His clothes swamped him: his neck swam in his collar; his wrists looked like sticks at the end of his sleeves.

'How do I look, ladies?' He patted his hair down.

'Dapper,' said Cassie.

He laughed. 'You're a terrible liar. Thank God you're a better nurse.'

She laughed and picked up her bag to leave. 'Have a nice lunch. See you on Tuesday. Greta will be in tomorrow and Monday.'

Walter scowled.

'That's enough of that,' said Cassie and she shut the door behind her.

'Greta is a Russian shot putter,' said Walter. 'Huge and brutal.'

'Well, at least you've got me now too. I'll take her on, if need be,' I said. 'Although I'm sure she's putty in your hands, really.'

Walter harrumphed.

Ellen burst in, a vase of flowers in her hands.

'I thought you could do with some colour in here.'

'Thank you, darling, very thoughtful.'

She gave Walter a kiss and sat next to him. I saw her take in the suit and tie, and bite her lip. Then she pasted on a smile and asked how he was feeling. I took it as my cue to leave.

In the kitchen, Jeanette and Grace were standing on opposite sides of the table. Jeanette was red in the face.

'I told you I had a football match this morning,' said Grace.

'I don't remember everything you tell me. Damn it, Grace,

you know the family's coming for lunch. I can't go gallivanting all over the county this morning.'

'I'll take you, if you like. Where is it?' I said.

'It's okay, thanks, Hester. It's a home game. I can cycle.'

'Thank you, Hester,' said Jeanette at the same time. She carried on, 'Ellen can help with lunch, and you'll be home sooner if Hester drives you.' She looked pointedly at her daughter, who shrugged and took a bite of her toast.

'I'll get my things then,' she said, and left.

'Football in the summer?' I raised an eyebrow.

Jeanette shrugged. 'They play all year round for some reason. Most popular sport at the school. I blame *Bend It Like Beckham*. Both the girls were obsessed with the damn movie when they were younger, as were all their friends. I'm sure it single-handedly changed the face of women's sport in this country.'

I thought that was a bit of a stretch but didn't say anything.

Ten minutes later we were driving away, Grace chatting about school and her friends while managing to give me directions at the same time. I hadn't watched a game of football since Justin used to play. I'd never played team sports of course, and when Justin had started football, it took a long time for me to see any kind of purpose to it. Eleven little boys and girls running up and down a field, kicking a ball, while eleven other little kids tried to take it off them. It was cute, but seemed like a waste of time. But then I saw how his eyes gleamed when he talked about it, how the team celebrated together if one of them scored a goal or even, when they were starting out, just kicked the ball in the right direction. It was about doing something he loved with his friends. I became one of those mums who stood on the sidelines cheering them on, wind, rain or shine. I think I was more upset when he gave it up to concentrate on his A levels than he was.

'Here we are,' said Grace.

We turned up the school drive and passed playing fields where matches were already in progress.

'Park anywhere you can. We'll be playing on pitch one, just over there. Oh, and please don't shout and carry on. Daddy used to be so embarrassing I had to ban him from coming.'

I could imagine Walter on the sidelines giving his advice, whether or not he knew what was going on.

'I won't open my mouth,' I promised. 'I'll have a little walk around the grounds while you warm up.'

The school had once been a stately home judging by the look of it. Elizabethan chimneys with their ornate brickwork were clustered on the roof and the stone surrounds of the windows looked as if they'd been recently restored. To one side, several squat modern glass and red brick buildings detracted from the overall aesthetic. I walked around the sports fields, stopping every so often to watch, and then made my way back to pitch one. Grace and her team were in place, facing their opponents. And then the whistle blew and the game started.

Several parents stood along the sidelines, some chatting, others intent on the game. A young man ambled over and watched for a while. He was tall and good-looking, dark-haired, with hazel eyes and one of those beards that looked like two-day growth but was too neat to be laziness. Too young to be a father, perhaps a brother. Then I noticed his tie. It bore the same crest as Grace's schoolbag. A teacher?

'Hi, I'm Hester Rose,' I said. 'I'm staying with Grace and her family for a while.' I put my hand out and he shook it.

'Gavin Green,' he said. 'I'm a teacher here.'

'And you have to wear school uniform at the weekends?' I gestured to the tie.

He followed my gaze. 'Oh, this?' He ran his hand down it. 'Yes, at all times if the pupils are present.'

'Are you a sports teacher?'

'No, English and drama actually.'

'Then you're very dedicated to turn out on a Saturday morning. Do all the staff come to watch the girls play?'

He laughed. 'No, but I'm also head of one of the junior boys boarding houses so I'm here anyway. Most of my colleagues are probably still in bed reading the papers and drinking coffee right now.'

He didn't seem envious of the fact.

'I didn't realise it was a co-ed school.'

'Only the juniors, then the boys have to go elsewhere.'

Three teenage girls in mud-splattered sports uniforms came past.

'Good morning, Mr Green,' they chorused in bright sing-song voices. He turned and smiled at them; they all went beetroot red and ran off, giggling.

'The joys of being a male teacher at a girls' school,' I said.

He laughed. 'You get used to it. It isn't personal – I mean, they don't really fancy me, there's just no-one else to direct their hormones at.'

'So, being a drama teacher, are you directing the play Grace is in?'

His hand went to his hair, and he cleared his throat. 'Yes. Soon be over though. Performances are next week. She's a stoic is Grace, what with her father being ill and everything.'

'I think she wants to keep everything as normal as possible.'

He nodded and turned back to the game. I wondered what it was really like, being a male teacher in a girls' school and if there was any reason he was watching this particular match.

'Well,' he said suddenly, 'I'd better go and watch the under 14s for a while or they'll never let me hear the end of it. Nice meeting you.'

'You too,' I said and watched him saunter off, looking back over his shoulder at the game from time to time.

In the car on the way home, Grace asked what Mr Green had wanted.

'Why do you ask?'

'I just noticed you talking, that's all.' She wouldn't look me in the eye.

'We talked about you, actually.'

She whipped her head round, eyes wide.

'He thinks you're a stoic given your circumstances.'

She blew out her cheeks and let out a long slow breath. 'That's nice of him.'

She looked out the window and I changed the subject. For the rest of the drive home, we talked about the game.

When we got back to the house, she ran upstairs to shower and change while I went in to see Walter. He had slumped down in his chair and I realised we'd got him up too early. He'd struggle to sit through lunch.

'How about a lie down before the guests get here?'

With Walter lying on his bed for a rest, I ventured into the kitchen. Jeanette was making gravy while Ellen cut up melon to add to the fruit salad she was making.

'They like a three-course lunch,' said Jeanette when she saw me. She looked as if she might burst into tears.

'It'll be fine, Mum, really,' said Ellen, putting the dessert in the fridge. 'And it'll all be over soon.'

Jeanette gasped and stopped stirring the gravy. Tears gathered on her lower eyelashes.

'Mum, I didn't mean... just, you know, today. They won't stay forever.'

She looked to me for support, but Jeanette fled from the kitchen and we heard her running up the stairs.

'What's wrong with Mummy?' asked Grace, coming in, towelling her hair dry.

'Same old same old,' said Ellen. She turned to me. 'Sebastian and Anna, Dad's children with his first wife, hate Mum. These family lunches are always a trial.' She went out with a tray of cutlery to start setting the table. Grace shrugged, helped herself to some juice and followed her.

Half an hour later, a car pulled up outside the house and a man who was a younger, healthier version of Walter got out. He was tall, his thinning hair greying at the temples, brown eyes hidden behind black-framed glasses. He wore jeans and a short-sleeved shirt that stretched over his ample belly.

Jeanette opened the door. 'Sebastian, how lovely to see you,' she said, air kissing him.

He walked into the house, peering around as if to see if anything had changed since his last visit, if anyone had walked off with the family silver or some other heirloom. His wife, a well-groomed woman in a low-necked dress, followed him in. She looked like she'd had a bit of work done; at her age, no-one's breasts looked like hers did without help, and her lips were just a little bit too full.

'Deborah, welcome,' said Jeanette.

The woman smiled thinly as if acknowledging a serf rather than her hostess.

'Sebastian, Deborah,' said Ellen, coming out of the kitchen.

He nodded to her and looked at me, waiting to be introduced. Deborah said nothing.

'This is Hester, your father's doula.' Jeanette gestured in my direction but was already heading back into the kitchen.

'Pleased to meet you,' I said.

He stared at me. 'What on earth is a doula?' When we shook hands, he stood a bit too close.

Ellen took him by the arm and steered him into the drawing room. I heard her telling him I was helping Jeanette with a few things for a while. Deborah went into the cloakroom to comb her already immaculate hair.

Minutes later Anna and her husband, Jeff, arrived. She was wearing an expensive dress that, even though it was long-sleeved, didn't hide the fact she was severely underweight. Her hands had the mottled purplish colour of the long-term anorexic. After we'd introduced ourselves, they too were taken into the drawing room for a drink. I went to see if Walter was ready to get up and greet his offspring.

I found him trying to get himself off the bed and into his wheelchair.

'I'm bloody dying and they can't even be bothered to come in and say hello before they start guzzling my booze and scoffing my food. What would you do, Hester Rose?'

'About what?'

'Never mind. Just get me in there before they start pocketing my valuables.'

I pushed Walter into the drawing room where Sebastian lounged in a chair, a large whisky in his hand, holding forth about the state of the country and how the economy was being driven into the ground.

'We need a real leader, a strong man at the top,' he said. Then noticing Walter had arrived, he stood and said, 'Father, I was just about to come and see you. How are you feeling today?'

Anna rushed over and kissed him on the cheek. 'You look well, Father. Better than last time I saw you.'

'Liar,' said Walter and waved her away.

Grace came in and flopped down into the sofa next to Jeff, tucking her legs up under her. 'What's new, Jeffrey?' she asked and then pulled her phone out and started texting without waiting for his answer.

Jeanette entered and stood by Walter, her hand on his shoulder. There was an awkward silence until the doorbell rang again and Ellen came in with the last guest: Louise, daughter of Walter's second wife, Marie. She made her way straight over to her father and gave him a hug.

'Oh, Dad, you've lost more weight. Are you eating at all?'

Walter patted her hand. 'I take what I can.'

'You didn't bring the children, Lou?' Jeanette looked relieved.

'No, it's a long drive for them and I wasn't sure how... well, to be honest, I thought they'd be a bit of a handful.' She turned to Walter again. 'I'll bring them one day during the week when they can run around outside and let off a bit of steam and not bother you too much. They'd like to see you. They sent their love. They've drawn you some pictures too – remind me to give them to you after lunch.'

He smiled and nodded.

'Shall we eat?' said Jeanette, gesturing to the dining room. 'Everything's ready.'

I pushed Walter in and parked him at the head of the table. Sebastian and Anna rushed forward to take their places either side of him.

'She's here to look after me so I need her here.' Walter jabbed a finger at me and then at the chair next to him. He smiled as Sebastian threw me a look that might have floored someone who cared.

'Of course.' He pulled my chair out for me. Grace squeezed in next to me before he had a chance to move, so he ended up between her and Louise.

Ellen poured wine and Walter raised his glass of water.

'Happy families,' he said. I'm pretty sure he winked at me. The old bugger was enjoying himself.

Jeanette and Ellen served the starter: salmon mousse they had slaved over for much of the morning. Walter took some pills with a sip of water. He had a bowl of soup in front of him but hardly ate.

'I'm intrigued, Hester. What does a doula actually do?' asked Anna, taking a minute taste of the mousse before pushing the rest of it around her plate and hiding it under the toast.

'I provide general help to the family,' I said.

'Can't Jeanette cope?' Sebastian looked at her. 'It's not as if you have any other work to do, is it?'

Jeanette looked down at her plate, jaw clenched.

This man was a total shit. I wondered if he was always like this or if he was playing it up a bit for a new audience. Then I remembered what Walter had said about the family dynamics and decided he was probably just being his usual delightful self. 'It's not about Jeanette. It's what Walter wants,' I said.

'Ah. It always is, isn't it, Father?'

Walter ignored him and slurped a spoonful of soup. Sebastian grimaced and downed his wine.

'How are the boys, Louise?' asked Ellen. 'I haven't seen them for ages.'

'They're busy and boisterous. Alan's taken them to see his parents today.'

'I'll have to invite myself over for dinner one night to see them – and get a decent meal for once. College food is the worst.'

'That's right, ask about her children. What about Eva? None of you ask about her, do you?' Deborah's knuckles were turning white she was holding her cutlery so tight. A vein throbbed in her head.

'How is she, Deborah?' asked Jeanette.

Anna laughed. 'How would she know? I bet she hasn't seen her all year.'

Jeanette intervened. 'How about you, Sebastian?'

'As you well know, I visit her each week. She's doing very nicely.' Sebastian glared around the table as if challenging anyone to disagree.

'Have you managed to find a new home for her or is she still in the same awful one in town? The one the council wants to close down?' asked Ellen.

Deborah's lips drew into a thin line and she stared at Ellen, who carried on eating as if nothing had happened.

'It's not so bad, is it? I mean, the inmates are treated well, it's just the building that's the issue.' Grace looked around for support.

'They're called residents, not inmates. It's not a prison, is it, Deborah?' Anna said, all wide-eyed and innocent.

Walter leant in to me. 'Eva has special needs,' he said. 'She lives in a home.'

I nodded and thought I'd probably also want to live in a home if I had Sebastian and Deborah for parents.

'Eva is happy there and well looked after,' said Sebastian firmly.

'I heard they can't keep staff, so there must be something fishy going on.' Ellen took a sip of wine and looked around the table, smiling sweetly.

'That's enough, Ellen,' said Jeanette mildly.

Grace said, 'I'm The Queen of Hearts in the school play. We're doing *Alice in Wonderland.*'

'Glad you clarified. We'd have thought you were doing *The Taming of the Shrew* otherwise.' Sebastian's voice dripped with sarcasm. 'We didn't have the luxury of private schooling. Father thought it was unnecessary, didn't you?' Sebastian raised one eyebrow.

'Quite. There was a job waiting for you in the business.'

'But not for your princesses?'

'That's enough,' said Walter, glaring at his son.

Sebastian clenched his jaw, then he looked towards his father as if he was going to say more but decided against it. Instead, he held up his glass and waved it at Jeanette.

'Here, let me.' I took it from him, went to the sideboard and poured a small drink.

Sebastian looked at it, looked at me and drank it in one. I sat down and turned to Jeanette.

'Divine mousse, thank you.'

She smiled back at me.

'So, Father, what do the doctors say about how your treatment's going?' asked Sebastian.

Walter wiped his mouth with his napkin, which he then folded and placed next to his bowl. 'If you'd bothered to listen the last time you asked that question, you'd know I'm not receiving any treatment. I am having palliative care only.'

Anna intervened. 'But there must be something more they can do?'

'Is everyone ready for the main course?' Jeanette rose to her feet. 'I'll get the roast beef.'

We passed our plates to the end of the table and Ellen and Louise took them into the kitchen. Jeanette reappeared with the roast and the girls carried in dishes of vegetables.

'Will you carve, Sebastian?'

He made a great show of testing the sharpness of the blade and then cut thick slices of beef, which Grace served onto plates and handed round. For a while there was no sound other than the clinking of cutlery on china.

Walter sniffed the air. 'It smells perfect, my darling.' He smiled at his wife.

'It's delicious, Jeanette,' said Louise. 'I don't know how you do it. I've never managed to master the art of a roast dinner.'

'Another thing you haven't mastered then. The list must be rather long.' Sebastian said it under his breath but everyone at the table heard it, as they were no doubt meant to.

Louise ignored him and turned to Jeff. 'How was your holiday – I hear you went to Corfu?'

'That's right. Seems like ages ago already, but we only got back two weeks ago. Marvellous holiday, wasn't it, Anna?'

'It was okay. The hotel wasn't up to much and a nearby nightclub kept me awake.'

'I'd love to go to Greece,' said Grace. 'My friend Polly went last year and said it was rad.'

'Rad? What the hell does that mean?' asked Sebastian.

'You know, great weather and full of hot boys,' said Grace, not put off by his response.

'Sounds perfect,' said Ellen. 'I'll go with you.'

Conversation flowed for a while, with talk of holidays past and future. It seemed to be the only safe topic in this family. I watched and listened. Walter didn't say anything, but occasionally he smiled and nodded.

Jeanette fluttered between the kitchen and the dining room making sure everyone had what they needed. Ellen and Grace helped between stories of swimming naked in a hotel pool in Portugal (they had only been toddlers at the time) and pony rides on the beach in France. Their conversation was aimed at Walter, including him as much as possible. Sebastian glowered throughout and Anna's contributions were limited to how awful certain places and experiences had been.

When the fruit salad and clotted cream had been demolished, Jeanette suggested moving back to the drawing room for coffee.

'And liqueurs, I hope,' said Sebastian, who after my

unsuccessful attempt to slow his drinking had managed to down most of a bottle of wine. Anna had managed another. They were the only calories she'd allowed into her body.

'I haven't heard you thanking Jeanette for the wonderful lunch yet,' said Walter.

'Yes. Wonderful,' said Sebastian, getting up and taking his glass into the other room. Anna followed him, calling to Jeff to join them.

'I'm afraid I'll have to go. I'm meeting a friend this afternoon. Jeff and Anna will give Sebastian a lift home.' Deborah checked her still immaculate hair in her compact mirror, applied more lipstick, gave a little wave and was gone.

Louise, Grace and Ellen cleared the table and helped Jeanette with the coffee while I took Walter back to his room. He was exhausted and needed to lie down.

'Awful, aren't they?' he said as I pulled his shoes off.

'Sebastian and Anna don't seem to have much time for Louise or Jeanette,' I said.

'Hmm,' he said. 'Get me one of those yellow tablets, would you?'

'Are you in pain?'

'Of course I'm in bloody pain, I've got cancer.'

'Perhaps you overdid it, staying up for lunch.'

'Yes, but I wouldn't have missed it for the world, would you?'

'I can think of things I'd rather have done. Sitting in a pit of Gabon vipers, perhaps.'

'You just did. Didn't I warn you?' He laughed and lay back on his bed.

I settled him and left him dozing off. As I crossed the hall, I took my phone out and checked my messages. There was one from Justin inviting me up for a few days and asking how I was, and another from the nursing home where I worked sometimes, asking me to call. I went up to my room before calling back.

'Hi, it's Hester. You messaged me?'

'Hester, how are you?'

'Good. I'm doing a private job at the moment, so if it's about a shift I'll have to say no I'm afraid.'

'Not a shift, no. Some bad news, I'm afraid. Peggy's had a seizure of some sort. I know you're close so thought you'd want to know.'

I suddenly felt cold. 'Is she okay?'

'We're not sure. She's gone into the local hospital for some tests.'

'Thanks. I'll call them. Give my love to everyone.'

I rang off and sat on the end of my bed.

Peggy. I couldn't bear the idea of losing her. She'd been my saviour when I was a single mum. We'd moved into the housing co-op at the same time, had bedsits next to each other. She'd signed her house over to her son and daughter-in-law on the advice of her lawyer so they could avoid death duties. She'd planned to live there with them until she died but they had other ideas and kicked her out as soon as the ink was dry on the deeds. In her sixties, she was homeless and depressed.

I was a new mother of a beautiful baby boy who I hadn't the faintest idea how to look after. She showed me how to bath him, the best way to mush vegetables when he started on solids, babysat him while I went back to school to get some qualifications and then on to my nurse training. She was a grandmother to my son and a mother to me. When I thanked her for all she did, she waved it off, said we did far more for her than she could ever do for us. 'You gave me a reason to carry on when I'd lost hope,' she always said.

Taking a deep breath, I called the hospital and was put through to her ward.

'Are you a relative?'

'I'm Hester Rose, her next of kin,' I said.

'All I can tell you is she's stable. As you can appreciate, it's the weekend. She'll be having some tests on Monday. We'll know more then.'

'Thanks. I'll call back then. Please give her my love.'

Either the hospital had no money for full staffing at the weekends, like so many in the NHS, or Peggy wasn't so critical they needed to rush around doing tests on a Saturday. I wanted to believe the latter, but couldn't dismiss the former option. I sat with my eyes closed, calming myself for a few minutes, and then visualised Peggy getting better: propped up in bed, breathing easily, asking for a decent cup of tea and wanting to know when she could go home. It was the closest thing I had to prayer these days.

I tidied my hair, dashed some more lipstick on ready to head back into the fray. When I passed Jeanette's room, I heard a noise. Peering around the door I saw Anna rifling through the drawers of the dressing table.

'Can I help you?' I asked.

Anna turned guiltily, shutting the drawer with a quick shove.

'Just looking for a comb.' She ran her hand through her thin hair.

'There's one just there.' I pointed to the centre of the dressing table.

'Silly me.' She shrugged but didn't pick it up.

'Was there anything else?'

She looked me up and down. 'I don't know what you think you're doing here, but you're nothing, a nobody. If you're gold-digging, forget it.'

I laughed. 'Gold-digging? Oh, come on. You sound like something out of a bad movie. I'm here to look after your father while he's dying and help Jeanette in any way I can.'

'And I expect you're squeezing as much money out of them as you can for doing it.'

'I beg your pardon? What right do you think you have to accuse me of anything? I don't know what you're really doing in Jeanette's bedroom, but I think you should leave.'

She rolled her shoulders back and flounced out of the room. A small bottle fell out of her pocket as she went. I picked it up and checked the label. Valium. Jeanette's name on the label. I wasn't surprised she'd been prescribed them, and it certainly wasn't up to me to judge the woman – many people need a bit of a chemical help occasionally, especially when their husband is dying. What intrigued me was that Anna had been trying to steal them. I put the pills back in the drawer of the dressing table and closed the bedroom door behind me.

I heard Grace calling my name and went downstairs.

'Sorry, I know it's a lot to ask but Mummy wondered if you'd have a word with Sebastian. About Daddy. He's asked, apparently.'

'Of course,' I said, my heart sinking a little. 'Where is he?'

'On the patio having a cigar, I think.'

I joined him outside. He was lying on a sun lounger as if he was on holiday by the pool, drink in one hand, cigar in the other. I sat in an upright chair beside him.

He turned and looked at me. No – he evaluated me, his eyes starting at my feet and running slowly up my body, pausing for a few moments on my breasts, continuing to my face. Inside I was squirming, but I was determined not to let him see how he affected me, so I took deep breaths and waited, teeth clenched.

He had asked to speak to me, so he was going to have to start the conversation. One thing you get very good at when working with the dying is sitting in silence. 'Holding the space' they called it in our training. It's not an awkward silence, it's more like making room for whatever needs to emerge.

'Anna thinks you're a gold-digger.'

'I know. She told me.'

'Well, are you?'

'What a strange question. If I was, would I admit it?'

'I suppose not. Jeanette says Walter employed you.' He took a slug of his Scotch. 'How long's he got?'

'I can't say.'

'Can't or won't?'

'I am not a seer, Sebastian. I can't divine the future.'

'Are we talking days or weeks?'

'Why are you asking? Is there something you need to say to him before he dies? Anything you need to do?'

'Nothing like that. He knows how I feel about him. There's nothing left to say. I just need to know for the sake of the business. He's said nothing about who'll be left in charge. I'm running it at the moment, and I fully expect I'll be CEO when he goes, but the workers need some certainty.'

The workers, my foot.

'Why don't you ask Walter?' I asked.

'About when he's planning to pop his clogs?'

'About the business. So you can reassure the workers.'

'I have. He won't tell me. He's hinted at me taking over, of course, but I have nothing in writing.'

'And the employees need proof in writing, do they? Gosh, they do sound worried.'

Sebastian was either too thick or too wrapped up in himself to notice the sarcasm. Or both.

'I'm sorry I can't be of more help,' I said when he didn't respond. 'Is there anything else I can help you with, Sebastian?'

'Maybe. Do they give you any time off from sitting beside the death bed?'

'At the moment I can take an hour here and there when I need to.'

'That's good. You probably need to let your hair down. How about a drink with me one night?'

'No thanks. I need to be here. Nights are hard for Walter.'

'Well lunch then?'

'I can't ever say for sure when I'll be needed.' God alone knew why I was being so polite to him, the self-absorbed creep. I wished I hadn't dabbed on the lipstick. He probably thought it was for his benefit. I had no illusions. To a misogynist like Sebastian I was nothing more than a conquest. And anyway, if I could get away it wouldn't be to spend time with him, it would be to see Peggy.

He said nothing for a while.

'Was there anything else?' I asked.

'What? Are you still here?' He swatted at me as if I was an annoying insect. Clearly a man who didn't like being turned down.

'Get one of the girls to bring me another drink, there's a love,' he called after me as I walked back to the house.

'Ellen, Sebastian wants some water,' I said as I entered the kitchen.

She snorted. 'He thinks water's what you bathe in. He's never drank the stuff in his life. But I'll gladly take him some.' She filled a tumbler and went off to find him.

I poured myself some coffee and went to check on Walter – sleeping – before joining the others in the drawing room. Jeanette was sitting on the sofa with Louise, chatting quietly. She looked more relaxed than I'd seen her all day. Jeff was tucked away in the corner reading the newspaper. Ellen had returned and was deep in conversation with Grace by the window. They looked round when I came in. Grace smiled. Anna was nowhere to be seen. I sat down beside Jeff.

'I understand you work for Walter too?'

He sighed and I was almost knocked out by his whisky breath. He had a long face and a high forehead. His small eyes were deeply set and with his hooked nose, he looked a bit like a vulture. He wasn't a man who would inspire confidence.

'I'm head of marketing, for my sins,' he slurred.

'You don't enjoy it?'

'Would you?'

'I have no idea – I'm not even sure what people who work in marketing actually do, to be honest. But if you don't like it, can't you leave?'

He chuckled and poured himself another drink from the bottle beside him on the table. 'You've met Walter. Even now he has a hold over this family no-one is willing to challenge. Imagine what he was like before he became ill, when he was running the company.'

'He's certainly a force to be reckoned with. But I'm still not sure why you stay if you don't like it. Surely you could get another job?'

He shrugged. 'You wouldn't understand.'

'Try me,' I said, and I adopted my listening pose.

He said nothing for a while. Then he tapped the side of his nose and said in a conspiratorial voice, 'He's got dirt on everyone in the company. Family or not. It's how he's kept everyone in line over the years.'

I nodded. Oh, Walter, I thought, that's not very nice. If it's true.

We sat in silence for a while longer and then Jeff whispered, 'I was a little indiscreet with his secretary. It was years ago and didn't last long but he threatened to tell Anna about it if I left. It would ruin our marriage. Anna isn't a forgiving person and I love her, I don't want to lose her.'

I hardly heard what he said. I was much more interested in what Walter might have on Sebastian and whether it was the cause of their strained relationship.

'What are you two plotting?' asked Anna, coming in and sitting next to her husband.

He put his hand on her thigh. She removed it.

'We were commenting on how lovely the lunch was,' I said. 'And discussing whether I should make more coffee for you before you go. Jeff thought not.' I smiled at her.

She looked at her watch, its dainty gold band hanging round her scrawny wrist.

'Good idea. Go and find Sebastian, would you? Deborah's run off and we have to give him a lift home.'

'He's out on the patio,' I said, not moving. Anna took a deep breath and scowled. Then she got up and tottered unsteadily to the door.

Jeff whispered again. 'I'm not sure why I told you that. Must've been the drink talking. I'm sure you'll keep it mum, eh?'

'Of course,' I said. 'Confidentiality is my middle name.'

He nodded and got to his feet. 'Jeanette,' he said. 'A fine feast, thank you.'

In the hall, Anna took Jeff's arm. Sebastian looked like he'd just woken up, his hair sticking up, shirt coming untucked.

'Bye then,' he said with a general wave of the hand.

'Did you not want to look in on Walter before you go?' I asked, gesturing to his door.

'Oh, yes. Of course.'

Anna and her brother glanced at each other and then went to the door of Walter's room.

'Bye, Father,' they said in unison, and then they were off.

I wondered how any of them were going to drive in the state they were in, but didn't say anything.

Louise said she'd also better go. 'I have a long drive. But I would like to bring the boys to see Dad – do you think he'd be up to it?' She looked at Jeanette and then to me.

'I think we should ask Walter,' I said. Jeanette nodded.

'Yes, it's up to him. He does tire so easily these days.'

'I'll call then. And thanks again for a lovely lunch.' Louise went in to kiss Walter goodbye and then left.

Ellen, Grace, Jeanette and I went back into the drawing room and sank into the sofas.

'I don't know how you did it, Hester, but you managed to get rid of them all in record time,' said Grace. 'They usually hang around for supper as well and by then they're often far too drunk to drive home. This is heaven. We have the whole evening!'

Walter was restless and bad-tempered during the evening. He asked for one thing and then another, said he was in a lot of pain and demanded an extra dose of morphine. He settled a bit after it but there was no doubt the last two days had taken their toll on him and I'd noticed a decline in his health. He was beginning to look more jaundiced, and his breathing was becoming laboured, a sure sign he was going downhill.

Ellen went in to sit with him. I heard her telling him about the work she was doing at university and the courses she'd be taking in her third year.

I decided to see how Jeanette was. I found her in the garden with Milly at her feet.

'Come and join me,' she said as I approached. She rested her head against the back of the chair and closed her eyes. 'I'm so exhausted. How can those people be so thoroughly unpleasant?'

'You mean Sebastian and Anna? The others seemed okay.'

'Yes, Louise is lovely, isn't she? And Jeff is just a lapdog. I've never understood what he sees in Anna.' She paused, looking out over her beloved garden. 'Then again, there are a lot of people who never understood me falling for Walter, a man old enough to be my father. You never can tell who people will end up with can you?'

'You certainly can't,' I said.

'I sometimes wonder what Walter was like before we met. I think he must have mellowed with age.' Jeanette twisted a strand of hair round her fingers.

'We all do, I suppose. You think he was stricter with his first family?'

'Undoubtedly. And I've heard that Dorothy, Sebastian and Anna's mother, was quite a force to be reckoned with: haughty and exacting. She was the boss's daughter, you know. It's how Walter came to own the company. Old Mr Shoebridge had a massive heart attack and Walter stepped up.' She laughed. 'Mr Shoebridge had a shoe company. Couldn't have done anything else really, could he? Walter built the company from a small family business to an international concern, exporting shoes all over the world.'

'What happened to Dorothy?'

'She died. It seems heart attacks ran in the family, but she was quite young. Sebastian was about eleven and Anna nine when they lost their mum.'

'A hard time to lose a mother, I would imagine.'

'Is there ever a good time?'

'I suppose not.'

Jeanette was in a talkative mood in spite of her tiredness. 'Turns out Walter had been having an affair for a while before Dorothy died and Louise was the result. Walter married Marie and moved her and the baby into the house, but the marriage didn't survive Sebastian and Anna's anger. They never accepted Marie, and haven't forgiven Walter for bringing her into their home. And you saw how they treat Louise. It's disgusting.'

I nodded. This family was, as Cassie had warned me, complex. And fascinating.

We sat in silence for a few moments, enjoying the last of the sunset draping itself in mauve and orange over the village rooftops.

Jeanette sighed. 'You didn't come out here just to watch the sunset and chat, did you? I expect you want to talk to me about Walter.' She turned to me and braced herself.

Before I could say anything, she carried on. 'He doesn't have much time, does he? Every day I notice another small decline and today really knocked him for six.'

'It did.'

'But he's a fighter.'

'Yes, he is, but even the strongest fighters can't go on forever.'

A tear rolled down her cheek and she chewed her bottom lip. 'I love him so much.'

'I know. Tell him.'

She smiled. A small pained smile. 'He knows.'

'I'm sure he does, but I don't know anyone who ever tires of being told they are loved.'

She sat, hands clasped in her lap, taking deep breaths.

WALTER

I'm exhausted.

Jeanette worked so hard. Lunch was another one of her amazing affairs. I couldn't eat any of it, but the smells were good. Got the juices flowing but the body just couldn't do it.

The table looked beautiful with fresh-cut flowers that she'd grown herself. I was never one for the garden. That's always been her domain. I was just glad she had something she loved doing. I didn't want her working when the girls came along, and she wanted to be a full-time mum. Lucky girls.

Hester Rose was a match for Sebastian. I knew she would be. Someone needs to put my son in his place. I've tried to like him. He always was a mummy's boy. Of course, he took it hard when she died. So did Anna. They united against me. They didn't want anyone except each other.

Anna didn't eat anything as usual. Pushed her food around the plate, tried to hide it under a lettuce leaf. She thinks no-one notices. Some people do make it hard to love them. Like them, even. How can you not like the children you bring into the world? Am I a psychopath?

I expect I've just attended my last family event. Apart from my funeral. They'll all gather then to see me off. Circle around to see what's left.

I have a few surprises up my pyjama sleeve. If I have the energy.

It's all so hard now. Breathing. Moving. I keep trying to go on for my girls, but I can't stay alive on willpower alone.

I want to roar but instead I sigh. I want to get out of bed and go for a walk but the effort of turning over leaves me in a sweat. This once-strong body is a sack of tendons and bones, tumours flowering where organs should be.

Time was when Jeanette and I would debrief over a brandy after the family had been, and then fuck like bunnies to put it all behind us. I can't remember what it's like to feel her skin under my hands, her lips on mine. I dream about slipping my cock into her, the tiny groans she used to utter as I pushed in and pulled out slowly. Now my cock lies limp and my hands are empty. She doesn't want to touch me, or be touched. I can't blame her, but I wish she'd lie next to me, fit her curves along the angles of my body and let me pretend to be a man who is still able to satisfy his woman.

FOUR

Walter called for me in the night again. He said he'd had a nightmare but couldn't remember what it was about. He was bathed in sweat, so I helped him change into fresh pyjamas and sat him in a chair while I changed the sheets. Settled in bed again, he took my hand in both of his.

'Every day I feel weaker,' he said. 'I don't want to go like this, fading to nothingness. You won't reconsider your position?'

'I can't, Walter. I understand it's hard for you, but no, I can't help you on your way.'

'Bugger.' He turned away but didn't let go of my hand. 'Told you I'd keep asking, didn't I?'

'You did. Forewarned is forearmed, as they say.'

'What do they do in Sierra Leone – with the dying, I mean?'

I thought back to the village, the rainforest, the fecundity of the place.

'My father battled constantly for the souls of the people who had lived there for generations with their own beliefs and really had no need of another God. Even when they took Jesus into their hearts, they carried on with their ancestral practices. It drove him to distraction.'

'And death?'

'It was a natural part of life, I suppose. No drugs, although sometimes herbs and often poyo, a sweet palm wine, took the edge off any pain.'

'And after?'

I smiled, again thinking of my father and his frustration. 'The relatives would want a proper Christian burial but would also sacrifice a pig or a goat to appease their gods, to ensure their loved one was welcomed into Heaven. Old habits were hard to break. Father would rage and shake his staff at them, but they carried on doing what they thought was right. Hedging their bets.'

'You're angry with your father, aren't you?'

I was surprised by his comment. Either he was very astute or I wasn't as good at hiding it as I thought.

'Yes,' I said. 'I am.'

Fortunately, Walter didn't want to pursue that line of conversation.

'What did Sebastian want to talk to you about?'

I laughed. 'You don't miss a trick, do you? We all thought you were fast asleep.'

'I was but I have my spies. Important to always know what's going on. It's how to stay on top of things.'

I began to think maybe Jeff had been telling the truth about Walter gathering secrets as a way of binding people to him and the company.

'He talked about the business. He said the employees need certainty as to who's going to take over.'

'I'll bet he did. In my experience, employees don't give a damn about anything as long as they get paid each week. But what did he *ask* you? I'm sure he didn't just want to chat about staff morale. He wanted to know how long I've got, didn't he?'

'Yes. And I told him I'm not an oracle.'

Walter grunted. 'His wife, the beautiful Deborah, airhead extraordinaire, is having an affair, you know. That's why she left straight after lunch. Off to shag lover boy.'

I raised my eyebrows and extracted my hand from his. 'Can I get you anything, Walter?'

'What's the matter, are you a prude? Don't like hearing about such things?'

'It's none of my business what they do with their lives,' I said.

'And none of mine either, you think.'

I didn't say anything. Walter could be charming, and I had no doubt he loved his wife and younger children, but this was a side of him that made me cringe. I began to feel sorry for Sebastian and Anna. And Jeff.

'Off you go then, Hester Rose. Get some sleep. I'll be all right now.'

I lay in bed thinking about the man I was working for. A control freak. A man of power. Or had been. He wasn't painting a very pleasant picture of himself, and I wondered if it was some sort of test: Would I still be nice to him if he revealed his true colours? But why would he do that? What would it prove, except that he could still command a situation? Maybe in the end, that's what it was all about for him. It was all a game, and I was just another person to be manipulated. He didn't know any secrets about me, but he was paying me well for my time which, in its way, was just as binding.

Or did he just like to see people squirm?

In the morning the girls took Milly for a walk and Jeanette sat with Walter for a while. I put on the washing then hung it out, got lunch ready, did some ironing. Gladys Jenkins vacuumed and mopped, swept around the house hunting down dust to get rid of and cushions that needing plumping.

Jeanette was subdued when she came into the kitchen.

'He's asleep again. He sleeps more and more. And one day soon he'll sleep and he won't wake up.'

She sat down and burst into tears, head in hands.

Milly came bounding in and shoved her head into Jeanette's lap. The girls followed and when they saw Jeanette, their smiles faded.

'Is Dad...?'

'He's sleeping,' I said.

'Oh, thank God. I thought he'd gone,' said Ellen. She went across the hall to look in on her father. Grace sat beside her mother and took her hand. Soon she was in tears too and when Ellen came back, she joined in.

Eventually, Jeanette raised her head. The girls wiped their eyes, blew their noses and left: Grace to do some homework; Ellen to have a shower.

'It just comes over me. I can't imagine life without him,' said Jeanette. 'I mean, I know I'll survive but it won't be the same. He can be such a curmudgeon at times but such a loving man too.' She blinked more tears away. 'He always told me he'd live until he was ninety and although I knew there were no guarantees, I wanted to believe him. I feel cheated.'

'It's such a difficult time,' I said, knowing how inadequate it was.

But Jeanette took my hand. 'I knew you'd understand,' she said. 'I don't know what I'd do without you here.'

I had only been there a few days and done so little, but I was at least a presence, and someone who had seen death before. What she seemed to want was a guide and I would do my best.

'Shall we go and see how he is?' I asked after we'd had a cup of tea.

She nodded, and kept hold of my hand as we crossed the hall and sat ourselves down by Walter's bed. He stirred, his eyes opened, and he smiled. But then he closed them and sighed. Soon his breath settled into a steady rhythm, and he was asleep again.

'Is there anything you want to do or say to him in the next few days? It's important for both of you to take the opportunities you have.'

She bit her lip and closed her eyes for a second. 'There's always more to say, isn't there? But all the important things have been said.'

I thought for a moment, trying to decide whether to say what was on my mind. In the end, I went ahead. 'Jeanette, he's a stubborn man and he's really trying to hang on for you and the girls–'

'He's always wanted things his way, even now.'

'Which, of course, is natural – leopards don't change their spots, after all. I'm just wondering if it may be necessary at some stage in the not too distant future for you to give him permission to go.'

She gasped as if I'd just slapped her. 'I couldn't do that. Never.'

'Okay. I shouldn't have said anything. It's a personal thing.'

She stared at me, wide-eyed. 'Some people do that, do they?'

'Some, yes. Not all.'

'Am I being selfish?'

'Not at all.'

She looked at Walter, who was snoring gently. 'We all think we're immortal, don't we?'

When Greta from the palliative care team arrived to see how he was, she woke Walter gently and he smiled at her.

'I've got myself a doula,' he said, nodding his head in my direction. 'Hester Rose.'

'Pleased to meet you, Hester,' she said. She was a diminutive woman with long hair in a French braid. Hardly the Russian shot putter Walter had described.

'I'll go,' said Jeanette and she got up.

'No, stay. It's all right. I wanted to talk to both of you anyway. Cassie wrote in the notes that you might want to discuss a hospice?'

Jeanette gasped and looked at her husband.

Walter shook his head. 'That was last week, before I got myself a doula,' he said. 'Sorry, darling, I should have told you, but I didn't want to upset you. Anyway, it's off the agenda now.'

Jeanette took his hand. 'You're staying right here, with me.'

Greta asked if we might have a word and we went into the kitchen.

'He's worsened since I last saw him, and he's been using more pain relief. Have you talked to him about what he wants, at the end?'

'He has certain ideas.' It wouldn't do to be more specific. I knew Greta had to keep notes and I didn't want Walter's request documented. 'I've encouraged Jeanette to talk to him too, but she's not ready.'

'She's quite fragile, isn't she? I think it's great you're here. He hasn't got much longer.'

'Yesterday was a big day – the family gathered for lunch. He was exhausted by the end, which didn't help. But he has gone downhill fast in the last couple of days.'

'It's the nature of the disease, unfortunately. Better prepare the family as best we can.'

'I'll talk to them. Ellen's home this weekend so they're all here.'

She nodded.

I didn't have an opportunity to talk to the Baxter women immediately. Instead, Walter called me in and asked me to do something for him that he wanted kept from the family.

'Is it really time for secrets?' I asked.

'For this one, yes,' he said. 'I want to change my will, but I don't want to use my usual solicitor. He'd try and talk me out of it. I suppose I'll also have to have a shrink declare me of sound mind and rotting body.' He coughed, took some time to settle his breath again. 'I want you to find me the people I need and invite them to the house. You'll have to get them here when Jeanette's out. She has a pottery class in town on Tuesday mornings and a voluntary stint with the hospital library on Wednesday afternoon. Those would be good times.'

'Are you sure about this, Walter?'

'Absolutely. And I'll need you and Cassie to be witnesses.'

Add personal assistant to my job description, I thought.

I wanted to say no. It didn't feel right for Walter to be making decisions like this so close to the end. And yet, who was I to say what was right and what was wrong? I had no idea what was in his will and what changes he might want to make. I drew in a deep breath.

'All right. I'll do what I can.'

'That's my girl,' said Walter, and if I'd been closer, I think he would have patted my hand.

After lunch Ellen and Grace sat with him. He dozed and they chatted and played cards. I got my laptop out and started looking up local solicitors and private psychiatrists to call first thing in the morning. Time was short and although I had an uncomfortable feeling about this change of will, it wasn't up to me to go against Walter's wishes. All I hoped was that he hadn't suddenly decided to leave all his money to a home for injured badgers instead of the family.

I wondered what it would be like to have money to leave, or to be on the receiving end of an inheritance. I would certainly never have got any money from my parents even if they hadn't cast me out. They were as poor as the proverbial, and quite apt, church mice. They owned nothing except their clothes and the family Bible. I wondered what had happened to that Bible. I didn't want it, filled with make-believe as it was, but still I wondered. I hoped it had rotted into the African soil where it could do no more harm.

I used to write letters to my sister. I never got a response. Even before I heard they'd all been killed, I suspected my letters were intercepted by my father. I carried on after I knew she was dead. It felt like an act of defiance – not admitting she was gone. And I needed someone out there when my world was caving in. I would tell her about my new life and how much I missed her and Caleb. I almost had myself believing she was still there, going about her everyday life. In one of the letters I had asked if our parents ever mentioned me. But even if they were still there, living in the jungle, saving souls, why should they? I was their biggest failure: a daughter who fell in love with the wrong boy. They hadn't known they had a grandson. I had been afraid they would come and claim him, although it was probably paranoia on my part – they wouldn't have wanted a "half-caste" in the family, a constant reminder of the shame I had brought them. Still, I changed my name from Sarah Penrose to Hester Rose, just in case.

Thinking of Justin, I remembered his text from the day before. I grabbed my phone and replied.

> Love to see you, but doing a live-in at the mo and not sure how long it will go. How are you? Miss you, xxxx

I sat on my bed and thought of my beautiful son. He'd had a tough time at school, bullied because he was different: not white, not black, teenage mother and no father. It used to tear me apart. If I'd brought him up in London, a cosmopolitan city with its transient population and tolerance for difference, things might have been different. But I had gone to London from my grandparents' house when I discovered I was pregnant and knew I would no longer be welcome there. The city had terrified me. The buildings were so tall and close together, there were too many people moving too fast, the noise was an unbearable mix of traffic and music blaring out of shops, people shouting to be heard over road works, aeroplanes flying overhead. In my African village the air was filled with birdsong, insects, laughter, singing, a machete on wood, the pounding of grain in deep stone bowls. So I had left and sought somewhere smaller, more manageable. The destination decided by the distance I could travel with the money I had in my pocket, stolen from my grandfather's wallet. I'd ended up in Eastbourne.

In spite of the bullying, Justin grew up to be a caring boy, always ready to stand up for the underdog. He'd never got into any trouble, although he was no saint. In his teens there'd been some drinking and pot smoking, but nothing that ever felt like it would get out of hand. I knew I'd been lucky. Some of his friends had been seduced by drugs or had tried their hand at petty crime: bored teenagers needing to flex their muscles in small-town England, where the best they could hope for on a

Saturday night was a few pints and a kebab from the caravan in a lay-by on the main road. They'd all left eventually, like Justin. They needed space and a challenge. They came home from time to time to see family but were restless, as if afraid they would be asked to stay. I felt it in Justin, and I heard about it from friends: the mothers who had stood on the sidelines at football, who had manned the stalls at school fetes, who had shared their affairs and divorces, their parent's illnesses and deaths.

Right from the start I loved those people and the town. It felt safe. Somewhere that had all I needed and where I could bring up Jusu's son. A new name, a new place, a new start.

My phone pinged. A reply from Justin.

> All okay here. Flexible for visit. Hope all good with you xx

I smiled. My gorgeous boy.

Tempting though it was to stay in my room, I had to talk to the Baxter women. So I splashed some water on my face, pulled a comb through my disastrous hair (it badly needed a cut), and went in search of them.

Ellen was carrying a laundry basket and heading into the garden. I followed to help her bring in the washing.

'Thanks,' she said, putting the basket down.

'No problem,' I said. We worked in silence for a few moments.

'I've decided not to go back to uni tomorrow,' she said. 'I want to be here, with Dad and Mum and Grace. It's not going to be long now, is it?'

'A few days, I should think,' I said.

'What will it be like – will he be in pain?'

'No. Cassie will see to that.'

She paused, mangling a pillowcase in her hands. 'I always imagined him walking me up the aisle on my wedding day.' She looked over to the church spire rising above the treetops. 'He'd make me slow down so everyone had longer to gawk at my amazing dress. And then he'd make a terrible speech at the reception – it would be far too long and full of jokes that weren't funny and stories about me growing up that were meant to embarrass me. Who's going to do that now?'

I took the pillowcase from her and put it in the basket.

'Let's sit for a while, shall we?'

I led her to the bench, and we sat watching the sheets flap lazily in the breeze.

'I don't suppose I should be thinking about things as trivial as getting married when my dad's dying.' She shrugged, sniffed.

I was about to respond when she carried on. 'And I wanted to make him proud. He wasn't keen on me going to uni, but I was going to make him glad he'd changed his mind. And now it's all turned to shit.' She clenched her teeth together and narrowed her eyes, still gazing towards the village.

'In what way?'

She turned to me. 'Promise you won't tell Mum?'

Not another secret. This family had more things hidden from each other than a room full of politicians.

Ellen bit her lip and looked down at her hands. 'I did okay in first year. Quite well, in fact. I was thinking of switching to physiotherapy – I'm doing exercise physiology at the moment. Anyway, when Dad got diagnosed nothing seemed to matter anymore. I started missing lectures and tutorials, handed in work late when I bothered doing it at all.' She looked up. 'The fact is, I'm going to fail this term and I can't tell Mum – she'll be so disappointed.'

I thought about it for a moment. 'I think she'll understand.

She's got her own stuff going on. It's difficult to keep life in perspective when someone you love is dying. It's an incredibly emotional time for you all and everything sort of goes haywire. Priorities shift, don't they?'

Ellen sniffed. 'That's exactly how it feels. I wake up sometimes and can't be bothered doing anything. It's like there's no point if we're all going to die in the end anyway.'

'And yet we carry on. You do get up, you see your friends, you talk to your father, you hug your mother. It might feel like it's all happening in a bubble or you're removed from it all, but you do keep going.'

She closed her eyes, fighting back the tears glistening on her eyelashes and then she launched herself into my arms and sobbed. 'Tell me I'll feel okay again one day,' she said between shuddering breaths.

'You will. But there's a lot of sadness to get through before then. Let yourself feel it, it's better that way.'

'I don't want to cry in front of Dad.'

'It's okay, you know. He might cry with you. He's sad too. Letting go is very hard.'

She sat up again, wiped her eyes. 'I don't know how you do this – being with people who are dying all the time. And their families crying all over you.' She managed a weak smile.

I looked up at the puffy white clouds scudding across the sky. 'Death's a natural part of life. In the old days, people gathered to mourn but there were rituals to help, and it was a community thing rather than something to be done in private, behind closed doors.' I paused, not sure she was listening, but she nodded at me to continue. 'There was always a celebration of life too – acknowledgement of the contribution of the person who had died, and a grand send off to the life to come. Cultures all over the world have their own ways of doing things. But here in the West we've lost some of that. Death and sex, the big taboos.'

'I've never been to a funeral, but friends whose grandparents have died say they're very sombre affairs. Dad would hate that. He's always said he wants a party when he dies, and he'd like to be there too!'

'Well, you can invent your own way of doing things, do what you want, how you want. Make it up or borrow from the old ways.'

She lifted her head and looked me in the eye. 'And Dad can be part of planning it, can't he? He can help us decide what to do.'

'Absolutely. Great idea.'

Ellen slumped again. 'I just can't imagine talking to him about his own death.' She took a deep breath then let it out slowly. 'And yet it feels right.' She smiled, properly this time. 'Thank you, Hester. You'll help, won't you?'

'Whatever you want, I'm here.'

That evening, after Jeanette and the girls had had their dinner with Walter and we'd settled him for the night, we gathered round the kitchen table. A cooler wind had picked up in the afternoon, driving the warm temperatures away, but the kitchen was cosy with the Aga throwing out its constant heat.

Ellen's eyes were red, but she sat with an air of purpose.

'Hester and I were talking this afternoon.' She glanced at me. 'We think it's a good idea to talk to Dad about what he wants.'

Jeanette's face went white and she clasped her hands together in front of her. Grace stopped stroking Milly who'd snuck in and was sitting under the table.

'You mean, like for his funeral?' she asked.

Ellen looked at me again as if doing so gave her the strength she needed to carry on. I raised my eyebrows and gave a little nod of encouragement.

'And before,' she said.

I felt all eyes turn to me.

'I know it's not easy, knowing where to start,' I said.

'But it's about having a ritual, a sort of pathway to follow so we know where we're going,' Ellen finished.

'I couldn't have put it better myself,' I said, and she nodded her acknowledgement.

'So?' She looked from her mother to her sister. 'What do you think? We all have to agree, or it won't work.'

'I don't really know what you're getting at,' said Grace. 'I mean, what sort of things can we do?'

'Wait a moment,' said Ellen and she ran out the door and thundered up the stairs.

Jeanette still hadn't said anything.

'Are you okay?' I asked.

'I'm not sure,' she said, swallowing hard. 'I feel like I'm wading through treacle, every step is harder than the last and I can't see the end, yet I know it's near.' She closed her eyes, took a deep breath.

Ellen came back in and put a folder down on the table.

'Here's some info I've googled about different rituals from around the world, just to give us some ideas, but we can do whatever we want.'

I looked at Jeanette who was gazing out the window at the setting sun. Grace started reading through some of the research Ellen had printed off.

'Jewish people sit in the house for a week after someone dies and all their family and friends visit and talk about the person who died. Oh gosh, and in some places, people have an open casket in the house and people can come and say goodbye. I don't like the idea of that.'

Jeanette started rocking backwards and forwards on her chair, clutching herself around the waist. No sound escaped her lips, but tears fell down her cheeks.

Ellen gathered up her papers and tapped Grace on the shoulder, lifting her chin to indicate that they should leave.

Jeanette and I sat in silence for a few minutes.

'She's so grown up,' she said finally.

'She's a lovely young woman.'

'She is. And I know she needs her road map. And I think it's a good idea too, I just can't do it. I can't imagine the next few days. Sometimes I lie in bed in the morning and pretend everything's all right – that Walter's gone to work, the girls are still asleep. It's the best time of my day. Then reality seeps back in and my body turns to lead and my mind recoils from the truth. I want to scream and tear the sheets, rage at the unfairness of it all. But Ellen likes to plan.'

'Everyone has different needs.'

'But you think she's right. You said we should talk about what we want, how we want to say goodbye.' She looked at her hands. 'I feel like you're all ganging up on me.'

I took a few breaths. 'That isn't the intention. Ellen was floundering and I just told her about the way things are done in other places. She wants something to hold on to, while you need to let things take their course. I'm not judging you.'

'But you told her it's so much better in little villages in Africa where everyone dances and sings and lets it all hang out, I suppose. In your idyllic past with your idyllic fucking rituals and your perfect fucking family!' She spat the last words at me, pushed her chair back and ran out of the room.

I'm used to being the target of people's anger when they can't take it out on the person it's really aimed at, whoever it might be. But still my heart beat faster and I took a few deep breaths to calm myself. I know I'm far from perfect, and sometimes I get things really wrong. Timing is important, too. But sometimes there isn't enough time to take time.

I sat and thought about my perfect family. My perfectly dead family. Now it was me, Justin and Peggy. A family by choice rather than just blood. My heart clenched when I remembered it might soon be diminished by a third. I looked at my watch and decided to call the hospital.

The night nurse on her ward told me Peggy was doing well and was brighter than she had been the day before. I thanked her and went to bed, relief flooding my tired limbs and allowing me to sit awhile, thinking about families and wondering what the next day would bring for all of us.

WALTER

I heard Jeanette shouting. That's rare.

And swearing. Even rarer.

Probably about me. What else would it be?

I am the focus of all that goes on in this house now.

Wasn't always. Felt sidelined when the girls were small. Jeanette was such a good mother, so capable. So loving. Forgot me for a while.

But not forever.

I thought I saw Dorothy at the end of the bed. It scared me. Come to get me, I thought. But I'm not ready to go. And I don't want to go with her anyway.

In India the wives used to die with their husbands. Throw themselves on the funeral pyre. Or get thrown on by family. Cheaper than looking after a widow. Jeanette needn't worry. There's money for her. But it would be nice to have her with me.

Bollocks. I don't believe in all the crap about happily ever afters in the afterlife.

Shit, now I'm crying. Even my eyes are letting me down, leaking all over the place.

No control over anything. Pissed myself yesterday.

Hester Rose cleaned me up. Very business-like. But gentle.

Life without dignity. I never thought I'd see the day. Hoped I wouldn't.

So tired. Just have to see a solicitor. Rouse myself enough for that.

There's a dead weight on my chest, pushing me down.

It may be fear.

FIVE

It started raining during the night and the wind picked up. I was already awake when I heard Walter calling for me through the monitor. His voice sounded weak.

'Another nightmare?' I asked as I entered his room.

''Fraid so.' He clutched the sheet in one hand, his legs were restless under the blankets.

'Any pain?' I asked.

'No worse than usual. Unless you count the mental anguish. God, I hate this.'

'I'll get you some water,' I said, and lifted his head while he took a few sips.

He fell back against the pillows, his breath short.

'No candles,' he wheezed. 'At my funeral.'

'No candles. Okay. Too religious for you?'

'Yes. And no sad faces.'

'I'm not sure you can control that, but I'll pass the message on,' I said.

He smiled, the nightmare receding. His breath began to settle too. 'They'll be okay. But you promise to stay the two weeks after, to see them through.'

'Of course, whatever you want.'

He closed his eyes and within minutes, he was asleep. I watched for a while. He looked peaceful.

When I got up in the morning Jeanette was already in the kitchen making coffee.

'I'm sorry about last night.' She didn't look at me.

'No need to be.'

'No, I was rude. Even at a time like this it's important to be civil, isn't it? To be as normal as possible. And you're trying to help, I know that. And you are.'

I gave a small smile and changed the subject.

'Walter had another nightmare last night but settled quite quickly again.'

'I looked in on him just now. He's dozing. I was going to make him some scrambled eggs. He loves my scrambled eggs.'

'Good idea.'

While she tried to persuade him to eat, I made toast for us. She came back in with most of the eggs still on the plate.

'Three mouthfuls. Better than nothing,' she said as she scraped the leftovers into Milly's bowl. 'She'll get fat if I keep giving her Walter's meals.'

Milly didn't care about her waistline. She wolfed the eggs down and looked up for more, hope written all over her face.

'He said no candles,' she said.

'He mentioned that to me during the night too. And no sad faces. I said we could probably comply with the candle ban, but the sad faces might be more difficult.'

Jeanette laughed. 'A control freak to the end.'

'Can't change the habits of a lifetime,' I said.

'He's not a religious man. In fact, he's quite anti-religion. He'd probably prefer not to even have a funeral.'

I hesitated, not wanting to upset her again but in the end, felt I had to tell her the facts. 'He doesn't have to. There's no law saying there has to be any service of any kind. Not that funeral directors would tell you that.'

Jeanette put her cup down slowly and looked at me. 'So what would we do instead?'

And just like that, we were talking about what Walter and his immediate family might want.

'Under English law, there doesn't have to be a funeral. Walter can be buried where he likes, within reason – there are rules about proximity to waterways and things like that, but it doesn't have to be a churchyard. It could be in the garden, if you like.'

'I didn't know that. I suppose I've never had to think about it.'

Grace scooted in with her school shirt in her hand. 'I'm going to be late. I forgot to iron my shirt last night.'

'Since when have you ironed your own shirts?' asked Jeanette.

'Well, you know...'

'Hand it over. I'll do it,' I said, putting my hand out for it.

'You're officially a gem,' said Grace and threw it to me over the table.

'She's always been the same,' said Jeanette when her daughter had gone. 'Late for everything except meals!'

Shirt ironed, Grace pedalling down the drive, I checked on Walter and then excused myself to go and have a shower. While I was upstairs, I called the solicitor and the psychiatrist I'd identified as the most likely candidates for Walters's request. The only selection criterion was that they were local. If they weren't available, I'd have to work down the list I'd made.

'Johnstone, Heppel and Associates, can I help you?'

I outlined what I needed a solicitor for, and the circumstances.

'It's rather short notice, but I think Mr Johnstone Junior may be able to help you.'

Excellent. One down, one to go.

The receptionist at the psychiatric clinic wasn't quite as accommodating. Apparently, it was most unusual for a psychiatrist to do a home visit. It wasn't until I offered to pay double the normal consultation fee to allow for travel time that she discovered one of the doctors was available.

When I went downstairs, I heard Jeanette's voice as I walked past Walter's door. I continued on to the kitchen.

Ellen was eating breakfast. 'Mum's peeved I haven't gone back to university,' she said. 'I told her I wanted to be with Dad, but she thought it was more important I carry on as normal. I knew she wouldn't like it. Anyway, I'm not going. I was wondering if you'd talk to her if she gets uppity about it? You know, back me up.'

Before I had a chance to answer, she got up, put her cereal bowl in the dishwasher, and called Milly.

'I'll take her for a walk now the rain's stopped and when I get back, I'll have a chat with Dad.' That sounded ominous. I wondered what I'd unleashed in our talk the day before. It appeared she had her father's control genes.

'Walter wants to talk to you,' said Jeanette, coming in just as Ellen and Milly left.

'Okay.'

'I told him what you said about not having to have a funeral.' She didn't look happy.

'Come and sit down,' Walter said as I entered his room.

He was sitting up and although it would be a stretch to say he looked brighter, he did look more alert than he had the past couple of days.

'My wife tells me I don't have to have a funeral, but she doesn't know what the alternatives are. I suspect you do though, don't you, Hester Rose?' His gaze was still sharp as he looked at me.

'Do you want me to ask her to join us?'

'No. No need. Tell me.'

What was it with these people? Why did they find it so hard to be in the same room and share information? The whole family ran on secrets.

'Okay. Well, there are several options. You can donate your body to science, in which case there are no costs to the family, but they also have no grave to visit and that may be an issue.'

'You mean donate my organs?'

'Yes, or your whole body.'

'For medical students to practice on?'

'Yes.'

'No.'

'Okay, then you could have an organic burial, which essentially means no embalming, no coffin and it can be at a place of your choosing – within reason, of course.'

'I could be compost for the vegetables?'

'No. That's illegal. And Jeanette would probably never eat again. But you could choose somewhere in the grounds and perhaps have a tree planted above you.'

'I like that idea.'

'Or you could be cremated. It has to be in a recognised crematorium, but you don't need a religious service with it. The family could bring your ashes back here or scatter them wherever you wish – again, within reason.'

'They couldn't throw me over the wall of Buckingham Palace to fertilise the roses?'

I laughed. 'Not even you would get away with that, no.'

'Thank you, you've given me something to think about.'

'It is important you include Jeanette and the girls in any decision you make. Legally they don't have to follow your request even if you put it in your will.'

'I understand, but I want to have an opinion before I speak to them about it.'

A decision more like, I thought. And then he'd do his best to talk them into it if they didn't agree.

'And the other matter we spoke about?' he asked.

'Which one?'

'Well, both. But I meant the will.'

'Organised for tomorrow morning. I just hope Jeanette goes to her pottery class.'

'Leave it to me,' said Walter and he winked.

For a man who was dying, he was in fine spirits. As long as he had a plan and people to organise, Walter would somehow find the energy to carry on a while longer.

Ellen spent the afternoon with Walter. I suggested to Jeanette that I cook some meals to put in the freezer.

'You mean, for when–' She stopped and took a deep breath.

'Yes. No-one will feel like cooking.'

'Or eating.'

'Perhaps, but better to be prepared, just in case.'

'How do you do this, day in, day out, and remain positive?'

We were sitting at the table, cups of tea in front of us. I stared into mine for a long moment. It had been hard at the beginning. Especially living in with families staring death in the face. It's impossible not to absorb the emotions of others and I was always reminded of my own grief. But I had learned over the years to look after myself, to have time off between doula jobs, to reconnect with the living and nature. To remind myself there is a lot of life to be lived before death.

I took a deep breath. 'I see what I do as being as much about living as it is about dying, I suppose. Plus, Walter isn't my family and although I like him, I have more distance. A distance that, I hope, allows me to see what you and the girls need as well as Walter.'

She sighed. 'Life's shit sometimes, isn't it? I can't see beyond the next few days. There's a total blank where any idea of a future used to be. But I need to be strong for the girls. I won't be much good to them if I fall apart, will I?'

'I think you'll find they'll each deal with Walter's death in their own way and they won't expect you to look after them. You'll support each other, and Walter's asked me to stay for as long as you want me.'

'Let's do some cooking,' she said. Conversation over.

When Grace came in after school it was obvious she'd been crying. Jeanette was sitting with Walter and Ellen was madly googling away in her bedroom.

'Tea? There's cake in the tin.'

'Nothing,' she said, flopping into a chair at the kitchen table.

'Bad day?' I asked.

'The worst.' Her lips trembled.

I sat next to her and put my arm around her. 'Is it your father?'

She nodded and then shook her head. 'Sort of, I feel so mixed up.' She buried her head in her hands and wept.

I rubbed her back but didn't say anything.

Eventually she lifted her head. 'Can we talk? I mean, in private?'

'Of course,' I said. 'Shall we go upstairs?'

We settled ourselves in her room. It was large and messy, the bed unmade. She lay down and I sat beside her.

And sat.

And sat.

Eventually she shifted her position and leant against the pillows. She looked at me as if trying to decide how to begin.

'You know Mr Green, the teacher you were talking to at football?'

'I remember him,' I said.

'Did you like him?'

'I didn't talk to him long enough to find out. He seemed pleasant enough.'

'He's a total shit.' Tears started spilling down her cheeks again but she ignored them. 'He... we... and now...' She looked at me with her big blue eyes. Her face crumpled.

'How long has it been going on?' So, my hunch had been right. Unfortunately.

'Since the beginning of term. He was casting the play and Daddy was ill – I mean, he'd been diagnosed before, but he went downhill around then. Gavin – Mr Green – was so understanding. We talked a lot. He was the only person I could talk to at that time: Mummy had turned into the Valium queen; Ellen was busy at uni; my friends didn't know what to say.'

'And one thing led to another,' I said.

She nodded. 'I love him. I really do.' She sniffed and wiped her eyes but the tears kept falling.

'And now?' I asked.

'He says he feels like he's taking advantage of me at a vulnerable time and what I need is friends to talk to. He mentioned you – I should talk to you, that's what you're here for. And then he said it was too risky for us to keep seeing each other.' She clenched her jaw. 'That's what this is really about. He's afraid we'll be found out and he'll lose his job.' The tears stopped and she took a deep breath. 'He's totally gutless.'

She shredded a tissue and I waited.

'Did you guess?' she asked. 'I mean, when you saw him at football.'

How should I answer her question? If I said yes, she'd ask how, and I'd have to tell her he gave himself away following her round the football pitch with his puppy dog eyes and her hopes would be lifted; such is the power of first love that she would believe she could persuade him to carry on. If I said no, she would use it to prove to him there was no danger.

'I suspected his interest was not just in the game, but I didn't know who he was particularly observing.' I crossed my fingers behind my back. I've always hated lying.

'So–'

'If I guessed he was interested in a student after talking to him for less than five minutes, others are going to have their suspicions too.'

She slumped down the bed again, turning away from me. Her shoulders shook. I put my hand on her back, a reassuring weight.

Suddenly she sat up. 'You're on his side, aren't you?'

I met her gaze. 'I'm not on anyone's side. You think you love him–'

'I do love him! And he loves me, he told me.'

'And he knows what he's doing is wrong. Regardless of how he feels about you.'

'He's only thinking about himself and his stupid job.'

And she, as anyone would in the situation, was only thinking of herself and her feelings.

'Not just a job, his whole career if he's found out.'

'Well, maybe I *should* tell Mrs Lacey. It would serve him right.'

'Don't do anything you might regret. If you love this man as you say you do, you don't want the guilt of ruining his life on your conscience, do you?'

'Why not? He's ruined mine.' She stared at me defiantly. She was magnificent and I could see how a young teacher like Gavin Green would fall for her.

'Take some deep breaths and consider this: your heart is being broken and if he loves you as he says he does, he is hurting too. But you would lose nothing else if you revealed your relationship – you might even be seen as a victim in all this, the poor young woman taken advantage of by an older man. He would lose his future.'

The fight went out of her again.

'If you love each other maybe you can see each other again when you leave school.' I very much doubted it, but stranger things had happened.

'That's ages away. A whole year.'

'But just think how romantic your reunion would be.'

She shrugged. 'I don't think I can bear to see him right now, but I couldn't wait a year.'

'Perhaps he could get an understudy for the play.'

'I was wondering if I should suggest that anyway, seeing how Daddy is.'

I leant over and gave her a hug. 'That would probably be for the best.'

'Thanks for listening,' she said. 'I'm glad someone else knows but you won't tell anyone, will you?'

I had been hoping she wouldn't ask that particular question. I had no idea what to do. Wasn't it illegal for a teacher to have an affair with a pupil? I suspected there were rules about it.

'What about your mother?' I asked. 'Don't you think she should know?'

Grace shook her head. 'Definitely not. Please, Hester, don't tell her. She's upset enough about Daddy. She doesn't need anything else to worry about.'

Part of me had to agree, but I was getting fed up with all the secrets I was meant to be keeping. One day, I was sure, they'd all come pouring out.

WALTER

Funny how planning your own funeral can make you feel positive. Involved. In control again.

Courageous girl, my Ellen. Wasn't easy for her to bring it up. Hester Rose's idea probably. The death expert. Except she isn't because she hasn't been there. Grief expert. She's certainly been there.

Reminds me of my sister, Cynthia. No nonsense. Practical. Big heart.

When did I last see Cynthia? Forty years ago? Fifty? And Ma – Jeanette met her once before she died.

Who's left? Cynthia? Davey? Mikey? Susan? Maisy? Christopher?

Seven of us. Tough little scraps. Had to be.

Mikey in prison as soon as he was old enough to graduate from Borstal.

Davey on the drink.

Both of them shooting crap into their arms.

I don't know what happened to the girls. Ma never said after they got married.

I never asked.

Ma dead.

Don't even know who's alive and who's gone. How would I find out?

Why bother? It's too late.

Dorothy was back again. She won't leave me alone. Large as life and twice as annoying. I turned away but I knew she was still there.

Is there a day of reckoning? Is that what she's here for? Does she want an apology? An explanation? She's not getting either. I did what I did and there's the end to it.

I dreamed I was well. That was cruel.

SIX

When I went down to Walter in the middle of the night, Ellen was already there. He was trying to tell her something, but he was short of breath and couldn't get the words out.

'Walter, let's get you settled first and then you can tell us what you want, okay?' I said.

He squeezed his eyes tight shut and nodded.

'Are you in pain?'

He nodded again.

'Ellen, can you get some morphine for him? Have you given it before?'

She nodded and measured out a dose.

'Here we go, Walter,' I said as I sat him up a bit.

Ellen supported his head and held the small plastic cup to his lips. He looked into her eyes as he swallowed, and she smiled at him.

'That's better, isn't it, Dad?' Then she turned to me. 'How long does it take to work?'

'It's pretty quick. He should be feeling the effects in a few minutes.'

Soon Walter's breathing settled.

'I'll stay with him if you want to go back to bed,' said Ellen, and I agreed having been up the previous two nights and not managing to nap during the day. As I left, Ellen put the radio on quietly, tuned to a classical music station.

In the morning, I looked in to find Ellen asleep in the chair next to Walter, her head near his on the bed. I shook her awake gently and as she opened her eyes, put a finger to my lips. No point in disturbing her father who was sleeping peacefully. I thought he was looking more jaundiced and was glad Cassie would be in later.

'How was he?' I asked.

'All right. We listened to the radio for a few minutes and then he fell asleep again.'

She went off to bed to try and get more sleep and I went to start breakfast. Grace came in, her eyes puffy and red.

'How did you sleep?' I asked.

'I didn't. My mind kept going round in circles.'

'When I was your age, my parents found out I was seeing a local boy. We loved each other but they were furious, and we were both sent away. That's when I came here, to England. I was distraught. For a long time I thought I'd never be happy again, but one day I realised I hadn't cried in a while. And another day I heard myself laughing at something someone said. Slowly I began to feel more like myself again. Life looked brighter and I started making use of the opportunities that came my way.'

'Not going to happen.' Tears started brimming in her eyes again. 'No-one understands, not even you.'

I shrugged and turned back to the toaster. No use arguing.

'Did you ever see him again?' she asked in a small voice.

'No. I haven't been back to Sierra Leone since I left. I don't know what happened to him.' I couldn't tell her I thought he was dead.

'So did you fall in love with someone else?'

'There have been one or two others.' I smiled. I wasn't about to tell her the only other man I'd ever loved was my son. He had become my whole life, and I hadn't missed having anyone else while he was still at home.

'Do you have someone now?'

'No,' I said. 'Not at the moment.' I shook my head and turned away from her so she didn't see me clutching my stomach. At times the pain of loneliness was visceral and left me gasping for breath.

When Justin left for university, I'd tried dating. The men I met were all older than me, some quite a bit older, and mostly looking for sex without commitment. I was looking for companionship. The sex was nice, sometimes, but I wanted more than just a physical relationship. In the end I had decided it was easier to live without anyone than be disappointed in the men I met. I had girlfriends to go out with and Peggy to stay in with. As she got older and needed more help, I did her shopping and cooking. We ate together most nights. And then she went into the nursing home and I couldn't bear the idea of someone else living in her flat, so I moved. I didn't know anyone in the new building and became quite isolated for a while. Perhaps depressed. And then I decided, with Peggy's help, that I could feel sorry for myself or get out there and live my life. She'd always been good at giving me a kick up the bum when she thought I needed it, and I was good at recognising she was right. Resilience, some people call it. Survival, I say.

'You'll be okay, Grace. It may not feel like it right now, but you will survive to love another day.'

She sniffed. 'Says the all-knowing Hester.' She took a piece of toast off the plate and left. I stared after her. I probably deserved that.

'I'm not going to go to my pottery class this morning. I need to spend some time with Walter.' Jeanette took a sip of her coffee, and I tried not to look alarmed.

'Cassie will be in some time before lunch,' I said, 'and Walter seems to be more alert in the afternoons these days. Why don't you go to your class and spend some time with him later?'

'I can do both. If he's dozing, I can sit reading. I just want to be near him.' She took the rest of her coffee across the hall to his room.

Why did she have to choose that day of all days to feel strong enough to be able to spend time with him?

I could only hope Walter's plan to get her out of the house would work. Although perhaps it wouldn't matter if she was here, unless he really was planning to leave all his wealth to a badger sanctuary.

She came back moments later wiping her eyes.

'He told me I have to go to my class because he wants me to make an urn for his ashes. Ellen thought it would be a good idea, apparently, and she's going to come too. I feel like they're closing ranks. They've always been close.' She stood in the middle of the kitchen as if she couldn't decide which direction to move in and finally left again without another word.

Walter could certainly be an insensitive old codger at times. She might have been okay with the idea if he'd given her more time to get used to it, but this had come out of the blue and sounded more like an order than a request, judging by Jeanette's response. I felt sorry for her, but I also had to applaud his ingenuity. Asking her to do something for him was probably the only way to guarantee she'd go to her class.

Ellen rushed in and poured herself a coffee. 'Is Mum all right? Did Dad tell her our idea?'

'He certainly did. I think she'll be okay as long as you're there.'

'I'm keen. And I've booked us massages for after – well, Dad suggested it. It'll be good for Mum – she needs to relax a bit.'

Don't we all, I thought, but said, 'Sounds lovely.'

They had only just left – a bit late – when Dr Bailey arrived. I opened the front door and watched her get out of her car. She was younger than I'd expected, or maybe I'd got to the age when policemen look twelve and professional men and women look like teenagers.

'Mrs Baxter?' she asked, proffering a hand for shaking.

'No, I'm Hester Rose, the help.'

She looked past me at Mrs Jenkins who was polishing the bannisters and I saw her eyebrows rise. 'I see,' she said and withdrew her hand.

'This way,' I said, leading her into Walter's room. 'I suppose the receptionist explained what was required?'

'I'm to assess the patient to determine if he's in sound mind in order to make a will.'

'Correct. He's not at all well, but he is quite compos mentis.'

'Let me be the judge of that, will you?'

Supercilious cow.

'Of course.' I turned to the sleeping Walter and put a hand on his shoulder, feeling the hardness of his unpadded bones. 'Walter, Dr Bailey's here.'

He opened his eyes, the whites of which were now quite

yellow. 'Doctor,' he said, 'thank you for coming. Hester Rose, why don't you get us some tea?'

Dr Bailey declined the offer, but Walter insisted. He didn't want me to witness this inquisition. I left but didn't make tea: Walter wouldn't have drunk it, and I didn't much like Dr Bailey.

Minutes later, she entered the kitchen with a piece of paper in her hand. 'This is all you need. He's quite capable of rational thought. Give this to the solicitor.'

I almost felt like I should salute. Instead, I said, 'I'll show you out,' and got rid of her.

I was just giving Walter a bit of a tidy up when another car drove up.

Mr Johnstone Junior was a tall, lanky man in his mid to late forties. Kind eyes, dark floppy hair, a wide smile and dimples.

'Lovely day,' he said by way of greeting, and made a broad gesture encompassing the sky and gardens, the house and the village in the distance.

'Indeed,' I said, returning his smile. He was one of those people. You couldn't help but warm to him.

'I'll take you in to meet Walter. Mr Armstrong. Will you have some tea or coffee?'

'Coffee would be marvellous. Milk, no sugar. Thanks.'

I made the introductions and went to make the coffee, cut a large piece of banana cake and took it in on a tray. Mr Johnstone's eyes widened, and his ready smile lit up his face. Perhaps he hadn't had breakfast.

I left them to it. It was no business of mine what Walter did with his money. When Cassie arrived, we sat in the kitchen. I told her what had been happening since she'd last been: Walter's need for extra morphine, his jaundice, the nightmares. She asked about the family lunch.

'It was awful,' I said. 'I caught Anna stealing tranquilisers from

Jeanette's bedroom, and Sebastian – well, he's in a class of his own as far as unpleasantness is concerned. Neither of them had a kind word for anyone. And they treat Jeanette and the girls like servants. Worse than servants; unworthy of their attention. I can't think why Walter didn't drown them at birth, they're ghastly people.'

'Poor Jeanette. I bet she didn't expect that when she married into the family.'

'She'd have run a mile if she'd known what they were like, I'm sure. Or made Walter promise to live with her in Outer Mongolia.'

Cassie laughed. 'Well, she won't have to have anything to do with them after Walter dies.'

'That's the silver lining.'

We were on our second cup of coffee when Mr Johnstone came in.

'Ladies, would you be so good as to come and witness the signatures?'

'That was quick,' I said.

'Walter was very clear about what he wanted and it's all very straightforward. My kind of client.' He smiled and I felt myself blush.

After we'd done what was required of us, Cassie stayed to attend to Walter while I showed Mr Johnstone out.

'Please, call me Mark,' he said.

'And I'm Hester.'

'Hester. What a lovely name. Unusual.'

I blushed again like a thirteen-year-old. Fortunately, Mark didn't seem to notice.

'I'll see you again, Hester. Walter wants me to be his executor. He wants you to call me the day he dies. There is a document he wants opened then, and I'll come again to read the will. I understand you're staying on after his death?'

'Yes, for a while at least. He wants me to make sure his wife and daughters are okay.'

'I'm sure Mrs Armstrong will appreciate your support.'

'Mrs Baxter. Jeanette and the girls are all Baxters. Her small gesture towards feminism.'

He smiled and nodded. 'We'd better swap mobile numbers then. It'll be easier than using the home phone.'

My heart skipped a beat. How long had it been since an attractive man asked for my number? Get a grip, I reminded myself. This is strictly professional.

I leant against the door jamb and watched him drive off in his sensible family car, wondering if there was a Mrs Johnstone Junior and happy little Junior Johnstone Juniors. I couldn't imagine someone like him being single. The good ones never were.

Sighing, I went to join Cassie and Walter.

His breath was short. The morning's activities had obviously taken their toll. Cassie changed his fentanyl patch and he was asleep almost before we left the room.

'Not long now, I think. All his vital signs are worse and he's more jaundiced because his liver's packing up. This time last week I would have said he had a month. Now, it's more likely days.'

'I thought so. We've been talking about his wishes.'

'Good. Is Jeanette on board with it all?'

'That's the problem – even now he wants to make all the decisions and assumes she'll agree. He asked her to make him an urn at her pottery class today. She was distraught. He's keeping her busy and involved but not in any useful way. And you know this change of will is all a big secret? I hate it. It makes me feel disloyal to Jeanette, but Walter's my employer–'

'He is a forceful man, even now, isn't he? Anyway, sounds

like you're going to have your hands full in the next few days. Call me if you need more back-up.'

'We'll see how we go.'

When Jeanette and Ellen returned, relaxed after their massages, they spent the afternoon with Walter. I tidied, did some laundry and walked Milly. She must have been one of the most hopeful creatures I'd ever met. She'd chase anything that moved, never losing her boundless joy despite never achieving her goal. Unless for her the whole point was the running, her ears flapping, paws barely touching the ground. And perhaps hers was the better way to live life: completely in the moment, unaware and unconcerned about anything but now. For those of us who could imagine a future, all too often it proved inaccurate. Like Peggy.

She'd once told me that since her son had thrown her out, she'd started each day with a wish for how it might go. Nothing as firm as a plan but more detailed than a vague hope. That way she was rarely disappointed.

I called the hospital and was finally allowed to speak to her.

'Peggy, how are you?'

'Here to fight another day, love, but they want to keep me in for another day or two.'

'I've been thinking about you.'

'I know, love. The nurses told me you'd been ringing.'

'I just wanted to say thank you.'

'Now you're frightening me. Am I dying? Have they told you something they haven't told me?'

I laughed. 'No. It's just this family I'm with at the moment – they never tell each other what they really feel, you know? We've always been honest with each other, and I've been realising how much I appreciate that. And your sage advice over the years.'

'You're welcome, love. You're very special, never forget it.'

We finished the call, and I went down to start preparing dinner, singing the Monty Python song, 'Always Look on the Bright Side of Life' to myself. Peggy and I had sung it often when we needed to remind ourselves we didn't really have it so bad, not compared to refugees or drug addicts. Or someone about to be nailed to a cross.

I hadn't heard a car approach, so I was surprised to hear the back door open. And even more surprised to find Sebastian marching into the kitchen. I tried to muster a smile.

'I wanted to talk to you,' he said without preamble.

'Well, here I am.' I didn't offer him a drink.

He looked around and again I got the impression of someone checking on his possessions. I felt immediately protective of Jeanette and the girls.

'It's about my father.'

I nodded. What else would it be about?

'I think he's up to something.'

He looked at me, his gaze fixed and hard, his lips curled into a sneer.

'He's dying,' I said when I could bear his scrutiny no longer. 'That's what he's up to.'

He laughed. 'Yes, he is. But you don't know him. There's always something going on in that scheming brain of his.'

'Well, if there is, and he wanted you to know about it, he'd have told you, I'm sure.'

He gave me another of his penetrating looks and sighed. 'Oh, well. It was worth a try. He's always up to no good and while there's breath left in him, he'll be plotting. I thought with you being flavour of the month he might have shared it with you. Anyway, how about a drink – I'm parched.'

'I'll put the kettle on,' I said and went to fill it at the sink.

'Okay, I'll have a cup of tea now if you come out for a drink with me later. There's a little place I know not far away – very cosy. Very discreet.'

I must have looked as shocked as I felt because he went on, 'Oh, don't worry. Deborah and I have an understanding. She has her friends, I have mine. It works for both of us.'

I took a deep breath and spoke as calmly as I could. 'I don't care about your domestic arrangements. I'm just dismayed you think I'd want to go out with you.'

He laughed again. 'Oh, Hester. You have no idea how sexy you are when you're on your high horse.'

I wanted to tell him to fuck off and ride his own horse right out of there, but I didn't get the chance. At that moment, Ellen came in.

'Sebastian. What are you doing here?'

'Just came to see the old blighter. How is he?'

Ellen snorted and rolled her eyes. 'Well, you won't find him in the kitchen.'

'The lovely Hester offered me a cup of tea, seeing as you were with him.'

'I'm not with him anymore, so you can go in now,' she said.

He smiled thinly – a twitch of the lips that didn't reach his eyes.

Watching him go, Ellen shuddered. 'That man gives me the creeps.'

'Me too,' I said before I could stop myself.

Ten minutes later we heard the front door slam and the crunch of gravel as Sebastian drove off. Jeanette came into the kitchen and stood, hands on hips, taking deep breaths.

'Calm down, Mum, he's left. Don't let him get to you.'

'That man–' she said, jabbing a finger in the direction he'd gone. 'That man is a psychopath.'

'No argument from me,' said Ellen.

'He just sat at his dying father's bedside and talked about what he was going to do with the company once he's in charge. All I can say is, if he runs the business, we'd all better watch out. We'll be in the poorhouse within a year. Thank God Walter was asleep and didn't have to hear any of his bullshit.'

'Perhaps it was meant for your ears, not Walter's,' I said.

Jeanette looked at me, eyes narrowed. 'How so?'

'He's letting you know he expects to be the boss.'

'But it's a family trust. We all have a say.'

Ellen smiled. 'You reckon Sebastian is planting the idea he'll be taking over. Being the only one suited to the job, in his own mind at least.'

I nodded. 'Something like that.'

'Sneaky git,' she said.

Jeanette sat and I put a cup of tea in front of her. 'I think I'd prefer a gin and tonic. Join me?' she said, looking at Ellen and me.

Ellen nodded.

'I'd better not,' I said, but she ignored me and went to the lounge to get the gin. Then she poured three generous drinks and dropped ice cubes in.

'Cheers,' she said and we clinked glasses.

Grace came in. 'What am I missing?' She looked flushed I wondered whether it was from her cycle home or some other reason. I caught her eye and raised my eyebrows, but she looked away.

Dinner over and Walter settled, we adjourned to the drawing room. I wanted to discuss what to expect in the next few days, but Grace had other ideas. She had brought Cards Against Humanity with her and suggested we all play.

'Just a bit of fun. Daddy wouldn't want us to be gloomy all the time, would he?'

Jeanette hesitated.

'Come on, Mum,' said Ellen. 'Just a quick game. We'll hear if Dad needs us.'

'What do you think, Hester?'

'You don't need my permission, Jeanette.'

'No, but you've been in this situation before and we haven't. I don't know what's acceptable.'

I smiled. 'There are no rules. You have to do what feels right for you. Having a bit of fun is probably a great idea. It certainly can't do any harm.'

Half an hour later, my sides were hurting from all the laughing, matching silly answers to ordinary statements.

'I got ninety-nine problems but ... ain't one of them' elicited the responses, 'I got ninety-nine problems but menstrual rage ain't one of them.' Neither, apparently, was 'tentacle porn', whatever that is, or 'unfathomable stupidity'.

It was a ridiculous game but amusing and light and I hadn't seen Jeanette so involved in anything else before. For a little while she shed her sadness and allowed herself to have some fun.

When the girls had gone – Ellen to sit with her father and Grace to her room – Jeanette and I sat together on the sofa.

'This afternoon he said he wants to be cremated and his ashes buried in the garden, deep enough so Milly doesn't dig him up. He's still got his sense of humour.' Tears gathered in the corners of her eyes and she wiped them away with a tissue.

'Is that okay with you?' I asked.

'Yes, of course. I'll be able to go out and talk to him. But he also said he doesn't want a funeral, just a party for family and close friends.' She fiddled with her bracelet.

'You want something different?'

She frowned. 'I don't know. I've always just assumed people have funerals. I'm not sure everything will be properly finished without one.'

'But he isn't religious. You could have a formal part of the party – speeches, eulogies, invite people to say a few words – whatever you like, really.'

'I suppose so, but without a blessing or a vicar smiling down on everyone it won't feel right.'

'Sit with the idea for a while. See if your feelings about it change. Sometimes new ideas need a bit of time to take shape. And if you still want something different, that'll be the time to talk to Walter again.'

'You're right. Thank you, Hester. Our voice of reason.'

I smiled and hoped Walter would be up for the conversation should it be needed.

Before I went to bed, I checked the back door and found it open. Milly wasn't in her basket so I went out to call for her but there was no sign of her. Opening the gate into the walled garden I was leapt on and almost fell backwards as the dog jumped up, licking whichever part of my body she could get her tongue to, her hot breath moist on my skin.

'Settle, Milly,' I said, pushing her off, trying to make her keep all four paws on the ground. She obeyed, finally, but instead of following me back to the house she trotted off towards the other side of the garden to where what I had thought was a mound of earth revealed itself to be a person lying on the ground.

Milly ran between the body and me.

The night was clear and cold, the moon waning. In the dull light, Grace's features, blotchy and slack, looked grotesque, as if melting off her delicate bones.

Heart in my mouth I knelt down beside her to feel for a pulse, but she groaned suddenly and vomited. I turned her onto her side so she didn't choke, and the foul tang of vomit and alcohol wafted over me.

Oh, Grace, I thought, you little fool. An empty bottle of Dalmore single malt lay on the ground next to her. Jeanette's favourite tipple. I heard Walter's voice in my head. 'Got expensive taste, my wife. The whisky she likes is 300 pounds a bottle.'

'Grace,' I said loud enough for her to turn her unfocused gaze toward the sound. 'It's Hester.'

'Hester,' she slurred. A trail of vomit stretched from her lips to her shoulder. 'S'nice to see you.'

'I need to get you into the house. Do you think you can get up?'

''Course I can,' she said, making no attempt to move.

I sat back on my heels and looked around for something that might help, but there was nothing except a trug by the carrots and a fork leaning against the wall.

'Okay,' I said. 'Here's what we'll do. I want you to bend your knees and roll up onto all fours.'

She giggled. 'Yes, miss,' she said. Nothing happened.

'Right, I'm going to bend your knees and roll you over. One, two, three!'

I got her onto her hands and knees with some effort and held her there while I got my breath back. She wasn't heavy, but she wasn't helping either. Her body was limp, her long limbs uncoordinated. She vomited again, which was good. The more she could get out of her system the better. And then she started crying.

'I love him I just want to be with him it's not fair he's the one I know he is there's no-one else for me...' Her voice tailed off into sobs and her body slumped against mine.

'Grace!' I said sharply. 'Lift your head and shut your mouth. I need to get you to the house and into bed, and I'm guessing you'd rather your mother didn't see you like this. *I'd* certainly rather your mother didn't have to see you like this. You're going to have to help me. I'm going to put my hands under your arms and on the count of three, you're going to get up onto your feet. One, two, three.'

Between us we managed to get her upright, but she was still kneeling.

'You have to stand up, Grace, help me here.'

'I am standing,' she said, wide-eyed as she reeled unsteadily.

I had visions of carrying her in a fireman's lift and her vomiting down my back as I struggled under the weight and length of her, but she lost her balance and plonked down onto the ground again and took me with her. So there we were, sitting in the garden with midnight approaching and no way of transporting her into the house.

And then it started raining. Not heavily; a light, spring drizzle. She lifted her face to the sky and opened her mouth.

Somehow, I managed to get her to the house. A mixture of dragging her and supporting her with strength I didn't know I had.

She closed her eyes and screwed up her face against the light as we went inside, and I flopped her down onto a kitchen chair. Milly ran around her feet and jumped up to put her paws on her thighs, but Grace didn't respond. I made her drink several glasses of water and held a bucket while she threw up again and again. After half an hour she was able to hold her head up and focus her gaze.

'I'm sorry,' she said. 'I'm so sorry.'

'It's not me you have to apologise to,' I said. 'Do you want to talk about why you chose to drink a bottle of whisky?'

'Not a whole bottle. It wasn't full.' She hung her head. 'I went to see Gavin earlier.'

'When you said you were going to do some homework?'

'Yes. He says he doesn't love me. But I love him so much. I can't live without him. My whole life has turned to shit.'

'Nonsense,' I said, surprising myself as much as her. Usually I was more empathic. I softened my tone. 'You will get over him. I know it doesn't feel like it now, but people don't die of broken hearts. Although they can die of alcohol poisoning, and no-one is worth killing yourself over, not even Gavin Green.'

She started crying again. 'Yes he is.' She sniffed. 'He's my soul mate.'

'Oh, for goodness' sake,' I said, crossing my arms. 'If there was such a thing, which I doubt, it's hardly likely to be the first man you meet.'

'You don't know him.' She rubbed at her eyes with her fists. 'We are made for each other.'

'Grace, you're sounding like a bad movie script now. I think we'd better get you to bed and continue this conversation in the morning.'

'You're not going to tell Mummy, are you?' She looked at me with her big grey-green eyes, begging for my silence.

'Not this time. But do it again and I'll be writing it up for the local newspaper.'

'You're the best.'

She leant on the table, got to her feet and stood there for a few breaths. I took her arm and guided her towards the stairs. She stumbled a couple of times but managed to get up to the landing. As she aimed for the bathroom though, she tripped and fell, pulling a table on which stood family photographs with her.

Ellen's light went on and she came out of her room.

'What the hell?' she whispered, staring at her sister who was sprawled on the landing. 'It smells like a pub out here – what on earth have you been doing?'

'Grace is a little upset and had a drink or two to make herself feel better,' I said quietly. 'I'm just getting her into bed.'

'Is it Dad?' Ellen asked.

I looked down at Grace without saying a word. Ellen took that to be a yes.

'In that case, I'll forgive her. Let's get her into her room.'

With Ellen's help, I got Grace settled in bed. She closed her eyes and was asleep before we left the room.

'How much did she drink?'

'I don't know, but she's thrown most of it up now. She'll be all right. A bit of a hangover in the morning, that's all.'

'Thanks, Hester. Better if Mum doesn't know about it, okay?'

'Fine by me.' But someone would have to explain away the missing whisky and it wouldn't be me. And Mrs Jenkins and her mop would have a good workout in the morning.

WALTER

I am conscious most of the time, although I do have periods when I'm less so.

I listen. I hear things.

I don't always know if they're real though.

My mind plays tricks on me.

I hear Ma's voice.

'Walter. Go down to the shop and get us a twist of salt and a dab of lard.'

'Walter. Look after your sisters while I go to Betty's.'

'Walter. Take this to Mr Gordon. Now.'

Walter. Walter. Walter.

The others had to do things too. No-one got off.

But Walter was the responsible one.

The special one.

The oldest boy.

The man of the house.

The one who got away.

'Walter. You send us what you can.'

Good boy Walter sent them what he could. More money than they could spend, probably.

More money than they'd ever had.
He did it for years.
I did it for years.
And then I stopped.
Why?
I don't remember.
I do remember.
Never any thanks.
Didn't even know if it was getting to Ma.
Mikey and Davey drinking it or putting it in their veins.
Other things to do with my money.
A boat. Golf. Holidays. Wife. Children.
I had a lot of money.

I had a chat with Dorothy. She was just standing there at the end of the bed, arms crossed like she was angry with me.

'What do you want?' I asked.

She just looked at me and narrowed her eyes slightly in the way that said 'You know what I want'.

And I didn't. I don't.

'You can't keep turning up like this. I don't want to see you.'

I could have sworn I heard her foot tapping.

'It wasn't my fault.'

She rolled her eyes at that.

I shut mine and counted to a hundred.

When I opened them again, she'd gone.

SEVEN

Over the next few days as Walter declined, the house became quieter. Jeanette and the girls spoke in hushed voices even when they were nowhere near his room. Every utterance took on the guise of a secret, laden with meaning, hidden from view. Offers of food sounded somehow shameful, as if they were betraying Walter by eating, diminishing his significance in their lives. They crept about, heads down, barely making eye contact. As if they were too alive, too aware that they, unlike Walter, had a future.

I had seen all this before. Families cowed by death stalking their loved ones, but I spoke in my normal voice, walked with my usual tread. It wouldn't make any difference to Walter.

One afternoon, Jeanette and I sat with him. The radio was on low in the background and the sun shone across the carpet. He hadn't been awake for more than a few minutes in the last twenty-four hours. The palliative care physician had been with Cassie and reviewed his medications. He needed something to help with the side effects of the morphine now he was taking more.

'It's not going to be long now, is it?' Jeanette whispered.

'I don't think so,' I said.

She winced as if I'd shouted.

'Perhaps we should have a roster so there's always someone here with him.'

I didn't remind her I'd been sleeping in the chair in the corner for the last three nights. He hadn't been alone for more than a few minutes for days.

'Good idea. I've been reading him *Cairo Mon Amour*. There was a bookmark in it about halfway through, so I reckoned he might like to hear the end.'

'That's kind,' she whispered.

'You know, hearing is the last sense to go and I'm sure Walter would like to hear what we're saying.'

She lowered her head. 'It doesn't seem right. It's like rubbing his face in it that we're still able to do all the things he can't.'

'Would he really want you to feel guilty because you're still alive?'

Walter stirred. I turned to him.

'Are you agreeing with me?'

One side of his mouth lifted into a crooked smile. His eyelids fluttered but didn't open. Jeanette took his hand and I saw his fingers curl around hers lightly.

'It's me, darling,' she said.

'I know. I want to hear.' He coughed weakly and sank back into sleep.

She kept hold of his hand and we were silent for a while. When she next spoke, it was in a more normal voice.

'We'll ditch the funeral and have a party to celebrate your life, my darling. We'll have good whisky and huge platters of that dreadful stilton you like.'

He didn't respond.

Later in the day, Sebastian rang.

'Say you've changed your mind about having a drink with me, Hester. You won't be disappointed, I promise you.'

He was as stubborn as his father but less likeable.

'My duty is to your father, as you well know. I'm not about to leave him now.'

'Is he actually dying then? Should I come and pay my last respects?' He sounded almost eager.

I knew Jeanette had phoned him the day before to tell him his father was near the end and Sebastian had, with no thought for how Jeanette might be feeling, said, 'Good.'

'You probably should. Can you let Anna know as well? Come tomorrow morning if you can.'

'We'll be there.'

Jeanette had called Louise too. She lived in London with her husband and three young children. I hadn't had a chance to speak to her at the lunch, but she certainly seemed more compassionate than her older siblings. Perhaps not having been brought up in the big house with Sebastian and Anna had been her saving grace.

I told Jeanette that Sebastian and Anna would be over the next day.

'Thank you. I don't particularly want them here, but they have a right to see him.'

'We'll keep it short. A cup of tea, a few minutes with Walter and they'll be on their way.'

'Yes.' She rubbed her temples.

'Are you okay? Can I get you an aspirin?'

'No, I'm fine. Just tired. I'll sit with Walter and maybe have a little snooze.'

When they came the next day, Sebastian arrived empty-handed, Anna brought flowers and Louise handed Jeanette a freezer bag of meals she'd made to tide them over.

'I'm sorry the boys didn't get to see their grandfather again, but I thought it better not to bring them today.' She hugged Jeanette.

Sebastian and Anna had gone straight in to see Walter, so Louise had a cup of tea in the kitchen and chatted to Ellen. Jeanette couldn't settle and roamed between the kitchen and Walter's room, sighing deeply.

I looked in and found Anna in tears, clutching her father's hand against her cheek, rocking gently while Walter slept. Sebastian watched, his eyes dry, his face set in a mask of disdain.

'Oh, please, Anna. Don't get all sentimental now. He was a terrible father, a selfish, controlling man. When he's gone we can get on with our lives without him watching everything we do with that disapproving look on his face. And he won't be controlling the purse strings. Life's looking pretty good, all in all.'

Anna sniffed, wiped her eyes, and nodded. 'You're right but I'll still miss him.'

She got her compact out and wiped under her eyes with a tissue, put on some lipstick and pouted at herself.

'We'll be orphans,' she said.

'Spare me the drama. I'm nearly fifty and you're not far behind. It's not as if we'll be out on the streets with our begging bowls hoping some kind person will take pity on us and give us a home.'

'You don't have a feeling bone in your body, do you?'

Sebastian turned and saw me watching from the doorway.

'How long have you been there?' he asked.

'Just got here. I came to ask if you want a cup of tea.' And some strychnine, perhaps.

'Anna and I were just saying how much we'll miss the old boy, weren't we, Anna?' He turned back to his sister who nodded and looked away. I noticed she was crying again and warmed to her a little.

'I'll leave you to say your goodbyes then,' I said. 'Tea will be in the kitchen when you're ready.'

Ten minutes later they were drinking tea. Sebastian had added something to his from a hip flask. Anna had declined.

Louise and Jeanette had gone in to see Walter and left me with them.

'Is there anything you need? Any questions you have about what happens next?'

Anna bit her lip and then said, 'He won't be in any pain, will he?'

'No. I can promise you that. He'll sleep more and more and in the next day or two, he'll slip away. It'll be very peaceful.'

'Thank you.' She dabbed at her eyes again.

Sebastian drank his tea in silence.

He took the opportunity of Anna going to the bathroom to ask me out again.

'You won't be needed here when he's gone. Come and let your hair down with me – relax, have a few drinks.'

I couldn't think of anything I'd like less, except perhaps sitting in a pit of riled up spitting cobras.

'Your father is dying, his wife is grieving already, and my place is with her. And even if it wasn't, I wouldn't go out with you.'

'Too prudish to get it on with a married man, are you?' He actually thrust his hips a few times.

This was too much. He really didn't get the message.

'Not at all. I just find you quite unappealing.'

I walked out feeling less triumphant than I would have liked. I don't like conflict and I hate being rude to people. I'm more of a 'talk about it afterwards' person, spouting all the things I wish I'd said at the time. But he really had asked for it. What arrogance!

In his final days Walter had someone with him around the clock. Often we sat in his room chatting, reading – either to him or each other – eating. Grace and Ellen played cards. Jeanette resurrected a knitting project she'd abandoned the year before.

Ellen was the one who fussed over Walter the most, sitting beside him, gently wiping his mouth when he dribbled in his sleep, brushing the wispy grey hair off his forehead, patting down the already neat sheets.

I noticed Grace's visits to him becoming further apart and shorter. It was time to have a chat. Too often I'd seen people pull back in the last few days and regret it when it was too late.

I found her in her room, headphones on, laptop open, phone beside her. She jumped when I entered and quickly closed the computer. Pulling her headphones off, she waited for me to talk.

'Can I sit down?' I asked.

She shrugged. 'It's a free world.'

I smiled and sat next to her on the bed, not looking at her. 'It's a shitty time, isn't it?'

I felt the bed shift as she moved away from me.

'And it's hard to talk about it. There's a lot going on for you.'

'Suppose so,' she said.

I nodded and let the silence hold us.

Then I heard her breath catch and knew she was crying. I sat quietly.

Eventually she took some deep breaths and blew her nose. 'I hate this,' she said.

'I'm sure you do,' I said, waiting for more.

'Why can't he be in hospital like other people?'

'You don't like seeing him like this?'

'It's disgusting. It's not Daddy in that bed anymore, it's a– I don't know who he is, but he's not my father.'

'Dying isn't pretty.'

'Why can't the doctors do anything?'

I wondered if this was Grace's naïveté or whether she hadn't been told what was going on when Walter was diagnosed.

'By the time the cancer was found there was nothing to be done. That's the awful thing about the kind of cancer he has – it's usually too far advanced for treatment by the time it's discovered.'

'But they didn't try. He didn't have chemo or anything.'

'Your parents would have discussed the options with the oncologist and made a decision based on his advice and experience.'

'Why didn't they ask me and Ellen? Why didn't we have a say? They're so selfish. Sometimes I just want him to die.' She stopped. Gasped. Covered her mouth with her hand and stared at me, wide-eyed.

'I didn't mean that.' She started sobbing.

I put my hand on her back. 'I know.'

'I'd do anything to make him better,' she said through her tears.

We sat for some time, the silence punctuated by her sniffs.

'I'm scared,' she said.

'That's normal.'

'What will it be like, you know, when he–'

'You mean what will his death be like?'

She nodded.

'It'll be peaceful. He'll fall asleep and not wake up.'

'Does he know what's going on?'

'He knows he's dying, if that's what you mean. And he is still aware of the people around him. He can still hear, even if he doesn't respond.'

'Did he talk to you about it?'

'His death? Yes. He would prefer it wasn't happening because he loves you and doesn't want to leave you, but he knows there are no miracles.'

'Isn't he scared?'

I thought for a moment. 'No, not now. I think he was, but now he's ready.'

She took a deep breath, swept her hair away from her face and tied it in a ponytail. 'Okay. I want to see him.' She stood up. 'Will you come too?'

'Of course.'

We went into Walter's room. Ellen was curled up in the chair, reading. Walter was sleeping peacefully.

'I'll sit with him for a while now,' said Grace.

Ellen got up, put her book down and said she'd go and make some tea.

Grace pulled a chair up to the bedside. She looked at me and then at her father, and took his hand.

'Oh, Daddy. I don't want you to die, I just don't want you to be in pain. I can't imagine not having you around.'

Walter slept on. Grace sat quietly. I went to help Ellen with the tea thinking what amazing young women she and Grace were and what a lot of growing up they were doing in a short space of time.

The days went by and still Walter lived. The few minutes each day his eyes were open, he looked around but didn't speak. His breath was slow, loud, uneven. Cassie had brought oxygen but the first time we tried to put the mask over his face, he weakly fought us off and we hadn't tried again.

Late one night, after Jeanette had started falling asleep in her chair and Ellen had sent her to bed, Walter woke and seemed more alert than he had for days. He stared into the corner of the room, focused on something neither Ellen nor I could see, then he looked at his daughter, held her gaze a moment and closed his eyes.

'What do you think he was looking at?' she asked.

'It's not uncommon for the dying to see visions of people who have already died, as if they've come to collect them.'

'Does that mean– is he going now?'

'It won't be long, but not necessarily tonight.'

Ellen stroked her father's head, took one of his hands in hers. 'It must be a comfort, I suppose, imagining someone's come to show you the way.'

'I expect so.'

We sat in silence for a while, listening to Walter's breath and the lengthening pauses in between.

Suddenly, he clutched the sheets, his head turning from side to side. His eyes remained closed, but his jaw was clenched.

Ellen took his hand again, whispered words of comfort.

'I'm going to get the others,' I said. I'd seen this before and suspected that this might be Walter's time.

When I returned, Jeanette and Grace on my heels, Walter was calm. Ellen was still soothing him, tears on her cheeks.

The pauses between breaths lengthened. Several times we thought he'd gone, only for him to take another weak crackling inhalation.

Jeanette and the girls spoke to him, telling him what he meant to them, their hopes he would be happy and pain free wherever he was going, that they would miss him, but they would carry on and do their best to honour his memory. They shed tears as they said their goodbyes, and then Jeanette said, 'It's okay, my love. I know you need to go. I love you – we all love you – but you can go now.' She kissed him on the forehead; Ellen and Grace kissed his cheeks.

And then Jeanette started humming, and Ellen and Grace joined in with the words to 'Row, Row, Row Your Boat'. Their voices intertwined, creating a well of sound into which Walter's last breath was received.

Jeanette and the girls stopped singing and sat around the bed in silence. I waited in the background.

Dawn crept up on us, the light seeping round the edges of the curtains. Ellen got up and opened them, looked out over the dewy grass, and stretched.

'What happens now?' asked Jeanette.

'We let Cassie know. She'll bring Dr Gupta with her to sign the death certificate. And we can wash Walter's body. But there's no hurry.'

'I can't do that,' said Grace.

'That's fine, darling. I'll do it.' Jeanette took her daughter's hand, but Grace pulled away.

'I'm going to get some fresh air,' she said and left.

Jeanette stared after her.

'I'll go and make sure she's all right,' said Ellen.

Jeanette and I washed Walter's emaciated body and dressed him in fresh pyjamas, made neat his too-long hair, folded his hands over his chest. Jeanette hummed as she worked. Only once or twice did her voice crack.

Cassie and Dr Gupta came later in the morning. They spent some time with the family in Walter's room. I made tea and toast but was not surprised when the toast was uneaten.

I also rang Mark Johnstone as requested, and Grace's school to tell them her father had died and she wouldn't be in for a few days.

In the afternoon, Jeanette, dry-eyed but haggard-looking, sat in the drawing room calling family and friends to tell them the news. I overheard her telling someone they wanted no visits until the following day and silently cheered her for asserting herself.

Mark Johnstone arrived, briefcase in hand, later in the day as I prepared yet more tea to tempt the girls.

I took him into the kitchen where the family was sitting round the table and introduced him as Walter's solicitor. Jeanette raised her eyebrows in surprise.

'What about old Mr Hill?'

'Walter asked me to find someone else,' I said. 'He wanted to make some adjustments to his will.'

She looked from Mark to me, and back again.

'I'm so sorry for your loss,' he said to Jeanette and paused for a moment before continuing. 'I'm here today not about the will but to read you a letter Walter gave me the other day, written soon after his diagnosis, and to advise you of his wishes concerning his burial. He wanted me to come as soon as possible after his death.'

'His wishes?' said Ellen. 'I thought he'd told us what he wanted.'

'That may be, but he wanted them written down.'

'That's Daddy for you,' said Grace and she burst into tears. Ellen put her arm around her and pulled her close.

I put a plate of crumpets and jam on the table with the teapot and mugs. Sitting at the table, Mark looked fresh compared to the rest of us who had hardly slept in days. I was still in the clothes I'd been wearing the day before and suddenly felt self-conscious.

No-one took any food or drink, so I poured the tea and put a crumpet on each plate and handed them round.

'Walter wouldn't want you to starve,' I said.

'Thank you, Hester,' murmured Jeanette and she sipped her tea.

'So,' said Mark, reaching down to his briefcase and pulling out a folder, 'there are two documents: a letter and your husband's wishes concerning the, er, disposal of his body. He wanted me to read it out,' he held the letter out to them, 'but you might prefer to read it in your own time?'

'Read it, please, if it's what Walter wanted,' said Jeanette, and the girls nodded.

My darling girls, it started. Mark had a mellifluous voice. I could have listened to him all day.

You know I am a man of few words, and you've all accused me – repeatedly – of not showing my feelings. Well, here they are.

I'm sorry I am no longer with you all and we didn't get to do all the things we wanted to do, but I want you to do them anyway. I will be there in spirit. So buy your tickets for the trans-Canadian train, go and stay in a Scottish castle, drink ouzo on a Greek beach at midnight.

I have been the most fortunate of men to have been loved by you all, and to have loved you in return. I have made mistakes in my life, but you have had the best of me, and you made me happier than I had thought possible.

Don't cry for me. Instead, live your lives to the full, have adventures, take risks.

Always remember I love you.

We all wiped tears away. Even Mark was dewy-eyed.

The clock ticked loudly on the wall and Milly, in her basket by the Aga, snuffled in her sleep.

Ellen cleared her throat. 'Bossy to the last, telling us what to do.' She smiled.

'Yes, typical Daddy,' said Grace.

Jeanette took her daughter's hand and once again, Grace pulled away. Jeanette looked at her in confusion, but Grace turned away from her and got up from the table.

'A lovely letter,' said Jeanette, watching her daughter pour herself a glass of water. 'Thank you.'

I wasn't sure if she was thanking Walter for writing it, or Mark for reading it.

'Perhaps Hester would accompany me outside for a few minutes to give you some time together.' Mark put the letter down on the table.

Jeanette smiled and nodded.

I followed him out and we sat on the patio outside Walter's room.

'That was thoughtful,' I said.

He sighed. 'It was what I wanted when my father died, and what I didn't get. Everything was rushed and there was no time to sit and feel anything.'

'Still, it was kind,' I said, and he smiled.

'How long do you think you'll be here, Hester?'

'Walter asked me to stay a couple of weeks after he died. I'll help with the funeral or whatever it is Walter has requested and then see what Jeanette and the girls need. In the end, it's up to them.'

'Of course. They're lucky to have you here. It can't be easy for you either.'

'No. It's never just a job, but because Walter hired me earlier than most would have done, I've been here longer than I usually would have been, and it's hard not to love the women in this family. It's not easy seeing them grieve.'

'And Walter? What was he like?'

I looked out over the garden and imagined a young Walter in his domain. 'Opinionated, used to getting his way. I imagine he was a ruthless businessman and not an easy man to live with, but I think he'd probably mellowed over the years. He was likely spot on when he said Jeanette and the girls had the best of him.'

He nodded and smiled. 'I suppose a lot of people soften as they age.'

'Is the will contentious – is that why you wanted to know what he was like?' I asked.

'I can't tell you anything about it, the family must hear it first, but I think it's a good thing you're still here.'

I sucked my lips in and tried not to show my alarm. Had Walter cut someone out of his will? Surely he had provided generously for Jeanette and the girls? I thought about what Jeff had said about Walter knowing secrets concerning each of them, and my heart sank.

'I'd better go and read the second document now,' said Mark.

We walked back across the lawn and in through the kitchen door. Jeanette was holding the letter; she and Ellen sitting close. Grace was leaning against the kitchen bench. Milly lifted her head when she heard us and bounded over to greet me as if I was a favourite she hadn't seen for months.

'Are you ready to hear Walter's wishes concerning the disposal of his body?' said Mark. 'He wanted me to read them out to you.'

Jeanette nodded.

He took the document out of its envelope and cleared his throat.

I do not want a funeral. I wish to be cremated and buried in the centre of the walled garden in the beautiful urn you made. I'd like a Japanese maple planted over me. No other marker. Just the tree. And a party afterwards for anyone who would like to come and raise a glass with you. No speeches. No tears. No black. Music and dancing. Champagne.

In the years to come, it would give me great joy if you'd sit nearby sometimes, or talk to me as you tend your beloved garden.

Jeanette took a deep breath and looked up at the ceiling.

'I must add,' said Mark gently, 'that this is not legally binding. Walter knew that. He also knew there may be family members who would not want to go along with his ideas. He said if that was the case, he would leave it to your discretion as his wife and next of kin.'

'If this is what he wants, it's what he'll get,' she said. 'And the rest of the family can go and take a running jump if they don't like it.'

'Hear, hear,' said Ellen.

Grace stared at her and said nothing.

'If you need any assistance, please call me. Hester has my number.'

There was something in the way he said my name that felt more intimate than it should. I looked at him and caught him smiling at me. Feeling myself redden I smiled back.

'I'll leave you now,' he said, turning to Jeanette again. 'And once again, please accept my condolences.'

I saw him to his car, wanting to reach out and touch him at the same time as being aware the timing of this attraction could hardly have been worse.

He opened the car door and then turned to me. 'Please do call, Hester. Anytime.' He took my hand and I thought he was going to shake it, but he just held it for a long moment. And then he got into his car and drove away.

I walked back into the house slowly, not wanting to let go of what had just passed between us. Or had it? Had anything actually happened or was it just wishful thinking?

I heard voices as I entered the kitchen.

'I don't care. I don't like it.'

'Let's not argue about it. I'm not sure what happens now.' Jeanette turned to me as I took my seat at the table again. 'What do we do next?' she asked.

'Hester, we don't have to put Daddy in the middle of the garden, do we?' Grace was wide-eyed.

'I don't mind him being there,' said Jeanette.

'Well I do. It'll feel really weird. Creepy. Why couldn't he have a plaque in a memorial garden like a normal person?'

'Because Dad wasn't like other people,' said Ellen quietly.

'We don't have to agree to anything right now. But Grace, please don't set your mind against it completely. We can talk later.' Jeanette sighed and rubbed her hand across her forehead. Then she blinked several times, her eyes glistening.

WALTER

It's over.

And in the end, it was easy. Soft, I would say. Hester Rose went to get Jeanette and Grace, and my darling Ellen sat with me until they were all there, and I slid away from them. Drifted off. Peaceful.

Ma was there at the end too. Not old and haggard, but middle-aged, full-bodied. In her apron, as always. Hair swept up in an untidy bun. She never had any time for vanity. It was comforting to have her there. Just a presence. Not demanding. Waiting.

I had no strength left. Even if I had wanted to stay, I couldn't have. Not anymore. The fight had left me, and I was ready to go. I'm glad Jeanette knew. Strong, brave girl, my lovely wife.

I'm so proud of my girls, all of them. 'Row, row, row your boat'. Ha! We used to sing it in the car when we were on long trips with the girls when they were little to stop them asking 'Are we there yet?' every two minutes and how long it would be before the end of the journey. Very fitting.

Hester Rose was right. No pain. Just a little tug as the last breath left me. I knew that was it. My girls didn't realise immediately. They held my hands, kept singing to me in their beautiful voices but I'd gone. If there's a good way to go, that was it.

They're leaving me at home overnight. My body still lies on the bed. The undertakers will come tomorrow. That'll be weird. I'm not in my body anymore, but will I have to go with it?

It's a strange sensation, being dead. It's not the complete nothingness I thought it would be. But it's not beingness either. Something in between. I see my body but can't feel it. I have an impression of breathing, but perhaps it's just habit. It's like I've been released into a hinterland. No feeling, no physicality. Not floating. Not sinking. No heaven or hell. I'm still in the room. Ma has gone but I know she's nearby. It's the weirdest thing; we haven't seen each other for twenty years and I've hardly thought about her in all that time, yet she's here now. I like that.

Jeanette is crying. I didn't want tears, but I suppose it's not up to me.

Hester Rose will look after her, guide her through the next few days. I hope they'll become friends, not just employer and employee. Hester Rose is worth more than that. She's a tough one. I saw myself in her. Had her struggles but she didn't lose her compassion. Some would say I never had any compassion, and maybe they're right. I had to make tough decisions sometimes. I was a businessman after all. Fair as I could be, but business is business.

The local paper did a piece on me years ago – rags to riches story. Some people said I'd married money, that I didn't work for it. But I built the business from a small local firm to a factory supplying shoes to stores all over the UK and beyond. That was my work. My ideas. My plans.

It doesn't matter now. Nothing does. No worries, mate, Steve, the Australian barman at the golf club, would say. No wucking furries.

EIGHT

Sebastian, in spite of being asked to stay away until the following day, turned up at dinnertime. Not that anyone was eating.

'What's the plan then?' he asked. And without waiting for an answer said, 'We'll use the local undertaker, of course. Good man. He's in Rotary with me. He'll give us a good deal. I've already spoken to him. He'll be buried beside my mother in the family plot.'

'No,' said Jeanette.

'What do you mean, no? You won't get a better deal, and anyway, I've promised him the job.'

Jeanette flinched. 'Walter is not a job!'

'The funeral then,' he said, annunciating loud and clear, as if talking to an imbecile.

Jeanette took a deep breath, looked at me and raised her eyebrows.

'Dad had very specific wishes,' Ellen said. 'Which we plan to fulfil. Dad didn't want a funeral. He wanted a party and his ashes buried in the garden.'

Sebastian snorted. 'You can't be fucking serious! What kind of bollocks is that?'

'Dad's kind of bollocks,' said Ellen, looking him in the eye. 'And if you don't like it, you don't have to come.'

'Not come to see the old bastard buried? You must be kidding. I've been waiting for this for years.'

'I'd like you to leave now,' said Jeanette. 'This is my house and I don't want you in it.'

He leant in so his face was inches from hers. 'We'll see who the house belongs to when the will's read. It may well be me who's ordering you out. This was my mother's house, and don't you forget it.'

'I'll see you out, Sebastian,' I said, hands clenched into tight fists. Oh, how I would have loved to have punched the supercilious look off his face.

'Anna and I won't let you get away with this hippy idea of not having a funeral,' he said. 'Anyway, it's illegal.'

'No, it's not,' said Jeanette and Ellen in unison, and they both laughed.

'Now bugger off,' added Ellen.

He marched out, ramrod straight, and screeched away in his car.

Jeanette sank into a chair, her head in her hands.

'It's going to be a shit fight but I'm more determined than ever to give Walter what he wants, even if it kills me.'

'We'll help, Mum,' said Ellen, putting an arm around her shoulders. 'I think we should do exactly what Dad asked for.'

Jeanette lifted her head and smiled at her daughter. 'Thank you, darling.'

Grace stared into space, the expression on her face difficult to read.

We picked at our dinner. I had quite an appetite but would have felt uncomfortable eating in front of the others.

'I'm going in to say goodnight to Dad,' said Ellen.

'I'll come too,' said Grace.

Watching them go, Jeanette sighed. 'They're chalk and cheese but both such a tribute to him.'

Jeanette decided we must dress Walter in his favourite clothes for his cremation: grey slacks, button-down shirt, cashmere sweater. The stout brogues he'd bought in Scotland several years before. The cufflinks the girls had given him for his 70th birthday: little gold beetles. Of course, everything was far too big on him now, making him look like a child dressed up in his father's clothes.

Before the crematorium workers took him away, Jeanette and the girls kissed Walter on the forehead and whispered their last messages to him.

Jeanette looked at me and said, 'He's so cold, my poor love. He never could stand the cold.' She watched as he left the house for the last time. Ellen was next to her, standing tall. Dry-eyed. They squeezed each other's hands until their fingers went white. Grace stood apart, hugging herself.

Louise rang to see how everyone was bearing up and she and Jeanette spoke for quite a while. The door was open and I couldn't help but overhear some of the conversation. Jeanette was telling her about Walter's wishes. There was a short silence then she chuckled, and I wondered what Louise had said.

The conversation was cut short when Anna barged in, shrieking.

'Where is he? What have you done with him? Where's my father?'

I intercepted her in the hall and tried to steer her into the kitchen, but she slapped me away and went into the drawing room. I hovered in the hall: backup.

Standing over Jeanette, Anna yelled, 'I hope you're happy now. You drove a wedge between Sebastian and me and our father. You're nothing but a nasty little gold-digger.'

Jeanette was still holding the phone. 'I'll have to call you back, Louise. I'm sorry.' She put the receiver down and looked up at Anna. 'Shut up,' she said without raising her voice.

Anna stopped mid-sentence. 'Did you just tell me to shut up?'

Jeanette stood. They were the same height, but Anna was half Jeanette's width. And Jeanette wasn't big. Had it come to blows, I wouldn't have rated Anna's chances.

'I have never stopped you seeing your father. I welcomed you into this house and put up with your airs and graces because you had every right to be here. I rang you this morning as soon as I knew when Walter was going to be taken away. I gave you ample opportunity to come over and see him. Don't blame me because you chose not to get here in time.'

Anna drew back as if she'd been hit. It was possibly the first time Jeanette had ever stood up to her.

'I believe Walter will be at the crematorium for a day or two before he is cremated. You can go and see him there. Now, preferably.'

There was little to do after Anna left. Jeanette and the girls put on thick jackets – the early summer weather had deserted us again – and took Milly for a walk. I stripped Walter's bed and put the sheets in the washing machine, wiped the plastic mattress and pushed the bed into a corner to await its collection by the palliative care team.

Then I gazed around the room to check everything was

done. My eyes rested on the bedside table and something that had been in the back of my mind, a whisper of a memory, a tableau half seen, grew into a full picture. I smiled to myself.

'I'm worried about Grace,' said Jeanette the next day.

I wondered if she'd realised there was a bottle of whisky missing. 'Anything in particular?' I asked.

'She's so angry with me. She doesn't talk to me anymore, she hisses. Has she said anything to you? She likes you. She talks to you, I know she does.' She sighed. 'She used to talk to me.'

'A lot of people get angry when a loved one dies. I know I did when I found out about my family.'

'Would you have a chat with her? I think she needs to talk.'

'Of course.'

'Thanks, Hester. I'd be grateful. I know it's pathetic, but I can't deal with her right now.'

I found Grace putting her jacket on in the cloakroom.

'I'm going to take Milly out,' she said when she saw me.

Milly was the most walked dog in England these days. She was the best excuse to get out of the house.

'Mind if I come?'

She looked away for a moment and I thought she was going to say no, but she nodded. 'Okay.'

We went out the back gate of the property, onto a narrow lane banked with hawthorn hedges. Wildflowers peeked out from the steep verges: red campion, wild garlic, buttercups.

'I love this time of year in the countryside,' I said. 'These hedges are ancient. Look how high the banks are – that's all old growth. It builds up over the years, the new plants using the old as their foundation.'

Grace wore a puzzled look. 'How come you know so much about hedges?'

I laughed. 'I have a son who used to be obsessed with nature. Every time we went for a walk he'd have a hundred questions about animals and crops, grasses, trees – you name it, he wanted to know about it. We looked up a lot of stuff over the years.'

'What does he do now?'

'He's twenty-seven, works in IT and lives in the middle of Manchester. Not a blade of grass within miles!'

'Do you miss him?'

'I do. But I've got used to not having him around all the time. Took a while though.'

Grace didn't say anything. We kept walking, Milly trotting along, nose to the ground, sniffing everything and occasionally stopping, cocking her head to one side, eyes darting here and there, searching for a rabbit or a bird.

After half a mile or so, I said, 'How are you doing, Grace?'

'I'm fine,' she said too quickly. 'I've got friends I talk to about, you know, stuff.'

'That's good.'

'Milly! Milly, come back here!' she shouted.

We followed her into a field where she was rolling in a cow pat. Grace shouted her name and eventually a filthy Milly trotted towards us, tongue lolling out the side of her mouth. I swear she was grinning.

Grace told her she was a very naughty dog and put her on the lead. We resumed our walk.

'Did Mummy ask you to talk to me?'

I hesitated but there was no point in lying about it. 'She's worried about you.'

'I'm so angry with her I can hardly bear to look at her.'

'Why's that?'

'Did you hear her, when Daddy was dying? She basically

told him to fuck off and die, like she'd had enough of sitting around waiting. Those were the last words he heard. How could she?' She actually stamped her foot.

I took a deep breath and looked out over the fields; so green after the rain.

'Your mother was just letting him know she knew it was his time and she was ready.'

'But I wasn't. I didn't want him to die. I mean, I know I said I did, but I didn't mean it. I don't want him to be dead.' She was shouting. Milly started whining. 'Shut up, Milly!'

'It wasn't your mother's fault he died.'

'But it's the last thing he heard. Not "I love you" or "we'll always remember you" but "off you go so we can get on with our lives".'

I thought back to Walter's death. It was true, Jeanette's words had been the last spoken before his death. And then the singing.

'Your father died surrounded by the people he loved, in his own home. By most standards, that's a good way to go.'

Grace shrugged.

We walked back in silence. Just before we went into the house, she paused, turned to me and said, 'You can't make it all better, Hester. You think you can, but you can't.'

I went to my room. Grace's words had hit hard. It was my job to help people, and I did my best. I wasn't blind to my shortcomings or unrealistic enough to expect I would always succeed but it was hard to be accused of failure.

I looked out the window at the gentle scenery until I was calmer and then called Peggy on her mobile. She was back at the nursing home, and I interrupted her playing cards with one of the other residents.

'I'll call back later,' I said.

'No, it's all right, love. Mary's getting fed up of me winning. She owes me twenty-three pieces of pasta and she's just asked for double or quits.'

I laughed. 'What are you playing – poker?'

'No, rummy, but we bet on who's going to win each hand to make it more exciting.'

'Oh the fun you can have in a nursing home,' I said.

'Yes. But guess what?'

'Tell me.'

'Mavis Clarke and Howard Morgan are getting married!'

'You're kidding?' Mavis Clarke had been in the home for about two years and when she first came, she wouldn't even sit at the same table as Howard because he was Black.

'She's saying it was love at first sight, it just took her a long time to realise it.'

I thought about the two of them. She had MS and her family couldn't look after her at home anymore. Howard's wife had died and he'd had a stroke shortly after. With no family in England to look after him, he'd come into the nursing home. He had made progress in the last couple of years and was quite independent. But they made an odd couple. She was the barely literate daughter of a bookmaker; he had been an academic and written scholarly works on some obscure area of physics.

'Love is blind,' said Peggy.

'But it's lovely they can make each other happy,' I said.

'I don't know about that. She's a bossy one, that Mavis. She's got him wrapped round her little finger.'

'And that's how some relationships work,' I said. 'Who are we to judge? We're single!'

'True, but I'm happy this way and I thought you were too.'

'I was.'

'Was?' Peggy didn't miss a trick. There was nothing wrong

with her brain; it was her body giving out on her. 'Come on, spill the beans.'

I took a deep breath. I wanted to talk about it – about Mark – to someone who wasn't involved in Walter's death and the life I was living with the Baxter women. And I wanted Peggy's approval for this, whatever it might be.

'It's nothing. Well, nothing's happened, anyway. But I met someone I find attractive, and I think the feeling is mutual.'

'Ooh! Is he a relative of the man who died? I can't imagine you're out anywhere else to meet someone at the moment.'

'Not quite so close. His solicitor.'

'Ah! Attractive and wealthy then. Good choice.'

'I think you're getting ahead of yourself, Peg – we've only met on strictly professional terms so far. Stay tuned. I'll let you know if anything happens. How are you, anyway?'

'Not so fast, my girl. You can't tell me you've met someone and then change the subject. What's he like? I want to know everything.'

I laughed. 'He's tall, handsome, caring. Drives a blue car and does people's wills. That really is all I know about him. I promise I'll give you more details as soon as I have them!'

'Just you make sure you do. Apart from the wedding of the year, we don't get much good news in here.'

We chatted about her and about the wedding plans, which were the talk of the nursing home, and ended with a promise to talk again soon.

Admitting to Peggy that I was attracted to Mark made it more real and I allowed myself a little fantasy of dining with him in a local pub and walking hand in hand with him afterwards, towards his house. I didn't know where he lived but imagined a cosy but well-kept cottage with a light-filled bedroom and a king-sized bed with crisp freshly laundered sheets.

I decided to call him. Actually, it wasn't as conscious as a decision. My fingers tapped my phone and his started ringing.

'Hello?'

'It's Hester,' I said.

'Hester! How are you? Is everything all right?'

'Yes.'

My tongue had tied itself in knots and wouldn't allow me to speak a full sentence. Talk about blushing teenager.

'Can I help you with anything?'

'I don't know.'

There was a pause in which I was aware of Mrs Jenkins vacuuming the life out of the carpet just outside my room.

'Would it be easier to talk in person?'

Oh Lord. In person. Face to face.

'Yes?' It came out as a question, as if he'd know better than me.

'How about we meet at the King's Head in the village for a spot of lunch? Can you get away?'

Lunch, a stroll back to his cottage, his crisp sheets... Now who was getting ahead of herself?

'Great,' I said. 'See you there.'

After we'd finished the call, I sank onto my bed and then jumped up and looked out the window towards the village. In half an hour I would be sitting in the pub opposite Mark Johnstone Junior. I changed into a dress, daubed on some make-up and then washed it off again and got back into my jeans. This wasn't a date. I'd said I needed to talk to him and now I had to think of a question, but my mind had gone blank.

I smiled at Mrs Jenkins as I left my room, but she turned her back to me and pushed the hoover along the hall.

'I'm going to the village. Anything I can get for you?' I said to Jeanette as I was leaving.

'The village?' She sounded surprised. As well she might. I hadn't left the house apart from walking the dog since I'd arrived.

'Yes. You don't mind, do you? I won't be long.'

'Not at all. We might need some bread, but I don't really know. There isn't much in the village really. If you want proper shops you'll need to go into town.'

'Oh no, I just thought I'd have a mosey. I'm not looking for anything in particular.'

Such a liar. Omitter of the truth. To save Jeanette's feelings. How would I feel if I'd lost my husband and the hired help was off after a man? And not just any man. The dead man's solicitor. What was I doing?

I paused outside the pub, made one last attempt to tame my hair into its clip and smoothed down my top. Then taking a deep breath, in I went.

He was already there sitting in a nook, a pint in front of him and a book in his hand.

'What are you reading?' I asked.

He looked up and smiled, turned the book for me to read the title: *Knowing Simone*.

'Sounds raunchy,' I said.

He laughed. 'It has its moments, but it's historical fiction, set in France. Interesting times. Anyway, let me get you a drink, what'll you have?'

He went to the bar and I looked round the cosy pub with its horse brasses and low beams. No gastro-pub this, it was a real local's local.

Over our drinks we chatted about books, and he asked about me and my life. He was easy to talk to and a good listener. We both chose the ploughman's lunch, with huge wedges of sharp cheddar, home-made chutney and fresh rolls, and we chatted on. I had almost forgotten this wasn't a date, that he was expecting me to ask for some advice or his professional opinion.

He wiped his mouth and scrunched up his napkin. 'So,' he said, looking at me, eyebrows raised.

I felt the blush rise up my neck.

'I... er...'

'I'm glad you called. I was going to phone to ask how you were all bearing up.'

'Oh, yes. Good. Well, not good, but as you'd expect. Jeanette and the girls are dealing with Walter's death differently, which is quite normal, but they're finding each other's reactions perplexing.'

'And you – you're looking after them all. How do you feel?'

My skin tingled and I smiled. People never asked how the doula was feeling.

'Tired. But okay.' I took a deep breath. 'Mark, I have a confession.'

'Sounds intriguing, but I'm not a priest.'

I fought back a giggle.

'I didn't call you in your professional capacity.' There, it was said. Now he would tell me he had a Mrs Johnstone and a brace of Junior Johnstones at home and that would be it. I'd leave with a red face and my tail between my legs, and we'd be formal with each other when we met at the funeral that wasn't a funeral but had no other name. I was so caught up in my thoughts I didn't catch what he said.

'Oh, that's okay,' I said, burning with shame.

He looked confused. 'Sorry?'

'No, I'm the one who's sorry. I shouldn't have said anything.'
He frowned. 'I'm glad you did.'
'Yes, well, I suppose everything's clear now at least. I should probably go.' I started getting up.
'Hester, I think there's been a misunderstanding.'
'Yes, there has. I really am sorry.'
'No, I mean I don't think you heard what I said.'
I sat down again but I couldn't look at him.
'I said I was hoping that was the case. That you hadn't asked me here for my professional opinion, I mean.'

His words slowly seeped through the embarrassment I was feeling, and I looked up to see him smiling at me. 'That's why I suggested the pub not the office. And because it's closer to the house and meant you didn't have to drive all the way to town.'

'That was very thoughtful,' I said as relief washed over me. I wanted to reach over the table and take his hand.

Instead, he reached over the table and took mine.

Mark had to go back to work, and I skipped back to the house.

I'd forgotten to buy bread, so we had Ryvitas with our soup that night. Nobody cared. Meals were a necessity rather than something to be savoured.

'The crematorium rang this afternoon,' said Jeanette as we sat at the table.

Grace tensed and put her spoon down.

Ellen looked at her mother.

'Walter's going to be cremated tomorrow. We can go to say our last goodbyes if we want but, as requested, there won't be any ceremony or anything.' She stopped, bit her lip.

Grace pushed her chair back and stormed out of the room. We watched her go, and Jeanette sighed.

'I'll go to the crematorium, Mum,' said Ellen.

'You don't have to, darling. Only if you want to.'

'I do.'

Jeanette took her half-full bowl to the sink. 'I'll go and see if Grace will talk to me.'

When we were on our own, Ellen said, 'What's going on with Grace? She's being such a little bitch.'

I shook my head. 'Everyone responds differently at times like this—'

'I know, but she's acting really out of character. I've never known her be so horrible. It's like it's all about her and no-one else matters, but we've all lost Dad.' Tears welled in her eyes and she stopped to wipe them away. 'She's not the only one who's sad.'

'I know,' I said, putting my arm around her.

We sat quietly until Jeanette came back and sat at the table. We both turned to her.

She shook her head.

'Don't take it personally, Mum.'

'It's hard not to.'

Jeanette looked at her hands that were clasped in front of her on the table.

'I don't think she's ready to let it go yet,' I said. 'Of her father or her anger. They go hand in hand. If she isn't angry, it means she didn't love him.'

'So we just have to let her be angry? It's exhausting,' said Ellen.

I shrugged.

'My poor Gracie,' said Jeanette and she let her head rest on her hands. Her shoulders started shaking and as Ellen put her arms around her, she turned towards her daughter. 'Nothing's ever going to be the same again, is it? We'll always be yearning for something we can't have anymore.'

Ellen nodded. 'It's like being homesick: We know what we've left behind and we don't like where we are.'

I left quietly. They didn't need me, so I went to my room and thought about Mark.

WALTER

Hester Rose has her work cut out for her, looking after my girls. She'll manage though.

As for me, I'm here and not here. My body has been taken away but I'm still hanging around. Well, not exactly hanging around, but conscious of what's going on. It's like being a fly on the wall.

I'm not a ghost. They aren't aware of me, nor would I want them to be. They'd freak out and get self-conscious. I don't know what I am though. Still this in-between thing.

Time means nothing. There is no heat or cold, no hard or soft, no up or down. I, whatever I am now, am weightless, formless. I sense rather than see or hear. I'm in the walls and the furniture and the air. But I do have a sense of an I. Milly looked at me, or at least at the point from which I sensed her, and barked. They say animals are more attuned to this sort of thing.

I wonder why I'm here still. And how. Is it the same for everyone? Perhaps I'm special. I always thought I was put on Earth for a purpose. When I was a kid I imagined a camera following me around, filming my life. Every moment worthy of being captured. It made me behave myself, believing I was being watched, recorded. Made me a better person. Some of the time at least.

Ma hasn't been back. Perhaps she'll return when it's time for me to leave.

I had another chat with Dorothy. I'm beginning to wonder if she's the reason I'm still here – that there's something to sort out between us.

When I say chat, I mean she stands there looking disapproving, and I think about the things I would say to her.

Perhaps I wasn't the best husband to her, but I did love her, at the beginning at least. She was bright and gay – in the old sense of the word – and she laughed a lot. I'd never met anyone like her. People said I was attracted to the money more than to her but it's not true. Although the money didn't hurt.

When we met, she was engaged to some boring wanker who worked for her father. Arrogant sort of bloke who saw himself marrying the boss's daughter and taking over the company. But no ambition, no plans for the future. So I made myself visible. Me, the lowest of the low back then. But I was good-looking and I had a vision for the future and an eye for a pretty girl. Didn't take long for Dorothy to drop old Cecil for young Walter.

Is that what this is about? Do you regret taking up with me, Dorothy? Is that what you've come to tell me? Bit late now.

I can't be bothered with it all. Dorothy died so long ago.

Will I feel anything when they cremate me? Is it me they've got there in the box? It can't be if my consciousness is here, surely? It worries me though, that I might feel the heat as my carcass is blistering, the skin lifting off the bones, the muscles – what was left of them – cooking and then shrivelling to ash. Never did like barbecues.

Problem with still being around is that I know what's going

on, how my girls are feeling, but I can't do anything about it. If I could tell them this dying lark isn't so bad perhaps they'd be happier. Not happy, exactly. Less sad. The part of them that's sad for me. I know they have to be sad for themselves, for the space I occupied in their lives. It's a complicated thing, grief, I suppose. Have to separate out what's what.

Don't be sad for me!

Don't worry about me!

I shout, but they are oblivious.

Forgive your mother for what she said, Grace. It didn't make any difference to me, nor did it make me love her less. I was glad she was ready to let me go but I was going anyway. It was my time. Ellen knew it too.

Hester Rose is a sensible woman. Sees what's what more clearly than anyone I've known. Wish I'd met her earlier. I'd have employed her as head of HR.

NINE

Grace wasn't talking to any of us, but Jeanette had asked me if I'd accompany her and Ellen to the crematorium. So there we were, in a small spartan office waiting for the man in charge to come and talk us through the process when Sebastian stormed in.

'I can't let you go through with this.'

'How did you know we were here?'

'Grace rang me. She's very upset, naturally. The whole idea of burning Father and then putting him in the vegetable patch is preposterous. I've booked a church and got an undertaker coming...' he looked at his watch '...in about twenty minutes.' He gave us a smug smile.

Ellen looked as if she was about to hit him, but Jeanette said, very calmly, 'That's not going to happen, Sebastian. I'm Walter's next of kin and he gave strict instructions, as you know, about his farewell.'

Mother and daughter stood shoulder to shoulder, facing him down.

The crematorium official came in and asked if they were ready.

'We are,' said Jeanette.

'This is not going to happen,' said Sebastian at the same time.

The official looked from one to the other.

I slipped out and called Mark to tell him what was happening.

'Oh, hello you,' he said. 'I enjoyed yesterday.'

'Me too,' I said, heart skipping a beat. 'But I'm afraid I really have called you in your professional capacity this time.'

'That's a shame, but fire away.'

I told him what was happening. 'What can we do?' I asked.

'Let me talk to Sebastian, would you?'

'Can I put you on speakerphone?'

'Good idea. You should all hear this.'

I went back in and told everyone I had Walter's solicitor on the phone. 'He wants to talk to us all,' I said and switched to speaker. 'We're ready when you are, Mark.'

'Mark?' said Sebastian. 'What's happened to Mr Hill?'

'Walter asked to see me in the week before he died. He wanted to make a statement about the disposal of his body.' Mark sounded very formal.

'Like bloody hell he did! He was off his head on painkillers – no-one would accept a statement made under those circumstances.'

Jeanette looked at me and blanched.

'Actually,' I cut in, 'Walter also asked for a psychiatrist to be present to assess whether he was mentally fit to do just that.' I couldn't suppress a smile. Jeanette sighed in relief.

'Jesus H Christ. I don't believe this. What else are you going to spring on me?'

'Can we stay on topic,' said Mark. 'I have a client waiting. Mr Armstrong, the fact of the matter is your father was declared mentally fit to make decisions and although they aren't legally binding–'

'Ha! There you are then.' Sebastian sneered at Jeanette.

'Although they aren't legally binding, as Executor I have the final say in the arrangements.'

'Now wait one bloody minute – you – the Executor?'

'Yes. That was also changed. So, as his Executor I say his wishes, while unusual, are within the law. Jeanette, are you there?'

'Yes.'

'I believe as his next of kin you're happy to comply with Walter's wishes?'

'Absolutely.' She stared at Sebastian as she said it. He glared at her.

'It's agreed then. Walter gets the send off he wanted in the way he wanted it. Now, I'm afraid I must go.'

'Thank you,' said Jeanette and Ellen in unison.

Sebastian scowled at us then turned on his heel. He swung back around as he reached the door. 'You haven't heard the last of this,' he said as he stomped out.

Jeanette turned to the crematorium official who was waiting quietly in the corner. He'd probably seen this all before. Death and funerals can bring out the worst in people, widening the cracks in families and letting all the old anger and resentments flood out. And the cracks had already been pretty wide in the Armstrong-Baxter family.

There wasn't a lot to it after that. Jeanette had to sign some papers. Walter's shrouded body was brought into the room and Jeanette and Ellen said their last goodbyes, teary-eyed but firm of voice. Then he was taken away to be cremated. Jeanette winced at the final clunk of the door closing behind him and almost ran out of the place, Ellen close behind. I thanked the official and followed them. They were already in the car by the time I got there and as I got in the back, Ellen drove off before I had the door shut.

'Thanks for calling Mr Johnstone,' said Jeanette. 'I don't know what we'd have done otherwise.'

I'm sure I blushed at his name, but Jeanette didn't notice, because at that moment Ellen swerved to avoid an empty hearse coming the other way up the drive. 'Haha, suckers! You're not getting my dad's body!'

Jeanette laughed. In fact, we all did. Ellen pulled over and we sat clutching our sides as if a hearse not collecting Walter's body was the funniest thing that had ever happened.

Grace was out when we got home. Laying low after her betrayal.

'I'm going to lie down for a while,' said Jeanette.

'I'll take Milly out,' said Ellen. 'I can't seem to settle to anything. Anyway, she's getting fat with all of us slipping our dinner to her under the table.'

My phone rang.

'Mark,' I said.

'Hi, Hester. I just wanted to make sure everything went okay. Sorry I had to go so abruptly.'

'No, it was fine. Thank you for sorting it out. You should have seen Sebastian's face. He was livid but he left, and Walter got his cremation.'

'I'm glad.' He paused. 'I meant it when I said I enjoyed our lunch yesterday.'

'Me too,' I said, feeling suddenly warm.

'Perhaps we could go out for dinner one night?'

'I'd love to, but can we leave it as an open invitation? Jeanette was rattled by what happened today and Grace is... well, I need to make sure she's okay.'

'I understand. My only regular commitments are on Monday and Thursday nights, so any other time, just let me know.'

'I will. And thanks again for today.'

I wondered what he did on Monday and Thursday nights. An evening class? Choir? Tiddlywinks?

Grace stayed out until early evening. I was in the kitchen when she tried to slip in unnoticed through the back door.

'Are you all right?' I asked.

'Why shouldn't I be?'

Because you've just had your heart broken and your father has died.

'Just wondered,' I said.

'I'm fine.'

She looked brittle, as if it was taking all her energy to walk and breathe. I decided not to push it, but she hovered just outside the door as if she wanted to say something.

I waited, feigning interest in drying a saucepan. My job involves a lot of waiting and looking as if I'm not. It'll be my epitaph: Hester Rose watched and waited.

Grace came back into the kitchen and opened the fridge.

'There's no juice,' she said, as if the world always disappointed her and she just had to accept it. I wondered where her anger had gone. I *worried* about where her anger had gone. I didn't like this apathetic version of her.

'Grace,' I said, carefully, 'the worst thing about grief is that you have to suffer through it. No-one can do it for you, and no-one is going to do it the same as you.'

She didn't look me in the eye, but she poured herself a glass of milk and sat at the table. I remained standing at the sink, earning my epitaph.

'The trouble is, Hester,' she whispered, 'I don't know if I feel worse about Daddy dying or the dickhead dumping me.' She sighed from the depths of her belly and started absent-mindedly spooning sugar into her milk.

'It's all such a jumble in my head and all I know is I'm really sad and really angry, but I don't know who I'm sadder about or angrier with.' Her shoulders slumped. She was still adding sugar to her glass. I watched, half of me wanting to laugh, the other half wanting to wrap her in my arms.

'I mean, I'm really pissed off with Mummy, obviously, because she was such a bitch and she wants to bury Daddy in the garden, which is really weird, but I'm angry with Mr Dickhead for being a coward and Daddy for dying, which doesn't make sense because he didn't choose to get cancer and leave us and none of my friends know what to say to me any more so they stay away or don't mention Daddy and they don't know about Mr Dickhead and that makes it worse because I can't talk to anyone about him and–'

I sat down next to her, put a hand on her forearm. 'Slow down, Grace. Take a breath.'

She sniffed and lay her head on my shoulder.

'It's normal to be confused and angry and sad and all sorts of other things right now.'

'Really? Nothing feels normal. I keep thinking it's all some awful joke and I'm waiting for the punchline – the moment when I'm told Daddy's alive and well and in the next room and Mr Dickhead loves me and wants us to be together.'

She sighed again and then she started crying, as if one deeper breath had given her tears the energy they needed to gather and fall.

Holding her, feeling her body shudder with sobs, there was nothing more to say.

On my way to bed later, I noticed Jeanette's door was open and her light on. I knocked and stuck my head around the door.

She was sitting at her dressing table, staring at her reflection.

'Anything I can get you?' I asked.

She didn't turn, instead she refocused to look at me in the mirror. Her face was gaunt, her eyes red. Lines that hadn't been there days before stretched from the sides of her nose to the edges of her mouth.

'I feel like I'm in suspended animation.' She looked back at her own reflection and lifted the flesh of her cheeks with her fingertips then let it drop. 'I don't know what to do without him. I don't know who I am. Even my body feels different without his to fit around. I don't mean just in bed. More generally. His absence makes me aware of how I used to adjust to his presence.'

I nodded, thinking about how it had been when Justin left home. All the space, all the time, all the longing. I'd had to redefine myself. I was suddenly the mother of an adult who didn't need me anymore. I was redundant, my job done. And although that was how it should be and I was proud of my independent son, the pain and the sense of loss were real.

Jeanette gave a half laugh. 'I thought I saw Walter just now. Over by the wardrobes. I often catch him out of the corner of my eye. When I realised it couldn't be him, I felt flattened. Hollowed out.' She rubbed her eyes and took a deep breath. 'I try to tell myself I'll feel better one day. Not better – different. The pain won't be so acute.'

'And that's the truth. The pain changes, softens.'

'Thank you, Hester. I'm glad you're here.' She opened the drawer and took out her Valium.

'Goodnight,' I said.

I was tired but when I got into bed, I thought about what I'd said to Jeanette. It was true grief changed over time, but when I thought about my sister and brother and their senseless violent deaths, sharp blades of anger and pain still pierced me. And guilt. Why had I been saved when they hadn't? Why was I allowed to have a life when theirs were cut short? Thinking about it left me floundering around in the same old emotional swamp. It was easier to shut it all out. I put a podcast on and got into bed.

I was so much better at dealing with other people's grief.

Two days later we collected Walter's ashes from the crematorium. They were in a cardboard box that Jeanette carried into the house and put on the kitchen table.

'I suppose we can set a date for the funeral now,' she said, stroking the container.

'The Not Funeral, you mean.' Ellen smiled.

'Party. Yes. Walter's last party.' She bowed her head and took a few breaths. 'The forecast for next week is good. Maybe Saturday?'

'Is it a bit soon? It doesn't give people much time to make arrangements, and can we get everything ready by then?'

'What's to do? Buy some food and drink, dig a hole–' She gasped and whirled round to face me. 'I can't do it. I can't put him in the ground. I'm not ready.'

'Then wait,' I said. 'There's no rush.'

'Grace apologised to me yesterday.'

'Oh yes?' I was used to abrupt topic changes in the bereaved. They'd step up to the unbearable and step away again. We all do it.

'She said she'd spoken to you. Thank you.'

'She's finding her way.'

'We'll do it on Saturday. I'll start making a list but perhaps you'd do the shopping? I'll need to make the phone calls. And

Hester, could you call Mr Johnstone and see if he'd come and read the will the same day – maybe late afternoon?'

'Of course.'

'I'd like to get it done. I don't want to see Sebastian any more than I have to. In fact, I'm hoping never to see him again after Saturday.'

She was probably being naïve thinking she'd never see him again, but I wasn't about to burst her bubble. We all need a silver lining sometimes.

I had to go to town for the shopping and took the opportunity to call Mark and see if he was free for lunch.

We arranged to meet in an Italian restaurant on the main street, squeezed in between an Oxfam shop and a men's outfitter. I wondered if Mark shopped for his suits there.

'Last time we met you grilled me about my life, so this time you have to tell me about you,' I said over the antipasto.

'I hope it didn't really feel like a grilling.' He smiled. 'It certainly wasn't meant to be.'

'Apology accepted.' I laughed and took a sip of my drink. 'But it is your turn now.'

He shrugged. 'Not much to tell really. I'm afraid my life has been quite tame. Nothing like yours in Africa. I was born not far from here, went to the local school, university in London and a couple of years working there. I married a girl I met at university, but it quickly became apparent she was much more ambitious than me. I think I was a disappointment to her. We divorced, and I came back to join the family firm. We're still in touch. She's a partner in a big law firm, married to the job.'

'I'm sorry it didn't work out.'

Mark gave a little shrug and smiled. 'It was better to find out early it wasn't going to work, before children came along. It was all quite amicable.'

'You didn't like London?'

'Not really. I think I'm a country boy at heart. The city was too impersonal, the people too transient. And big law firms are not nice places – they're full of people cutting and slashing their way to the partnerships. That wasn't me.'

I smiled.

'What's so amusing?' he asked.

'I was trying to imagine you in a place like that. The cut-throat world of law. Sounds awful.' Actually, I was imagining him in a Tarzan-style loincloth wielding a machete, but I thought it was too early in our acquaintance to let him in on my weird and wonderful fantasy life.

'It was. I had nightmares about morphing into one of them, of losing my humanity and running over mountains chasing a pot of gold.'

'I'm glad you got out.'

'Me too. I'm much happier in a small firm where we get to know most of our clients well and actually feel like we're doing something worthwhile.'

'And your mysterious Monday and Thursday nights?' I tried to sound nonchalant, but really, I was intrigued.

'Not so mysterious. I visit my mother. She went into a nursing home last year. She has Alzheimer's and my father couldn't look after her at home anymore. And then he died not long after.'

'I'm sorry.'

'Don't be. Dad hated living alone and he always said he wanted a massive stroke or heart attack to take him, so he got his wish, no suffering. And Mum's as happy as can be – she thinks all the other residents are her brothers and sisters and loves having lots of staff to look after her! She's like the Dowager Duchess from *Downton Abbey*.'

'And she still recognises you?'

'She knows me but not quite how I fit into her family. She tells me all about her little children, Mark and Hannah, but also knows I'm Mark. Time slips for people with dementia. Anyway, let's talk about something more interesting. How long can you stay out today? I don't have anything in my diary until three thirty, so we could do something after lunch, if you like?'

'I like,' I said and raised my glass.

We walked along the river, got chased by a hissing swan – those birds can move— and were caught in a sudden downpour. Mark took my hand and together we sheltered under a chestnut tree. He kept hold of my hand and pulled me towards him.

'We're not too old for this, are we?' he asked, looking into my eyes and smiling.

'I don't think so – right this moment I feel like a blushing teenager.'

'Me too.'

Kissing him was like arriving home after a long day and discovering your favourite dessert waiting for you. It was exciting and comforting at the same time, new and surprisingly familiar.

'I like kissing,' he said. 'As a pastime, I think it's hugely underrated.'

'I agree,' I said, and we kissed again.

WALTER

My poor Gracie. Some unworthy bastard has broken her heart. If I was still alive, I'd give him a piece of my mind, hurting her like that. Or a leather belt to the arse. I'm glad she's got Hester Rose to talk to.

Although if I was still alive, I'd likely know nothing about it. I'm learning all sorts about the family now I'm dead.

It turns out I can't leave the house. I sort of float – or more accurately, spread – because I can sense what's happening in more than one place at a time. And I hover about the same height above the floor as my eyes used to be, so I have the same perspective on things. Consciousness is weightless, of course, so hovering makes sense. There's probably a formula to describe what I'm doing. Ellen would know, she's good at science.

I like that Jeanette sees me. I know she doesn't really and it's just her grief making her think she does, but I want to put my arms around her and tell her I'm still here. Would it be a comfort to her? I don't know.

So, Jeanette, Ellen and Hester Rose went off to the crematorium to say their final farewells and make sure they burned the right body. I've been turned to ash and lumpy bits of bone. I'm relieved I didn't feel anything when they bunged me into the furnace. Total separation of body and consciousness. Thank God. Two days later they delivered me back to the house in a cardboard box. That's all very well – glad to be biodegradable.

Bloody Sebastian, turning up and trying to stop them from carrying out my wishes. He's such a fuck-knuckle. Blundering around pretending to be the head of the family now, I suppose, with no regard for anyone or anything but his own ego. Sometimes I wonder if I could have done things differently with him. Dorothy was an indulgent mother. I was working hard to build the business. He could have done with some discipline. A wooden spoon to the backside every so often to teach him right from wrong, whack the sense of entitlement out of him. I should have seen to it.

Sounds like the girls saw him off, though. They were still laughing about it when they got home. Nice to hear them laugh.

Dead. Sounds so final when you're dreading it, and then you discover it's not. I don't know how long I'll be hanging around or what'll happen next but even if this is just a transition, it's a good one. So far, anyway. Might not think so if I'm still here for the Not-the-Funeral Party. They've fixed the date for Saturday. I think that's four days away. Depending on who comes I might hear some less than loving words about myself. I can't wait!

In the meantime, I'm still having to deal with bloody Dorothy. Always was persistent.

I'm getting to the point where I'll apologise just to get rid of her. But knowing her, it wouldn't work. I know she was annoyed with me when I sacked old arse-face Cecil, but he was shit at his job and he should have had the balls to leave when Dorothy broke it off with him. Instead, he stayed on, watching me and waiting for me to fuck up. But I didn't. I was good at what I did, and he got more and more pissed off about it. Last straw was when I caught him trying to sabotage a shipment, thinking I'd get the blame for it. Always was stupid. It was so satisfying kicking him out. Dorothy tried to plead his case. I don't think she was still sweet on him, but she always went for the underdog. By then I was the rising star and he was a useless has-been. I made sure he didn't get another job in our area – I had contacts by then and I used them. That's business.

TEN

I found Jeanette in the kitchen the next morning, sitting at the table looking at the cardboard box containing Walter's ashes. The urn she'd made for him in her pottery class was next to it.

'We have to transfer Walter from here,' she pointed to the box, 'to here.' She tapped the urn then put her hands back in her lap and stared at the cardboard container. 'I can't believe all that remains of my husband is in there.'

'All that physically remains.'

'Yes, I suppose what matters is in here.' She put her hand over her heart and let out a long slow breath.

Then she sat up straighter. 'I don't think I can do it. I can't look at what's in the box.'

'I'll do it. Why don't you go and have a shower or something?'

She nodded, rose like an automaton and walked out of the room.

As I was wondering how best to get Walter's ashes into the urn, Ellen came in.

'Oh, are you doing what I think you're doing?'

'If you think I'm putting Walter in his beautiful urn, then yes, that's what I'm doing.'

She bit her bottom lip and looked at the box. 'I'll help.'

'The thing is, I reckon it's too small.'

She looked at the two containers. 'Shit. You're right. What are we going to do?'

'I think we should get what we can into the urn and see how much is left.'

'Okay.' She rummaged around in one of the kitchen drawers and found a funnel. 'This'll help.'

I smiled. The practical one, like her father.

As we lifted the lid off the box, the back door opened and Grace came in followed by a very excited Milly. The gush of wind that accompanied them blew a fine cloud of the ashes out of the box and onto the table and floor.

Quick as a flash, Milly was onto them, licking them up.

'Milly! Stop. Away.' Ellen grabbed her and pulled her back. 'Shitshitshit.'

'What the–' said Grace.

'Shit,' I echoed Ellen, hands flying to my face. Then I took a deep breath and busied myself scraping up the ashes from the table and funnelling them into the urn, adding what was in the box and tapping it to make sure there were no ashes left in the corners. Then I turned to the girls.

'They just fit.'

'Only because–' began Ellen.

'Mummy must never know,' said Grace, wide-eyed. 'Ever.'

We looked at Milly who was wagging her tail as always, unaware of what she'd just done.

'Are we agreed?' said Grace.

'Agreed about what?' asked Jeanette, coming into the kitchen, a towel wrapped round her head.

'That we need to seal the urn with wax or something,' said Ellen, 'to stop the lid coming off.'

'Good idea, darling. I think there's some sealing wax in the craft box. Remember when you did that project for school? The scrolls and treasure maps you made and then poured tea over to make them look old? We had to go all over the place to find sealing wax and then your father found some somewhere.'

'I'll get it,' said Grace, running out of the room.

Jeanette sat at the table, one hand on the urn.

'I'll make some tea,' I said and as I turned away, I noticed another dusting of ashes on the floor both Milly and I had missed. I caught Ellen's eye and looked from her to them. She gasped and her eyebrows shot up towards her hairline.

'Hey, Mum, why don't I blow dry your hair for you while Hester makes tea?'

'Excellent idea,' I said. 'I'll bring it through when it's made.'

'Thank you, that would be lovely.'

As they left, Ellen looked back over her shoulder at me then at Milly, and shook her head slightly.

I looked at the dog and wondered if she'd start channelling Walter now she'd ingested some of him. Springer spaniel meets shoe company executive. Would it make her more responsible: less ditsy dog and more mature mutt? Or would she now fixate on leather instead of underwear?

I laughed and shook my head. Sometimes, even I was alarmed by where my thoughts could take me. Milly, aware of my gaze, wagged her tail and looked at me hopefully. She probably wanted something to take the awful taste out of her mouth.

Later, as I was folding washing, there was a thud from upstairs followed by several more thumps. I looked up at the ceiling as if

I had X-ray vision and would be able to see what was going on. Another thud and then Jeanette's voice: 'Shit!'

I ran up the stairs to find her in her room, Walter's clothes strewn around. A lamp had been knocked over and there were books in a heap by the bedside table. Jeanette was flinging suits and shirts out of the built-in wardrobes onto the bed.

She hadn't seen me, so I knocked on the door.

She spun around, a mustard-coloured waistcoat in her hand. 'I'm sorting,' she said.

'I see.'

'I'm going to take it all to the charity shop in town.'

'Want a hand?'

'I just want it all gone.'

I didn't say anything.

'You think it's too soon,' she said.

'I think you're upset,' I said, 'and later you might regret throwing everything out so quickly.'

'I'm not throwing it out. I'm giving it to the poor and needy.'

'Even so,' I said. 'Giving it all away, while very noble, may not be the best thing right now.'

She looked at the waistcoat and sank onto the bed.

'It was his favourite. We all hated it, said it made him look like Toad of Toad Hall, but he just laughed at us and wore it more. That's what he was like – his own person. Didn't care what anyone else thought.' Slowly she put one arm and then the other into the waistcoat and wrapped herself in it. 'I can't forgive him for dying,' she said quietly. 'And I feel guilty because I'm so angry with him I want to scream.'

Her breath shuddered, and for a moment I thought she might be building up to that very thing, but she held her feelings in, hugged herself and keeled over so she was lying on the bed.

'I'd rather be alone,' she said.

Grace knocked on my bedroom door.

'Mummy's in a state,' she said, flopping down onto my bed.

'How about you? How are you doing?'

'Up and down. One minute I feel fine and the next I remember what's happened and I'm all over the place – sad about Daddy and feeling guilty I'm not crying all the time.'

'That's how grief goes.'

'Really? No-one tells you these things, do they? I thought I was a real cow for being able to still laugh at things.'

'And dare I ask how you're feeling about Ga–?'

'Mr Dickhead, you mean? Kind of switched off. It's like I can't be sad about Daddy and think about him too. Maybe I'll fall apart some time but at the moment I'm managing.'

'I'm glad. You're a remarkable young woman, Grace.'

She looked puzzled. 'Really?'

'Yes. You're sorting things out so well.'

She smiled and got up. 'I'm also starving. I'm going to make a sandwich – want one?'

When she'd gone, I sat thinking. I was glad she wasn't still pining for Gavin Green and hoped it would continue that way. When I'd been banished to England and didn't know what had happened to Jusu, I was bereft for weeks, unable to contain all my feelings: my anger at my father, the betrayal by my mother who should have stood up for me instead of agreeing with him, the loss of the boy I loved and didn't know what had happened to, being separated from my sister and brother and my home. I'd been unable from one moment to the next to work out what I was feeling and for whom.

In the cold bedroom in the cold house in the cold town where my grandparents lived, I wept, shouted, stared in silence at the walls, lay awake unable to form a coherent thought, wrote letters only to tear them up or scrunch them into tiny balls and flick them out the window. I couldn't eat, didn't talk, felt constantly sick – which was as much to do with my pregnancy as my inner turmoil, although I didn't know it at the time. I walked the damp grey streets of that northern town scowling at anyone who looked my way, searching for something familiar: a tree, a plant, the shape of a window in the façade of a house. Along the riverbank I found tiny pink flowers and sat looking at them for hours, willing them to become orchids growing at the base of an okuome tree. At my grandparents' house I paced, ran for the door every time the postman came, hoping for news, for an apology, for forgiveness, for an invitation to return home.

I had a sudden urge to see Peggy. Thinking of the past often had that effect. There was nothing specific required of me that afternoon, so I asked Mrs Jenkins, who was polishing the cupboard handles in the kitchen, to tell Jeanette I'd be gone for a couple of hours.

As I drove away, my shoulders relaxed and my breath settled. I hadn't realised how tense I'd been feeling. I sang along to Simon and Garfunkel, out of tune, out of time but happy. As I always did after I'd let myself think about my family, I counted my blessings: I had a beautiful son, had built myself a life I loved, had friends who made me laugh but also let me cry and I was going to see Peggy who grounded me and kept me sane.

She was in the lounge when I arrived, having a cup of tea with Gloria, her bridge partner. When she saw me, she smiled and started to get up.

'Don't,' I said, sitting next to her. 'Mind if I join you?'

'Are you working?' asked Gloria.

'No, just come to visit you. I need to let my hair down for a while.'

Peggy laughed. 'Well, you've come to the right place. Noel

the diversional therapist is coming in soon to do some dancing. Kick up those heels, Hester. We'll watch!'

'I thought maybe I could bust you out of here and take you for tea and cake.'

'Now you're talking,' said Peggy. 'Coming, Gloria?'

'No, you two go. I'll give Noel a run for his money.' Gloria wiggled her hips in her chair and her ample bosom jiggled. 'I'd better go and put my lipstick on,' she said and heaved herself out of her seat, grasped her Zimmer frame and limped off.

Peggy told the staff she was going out. As soon as we were settled in a café in town, Peggy asked about Mark.

'Tell me the latest. Have you been out yet?'

'Sort of. We had lunch and went for a walk.'

'And?'

'And nothing. He's nice. We get on well.'

'I do declare you're blushing, my girl. What else happened?'

I put a hand to my cheek. It was warm. 'You're like a pit bull, Peggy! We kissed. Okay? Now you know everything.'

'I knew it! When are you seeing him again?'

'He'll be at the interment of Walter's ashes on Saturday.'

'Ooh, how romantic.'

'And that's enough.' I smiled. 'How are you?'

'Better for seeing you, dear. I'm all right. The doctor gave me something for my ankles – you know how they swell up. Seems to be working but I have to go to the toilet all the time. Anyway, enough about me. Tell me about Justin. He rang the other day, but I didn't have my phone with me. He left a message saying he was going to come down soon.' She stopped and put a hand over her mouth. 'I wasn't meant to tell you. It was going to be a surprise.'

I laughed. 'If he didn't want me to know he should never have told you – you're the world's worst secret keeper. Did he say when?'

'No. Just that it would be soon.'

We drank our tea and ate too-sweet vanilla slices. When I dropped her back at the nursing home, I watched Peggy negotiate the front steps. She was leaning heavily on the handrail and I wondered if I should have probed more about her health. She'd lost weight since I'd last seen her. She'd always been one to minimise her suffering, preferring to soldier on without complaint, but at her age it was better to know exactly what was going on. I promised myself I'd interrogate her next time.

I sang my way back to the Baxters, wondering when Justin would be down, and looking forward to seeing him.

Ellen greeted me at the door.

'Oh, thank God you're back,' she said.

'What's the matter?'

'It's Mum – she's gone mad. I went up to see if she was okay and she threatened me with a golf club!'

My heart skipped a beat. I thought back to Jeanette throwing Walter's clothes around earlier and wondered if I'd missed something. She hadn't appeared frenzied; it was more a desire to clear out physically what she couldn't emotionally. Or so I had thought.

'Where's Grace?'

'She went to see one of her friends, I think.'

'Right. Where's Jeanette?'

'In the lounge.'

She hovered on the doorstep, so I went in past her and headed for the living room. There were noises coming from behind the closed door: the clinking of glasses.

I turned to Ellen who was at my shoulder.

'Does she have anyone in there with her?'

She shook her head. 'She's been talking to herself though.'

I knocked and entered without waiting for a response. Jeanette was standing by the drinks cabinet. I was glad to see she was holding a nearly full bottle of brandy instead of the golf club. She turned away as I approached.

'A little early for that, isn't it?' I asked.

She hugged the bottle to her chest.

'How about you sit down for a minute, you look done in,' I said. I had no idea how she looked as she still wasn't facing me, but it was as good a guess as any.

Still clenching the bottle, she sank into an armchair. I saw her face then – her jaw was hard and her lips tight. Her eyes were glassy in her thin face. She didn't so much look done in as half dead.

I glanced around the room. On the coffee table there was an assortment of objects: a cut-crystal glass; *Cairo Mon Amour*, the book we'd been reading to Walter but hadn't finished; a shirt; a pair of glasses; a mobile phone; and the golf club.

Jeanette got up and added the bottle of brandy to the collection. She remained standing, swaying slightly. I wondered for a moment if she was drunk but there was no smell of alcohol on her breath. Suddenly, she screamed. A high-pitched prolonged cry of anguish. Her hands clenched by her sides, her head thrown back, eyes closed. She kept on and on, getting louder, sucking in sharp breaths and shrieking some more.

Ellen appeared at the door, but I waved her away. Jeanette needed this and had her daughter come in she would have stopped to look after her instead of doing what she needed to do. The work of grief, of claiming the voice of her pain.

Finally, she quietened and sat again, limp, head bowed, spent. Breath coming in gasps, shudders. I knelt beside her and put my hand on her knee.

She gestured to the table. 'They're all things he'll never

finish or need again. The book – he'll never know how it ended. He died not knowing. The shirt was in the mending basket waiting for a button it won't need now. His favourite glass, the bottle of brandy he won't get to drink, the golf club I bought him for his birthday just days before he was diagnosed.'

She turned to me. 'What's it all for, Hester? Can you tell me that? What's it all bloody well for?' Her voice rose, a hysterical edge to it.

'I don't know, Jeanette. I don't know what it's all for.'

'It's a fucking farce. It's all for nothing. NOTHING!' she yelled. Jumping to her feet again, she began pacing the room.

'This cabinet? We found it in a second-hand shop in Paris and had it shipped back. The sofas? It took years to find exactly what we wanted. The curtains – months of looking at fabrics and disagreeing about the one we liked. For what? None of it matters a jot anymore.'

She picked up the crystal glass and held it in her hand as if assessing the weight of it, then she hurled it into the fireplace and watched it shatter against the stone. She stared, silent, unmoving, and then looked at the hand that had held the glass as if she couldn't understand what had happened. Then she crumpled, falling onto the sofa clutching herself and weeping.

I went to the door and found Ellen, wide-eyed, in the hall.

'She needs you now.'

I left them lying on the sofa holding each other, Ellen stroking her mother's hair and whispering words of comfort.

Grace got back while Ellen and Jeanette were still in the lounge, and I was boiling water for the pasta. She breezed in looking more cheerful than I'd seen her; getting away from the house had been good for her.

'Nice afternoon?' I asked.

She nodded and took an apple out of the fruit bowl, then disappeared to her room.

Jeanette didn't join us for dinner, but Grace and Ellen were hungry for a change, and chatty. Ellen had phoned the university about her absence and had good news.

'I've got a second chance. I told my tutor about Dad being ill all year and he gave me a rap over the knuckles for not telling him sooner. Basically, they're going to let me carry on, subject to pulling my finger out next term and getting a credit average.'

'And?'

'It's doable.' She took a mouthful of pasta and chewed for a while, looking thoughtful. 'I actually feel excited about going back. I haven't felt this way for months. It isn't that I'll stop missing Dad, but he isn't connected with the place in my mind, so I think I'll be able to kind of switch off from all that's happened and concentrate on my course again.'

'That's good.'

'I don't want to forget him or anything, but I do want to feel normal again. Does that sound awful?'

'No. People always think grief is a twenty-four hour a day, seven days a week process and you'll wake up one day and feel better. It's not like that at all. It comes and goes. It's sharp and it's soft. It flattens you one minute and disappears the next.' I paused. 'Like your mother today.'

Grace looked at me in alarm, her fork halfway to her mouth.

'What happened? Is she okay?'

'She's calmer now, but today was a difficult one for her.'

WALTER

I liked that glass. Stuart Crystal. A present from Dorothy. One of a pair. Not that I need it anymore. Jeanette could have used it. I seem to remember she broke the other one too, although that was an accident.

It's cruel seeing her suffer and not being able to do anything about it. I wanted to put my arms around her and soothe her like I used to when she was upset. Not that she got upset often. She's a strong woman. But compassionate too. The sorts of things she gets upset over are finding a litter of baby hedgehogs abandoned by their mother, or a bird with a broken wing. She'd be all practical and deal with whatever the problem was and then at night she'd cry in my arms. Once, she accidentally killed a vole when she was digging in the garden. You'd have thought she'd assassinated Mother Theresa.

And this morning in the kitchen – if I could have laughed, I would have pissed myself when Hester Rose was transferring me into my beautiful urn. I've always known Milly is the greediest mutt in the world but the rate at which she lapped me up from the floor was impressive, even for her. You'd have thought she hadn't been fed for a week. I don't think she was impressed with how I tasted – a bit dry too, I expect. She'd have preferred me mixed in with a bit of Chum. Maybe we should consider a dog-meat industry for the dead. Spend your life with your best friend and then be fodder for them when you die. Nice idea, but it won't catch on. People are too squeamish.

The girls are doing okay. Grace is a softie like her mother, but a sensible one. And Ellen, well, she's like me. She'll move on and get back into her studies. She'll go far, with her work ethic. She can get on with anyone, too. Both of them can. That's an asset these days.

I wish I could hold them all again. That's the only downside of being in this state. I can see and hear but I can't intervene in any way. Powerless. Is it my punishment?

Or is Dorothy my punishment? Still here. Still disapproving. Still don't know what she's waiting for.

We were married in spring, in the village church. Her father gave her away. Yes, he gave her to me. He hadn't been too impressed when she gave Cecil the heave-ho and he certainly wasn't in raptures over the fact she'd picked up with me, but we took it slowly and I worked hard, and he began to see my potential. Gave me more responsibility. Then gave me his daughter. And now she won't leave me alone.

ELEVEN

Saturday morning saw the sun peeping out from behind the clouds and the wind dropping to a light breeze. In the Baxter household we were up early, breakfasted and in our work clothes by just after seven.

'I'm going to go and dig,' said Jeanette.

We'd tried, over the last few days, to persuade her to get someone else to dig the hole for Walter's ashes, but Jeanette was adamant she wanted to do it, and do it on her own. And leave it until the last minute. I suspected she needed to do something physical before fronting the guests and steeling herself to get through the afternoon.

She held herself tall as she walked out, and I wondered what putting on this show of fortitude was costing her.

Turning to the girls, I said, 'Right, Ellen, Grace, you're with me. Mrs Jenkins will be here later to do some cleaning and help hand round food and drink, but there's a lot of preparation to do and we need to put some tables outside for the refreshments.'

Grace pulled a face.

'None of it will take long if we all help,' I said.

'I want to put some decorations up too,' said Ellen. 'Dad

loved Christmas. He always took us up to London to see the lights in Oxford Street and the window displays.'

'Good idea,' said Grace. 'And what about flowers?'

I closed my eyes for a moment and took a deep breath. When Jeanette had set the date for the Not Funeral, I'd suggested they think about what they wanted to do for it and prepare ahead of time and now here they were, with only a few hours to go until the guests arrived, planning the décor.

'Okay,' I said, trying not to sound as pissed off as I was. I knew they were grieving, but it shouldn't have stopped them doing any planning. 'I'll see to the food, you do the tables and decorations and perhaps you can come and help in the kitchen after you're done?'

'Thanks, Hester,' said Ellen. Grace blew me a kiss and they both rushed out.

I went to get clean hand towels for the bathrooms and make sure there was soap, then headed back to the kitchen to start on the food. Ellen and Grace were there, Christmas decorations all over. Glitter dusted the floor and table as it detached itself from baubles and a nativity scene. Heads down, the girls were trying to untangle the fairy lights.

'Damn!' said Grace, dropping her handful of lights. 'It's impossible. We'll have to get new ones.'

'And where, exactly, do you think you'll get Christmas lights around here in June?' I asked.

Their faces dropped.

'We'll borrow some.' Grace pulled out her phone and started texting, her fingers moving over the screen faster than the spiders that occasionally scrabbled across my bathroom wall.

'I don't want to put a dampener on your decorative genius, but there isn't much time – the guests will be arriving in a few hours, and there's still a lot to do.'

'It's fine, Hester,' said Ellen. 'Grace can take my car and get the lights and I'll cut some flowers and then help you with the food.'

'Why do you want lights, anyway? Everyone will be gone before it gets dark enough to put them on.' Most of the time I'm an accommodating person. I go along with other people's ideas, help them where I can, encourage when necessary. Today, though, I was annoyed. Jeanette was still digging, the girls were in la la land over their bloody fairy lights, and I was having to do everything. I wouldn't have time to have a shower, iron my dress and dab a bit of blusher and mascara on. Mark was coming and I wanted to look fresh and gorgeous. Now I'd end up looking like I'd been dragged through a hedge backwards, as usual.

'He'll know we did it for him, that we were thinking of him. Even if we don't turn them on. Anyway, we will. We'll still be here after dark, won't we?'

There was no answer to that. Short of aliens taking them away or a nuclear bomb going off nearby, they would still be there that night and for many nights after. If only they could have planned their exterior decorating sooner.

'Okay.' I sighed. I'm not a sigher usually, but I sighed then.

Grace nudged me with her shoulder. 'Thanks, Hester. You're a star.'

'A fading one right now,' I said, but I couldn't help smiling. 'Just hurry up, will you?'

There's comfort in routine work. Chopping vegetables, arranging cheeses and crackers on platters, polishing glasses, folding napkins. Ellen made a beautiful flower arrangement for the buffet table, and then cooked. She was focused and efficient in the kitchen, making mini quiches, sausage rolls, but not just any sausage roll – these were chorizo, gruyere and apple rolls and looked delicious – a white bean dip, finger sandwiches of salmon, cream cheese and dill.

'Nothing fancy,' she said as she popped yet another batch of pastries into the oven. 'We don't want the guests sticking around too long, do we?'

Definitely not. The day would be exhausting enough without people hanging around till all hours.

'I'll go and start setting up tables,' I said, taking the tablecloths with me. Mrs Jenkins had bleached and starched them, and they were dazzlingly white. She'd be finished with the cleaning soon and would be staying on to help hand out food and top up drinks.

Laying out glasses and cutlery on the table in the shade of the old chestnut tree, I could hear the regular strike of spade to earth in the distance.

And then, 'Oh, shit!' Jeanette's voice carrying on the warm air.

I waited for a moment to see if anything followed, but there was just the sound of digging so I carried on with my task, clamping the cloths to the tables so they wouldn't blow off as soon as the breeze picked up.

Grace screeched up the drive and rushed over with a large box under her arm.

'Tilda had some. Yards and yards of the things. And neatly wound. We'll have to do that this year when we take them off the tree.' She paused, gazed around as if disorientated. 'I suppose we'll have Christmas this year. I mean, with Daddy gone–' She took a deep breath and turned to me. 'Will we?' A tear made its way down her cheek.

'I'm sure you will.'

She wiped her eyes, opened the box and took out the lights. 'Well, tonight will look like Christmas. I'm going to get the ladder.'

And she was off, running towards the garage.

Milly followed her, getting between her feet so she almost fell. I called the dog back. This day was going to be tough enough without accidents happening.

Jeanette strolled over, dirt smearing her clothes and hands. She looked like she'd returned from the trenches. She had. But there was a lightness about her, as if the hard physical toil had helped her work something out. She wiped her forehead, smearing mud into her hair.

'I'll help with that,' she said to her daughter as she struggled with the ladder.

I looked at my watch. Less than an hour until people started arriving.

'Me too,' I said. 'All hands on deck.'

Milly pranced around us as we passed the lights up to Grace who strung them through the branches and along the hedge.

'I'll get the extension cord,' said Jeanette and she made her way back to the house. Minutes later, the lights were on but almost invisible against the sun streaming through the leaves.

'At least we know they work,' said Grace. Then she sprinted off to the kitchen to help Ellen with the final touches.

Jeanette and I looked at each other.

'Ready?' I asked.

'Never. But it has to be done. Walter deserves a good send off.' She looked up at the lights in the tree. 'He'd love this,' she said. 'I'm so glad the girls thought of it.' She took a deep breath and held her hand over her heart, closing her eyes. Tears streaked their way through the dirt on her face. Then she turned away and walked toward the house.

I finished laying out the crockery and cutlery then followed her in.

It was nothing less than miraculous. Ellen had managed to produce dozens of bite-sized quiches and sausage rolls and get them onto platters dressed with fresh salad leaves and herbs. The dips were in deep bowls and the crudités were standing in glasses next to them ready to go. How she'd managed to get everything done was a complete mystery to me.

She was red in the face and her hair was all over the place, but she gave a satisfied smile as she surveyed her handiwork.

'That'll do,' she said. 'Your cheese platters are ready to go and there's more of everything in the boot room to put out later.'

'Brilliant,' I said.

With that, we all left to shower and change and prepare ourselves for the Not Funeral party.

There must have been seventy or eighty people spread around the garden. I scanned the faces for Mark, but he hadn't arrived. Perhaps he was only coming later for the reading of the will. My heart sank at the idea; it would have been good to have him there to help corral Sebastian if he started playing up.

Jeanette and the girls were bearing up well as they accepted condolences from their guests, moving from one group to another, not allowing themselves to get stuck with anyone for too long.

Mrs Jenkins and I filled glasses, handed round the food and directed people to more on the laden table.

'And how did you know Walter?' asked a suited man with silvering sideburns.

'I'm a family friend,' I said, not wanting to have to explain further. 'And you?'

'Foreman of the factory. Ted Vines.'

'Have you been there long?'

'Thirty years come October.'

'That's a fair while. What was Walter like to work for?'

'Mr Armstrong was a demanding boss but always treated his workers well. There was never any trouble from the union, and that's saying something.'

'It certainly is,' I agreed. 'I expect you had a hand in it too, though. The link between management and shop floor?'

He reddened slightly and cleared his throat. 'Maybe. Once or twice.' He looked at his feet and then excused himself and went off to get some food. I watched him take a sandwich and stand eating it self-consciously until another man joined him and he relaxed and started chatting.

I wondered about Walter as a boss. He had been mine, too, but in such different circumstances. He might have been paying me, but I was a person he could rely on for help and guidance. I doubted he had ever let himself be in that position before.

Jeanette approached with a woman who obviously wanted to get more wear out of a fascinator she'd bought for going to the races. It was so out of place here I couldn't stop staring at it. She put a hand up to touch it.

'Lovely, isn't it?' she said.

I could only nod and glance at Jeanette, who was trying not to laugh.

I put my hand out. 'Hester,' I said.

She shook it. 'Pauline. Wife of–' She turned, scanned the guests and then pointed at a very tall man who was bending down to listen to something a petite blonde in a dress two sizes too small was saying. Pauline's mouth tightened momentarily and then she forced herself to carry on. 'Brian Coombes. One of Walter's golfing friends.' She cranked her face into a smile, excused herself and marched over to her husband, putting her arm through his in a proprietorial manner.

Jeanette laughed. 'Pauline Coombes. One of the most boring women I've ever met, married to one of the most interesting men. Funny, isn't it, who people end up with? He's in banking but loves gardening. He helped me a lot when I first decided to tackle the mess here. And he reads anything and everything so he's a great dinner party guest.' She paused and let her eyes roam over the people gathered on the lawn. 'I don't suppose I'll be having many dinner parties now. And these people – I'll never see most of them again.'

'Where are they all from?'

'The business.' She indicated a group standing near the hedge, chatting and looking sombre. 'Golf club.' She nodded towards Brian and Pauline and two other couples. 'Classic car club.' A cluster of men looking awkward. 'My close friends, Brigid and Juliet – we met at university.' Two women in summery dresses saw us looking at them and waved. Jeanette waved back and raised her glass.

'And village.' Jeanette smiled over at the men and women who were chatting easily with each other, occasionally laughing at something someone said. 'The one in the green dress is Marie, Louise's mother.'

'Gosh,' I said. 'I didn't realise she was a local. How was that for you?'

'Fine. Marie's a good friend. She wasn't at all bitter about Walter and was one of the first people to welcome me when I came to live here.'

'Like mother, like daughter, then,' I said, thinking of Louise at the family lunch.

'Exactly. Lovely women, both of them. They have given me a few tips about handling Sebastian and Anna over the years. And listened when I needed to offload.'

'Speak of the devil,' I said.

'Sebastian,' said Jeanette, chin raised.

'Jeanette. Hester.' He nodded to us curtly and then gestured to the assembly. 'I see the usual sycophants have crawled out of the woodwork to pay their respects.'

'They're Walter's friends and colleagues. He'd have been happy to see them all.'

Sebastian grunted.

'Is Deborah here?' I asked.

'She couldn't make it. Prior engagement.' He turned to Jeanette. 'You didn't give us a lot of warning.'

She smiled. 'Everyone makes their choices, don't they, Sebastian? I chose this weekend. The people here chose to come, some of them postponing other plans.'

He clenched his jaw.

'And Anna?' I asked.

'She's here, but you'll never see her at the food table.'

'Of course,' said Jeanette. 'She'll be by the drinks. I'll go and say hello.'

Sebastian watched her go; his mouth drawn into a thin line of distaste.

'So, how are you?' I asked.

He turned to me. 'How am I meant to be? I've been kept out of all the arrangements – no, more than that, my attempts to help have been rebuffed – and here I am talking to the hired help.'

Ouch. 'I won't keep you,' I said and started to walk off. He grabbed hold of my arm.

'Stop,' he said. 'That was rude.'

'Yes, it was.' I looked at his hand on my forearm. He loosened his grip.

'As you know, my father and I had little time for each other.'

I didn't reply.

'He was a shit of a father and a shit of a man.'

'Whatever you say.' I shook myself free and this time managed to walk away, leaving him standing by the table alone.

I grabbed a bottle of wine and mingled again, topping up drinks. As I went from group to group, I overheard snippets of what people were saying about Walter.

Ted Vines was chatting with some others from the factory. His staff thought he was a fair boss, a powerful negotiator, but at times rather stern and rigid. One man standing with them was tight-lipped as he listened to the others praising Walter. It was clear he had a different impression of his boss, and I wondered what it was. I dallied as long as I could, but he didn't say a word.

The friends from the golf and car clubs Walter had belonged to found him to be helpful, a good friend, an average golfer, generous, amusing. None of this surprised me.

I took an empty bottle back to the table and glanced around.

Grace was with a huddle of friends. Ellen had joined Jeanette who was greeting Louise, her willowy husband and three energetic boys, who had burst out of the car and now needed to run around. I went over.

After saying hello to Louise and her husband, Alan, I suggested to the boys that we go and find Milly, who had been locked in the house. Taking the youngest by the hand, I headed off, turning to make sure the other two were following. Louise smiled and nodded her thanks.

Opening the back door and entering the utility room, I knew instantly I had walked into a disaster. With the boys pressing in behind me I stopped and took stock of the scene in front of me. Milly, flakes of pastry decorating her muzzle, wagged her tail frantically, but didn't look at me, as if she knew she'd done a bad thing. A very bad thing. The trays on which the quiches and sausage rolls had been cooling were upturned on the floor. Half-eaten food scraps were decorating the tiles.

'What's happened?' asked the youngest boy, Rory, whose hand I was still holding.

That broke the spell.

'Milly has eaten all the food,' I said.

'Will she be sick?' asked Ben.

'Probably.' I looked at the dog and her distended abdomen.

'Cool,' said Tom. 'Our dog, Suki, once ate a whole chicken and she was sick all over the floor. It was gross.'

His brothers laughed and acted out Suki vomiting for my benefit.

I smiled, but I was worried about Milly who was looking as green around the gills as a brown and white spaniel can look. She'd stopped wagging her tail and had flopped down onto the ground and lay there panting.

'Let's get her some water and clean up this mess,' I said.

'I'll get the water,' said Ben, and his brothers followed him into the kitchen.

'Her bowl is by the pantry door,' I called after them.

Kneeling by the dog, I stroked her head. 'Silly fool, Milly. Greedy, greedy dog.' She looked up at me as if to say, 'I know. And I feel terrible.'

The boys came back, trailing a stream of water behind them, Ben carrying the bowl as carefully as he could, tongue sticking out between his teeth as he concentrated.

'There,' he said as he put it down by Milly. The boys sat by her and patted her gently, all their wild energy gone as they focused on the sick dog.

I swept the floor and threw away the scraps Milly had left, wondering how many quiches she'd eaten. A couple of dozen, I guessed. No wonder she felt so sorry for herself. There were still two trays of sandwiches and sausage rolls sitting on a shelf, so at least there was something to put out when the guests needed them.

At that moment, the door opened and Ellen came in. She stopped short when she saw us, looked around and then down at the dog. Then she started laughing, deep belly laughs. The boys looked at her and joined in. Milly lay her head on her paws and watched out of her big brown eyes.

When they'd all calmed down, I offered the boys a sandwich and then asked them to help me take the rest out and put them on the tables.

'Are you all right?' I asked Ellen.

'I'm fine. Dad would have laughed his head off at that. Always said Milly was the greediest dog he'd ever met. Anyway, there's plenty of food.' She bent down to stroke the dog, who wagged her tail weakly. 'Bet you feel awful, don't you, Mill? We'd better leave you to sleep it off and then run you round the fields later. Shall we?' she said, opening the door, and we followed the boys out.

From one disaster to another. As I exited the kitchen, two more guests were arriving: Gavin Green, accompanied by an older woman in a suit and high heels that kept sinking into the grass, making her walk like a drunk. They arrived at the food table, beside which was an easel where a portrait of Walter and his family was on display.

I intercepted them before they got anywhere near Grace.

'Good afternoon, I'm Hester.'

'Davina Lacey, headmistress of Grace's school.' She put out a hand to shake and then gestured to Gavin. 'And Gavin Green, one of her teachers. We thought we'd come and pay our respects.'

'Mr Green and I met at a football game a few weeks ago,' I said.

He nodded, keeping his eyes on the photo. Pale-faced, Gavin looked like he'd just been asked to clean out the shark tank at the local aquarium.

'Very thoughtful of you to come, Davina. Jeanette and the

girls are over near the tree,' I said, pointing. 'But I wonder if I might borrow you, Gavin, if you don't mind. I need some muscle.'

'Of course,' he said, looking relieved.

As Mrs Lacey walked off, I turned to Gavin. 'I'm surprised to see you here, to be honest.'

'Because?' He looked around, ran a finger round his collar.

'Grace told me about you and her. She was quite upset.'

'Ah.' He scratched his ear and sucked in his lips.

'It's okay, I haven't told anyone, but I don't think it's appropriate for you to be here today.'

'Neither do I, but being a house master and therefore available at weekends, Davina asked me to come. A bigger representation from the school and all that. She wouldn't take no for an answer.'

'I'll tell her you got oil on your clothes helping me with something and had to go back to school to change.'

He looked around briefly and retreated further into the shade of the house, then nodded. 'Good idea. And Hester, thanks. Is Grace okay? I didn't mean to hurt her, especially not at a time like this, but it couldn't continue. Christ, if I'd known–' He stopped. 'She's a lovely girl, though. But not in that way.'

'She'll live,' I said. I believed he really was sorry but now wasn't the time to indulge his guilt or hear his confession. Every minute he was at the house was a minute Grace might turn and see him.

'Now, off you go,' I said. He sighed and turned away. I watched as he practically ran off down the drive without looking back.

I was just congratulating myself on a calamity avoided when Grace grabbed me by the shoulder.

'Was that who I thought it was?'

'Yes. I told him to leave.'

Her nostrils flared. 'You had no right.'

'I was trying to avert a scene. No-one needs more stress today.'

She turned away and I saw resolve in her bearing.

'Grace, don't you dare think of going after him. This isn't the time.'

Just then Jeanette tapped the side of her glass with a spoon to get everyone's attention. All eyes turned to her. Grace let out a long hard breath and went over to join her. Ellen was already by her side.

'Thank you for coming,' she said, her voice shaky. 'We're here because of Walter. To remember him, to honour him. As a husband, a father, a colleague and a friend.' She looked around at the guests standing silently in front of her. 'He didn't want speeches. He didn't want tears.' She stopped to wipe hers away, took a deep shuddering breath. 'What he wanted was for us to gather and tell stories – about him or anything else. Just to be together for a while, bury his ashes and have a party.' Her voice broke but she carried on. 'So, in keeping with his wishes, please follow me into the walled garden where he will be laid to rest.'

She led them through the gate. The soil from the hole was heaped onto a tarpaulin to one side. A Japanese maple stood next to it in its pot, waiting to crown Walter once he'd been buried.

Everyone was sombre as they stood around the urn. The men had their hands crossed in front of them; the women clutched their bags. All eyes were downcast. Except for Jeanette's. She gazed around as if trying to gather strength from the assembly.

I noticed Mark slipping in through the gate and relaxed. His presence instilled confidence. Nothing would go wrong now. I saw him glance around, looking – I hoped – for me. I caught his eye and we smiled.

Jeanette lifted the urn and held it to her chest. 'Walter wanted this to be simple. I'm going to place him in the hole and invite anyone who wants to come and throw in a handful of soil and help plant the tree he requested.'

She kissed the lid of the urn and closed her eyes for a moment. Grace and Ellen did the same.

'I can't do this,' Jeanette whispered, head down, shoulders heaving.

Ellen gently took the urn from her and placed it on the ground. She and Grace put their arms around her, and they knelt there by the grave. The guests remained quiet.

Eventually, Jeanette lifted her head, blew her nose and picked up the urn again.

'Goodbye, my darling,' she said and settled Walter's ashes into the hole.

She stood, picked up a handful of soil and threw it in before stepping back to make room for others. The girls had tears in their eyes and weren't trying to stop them as they watched Sebastian step forward, followed by Anna, Louise and Marie. The boys chucked clods of earth in and chorused, 'Bye, Granddad!' before their father whisked them away to the main garden for lemonade, little Rory crying in his arms.

One by one, Walter's friends, staff and colleagues stepped up. When they'd finished Jeanette lifted the tree out of its pot and put it in the hole. Sebastian was nowhere to be seen, so Mark took the spade. He looked at her and she nodded. We all watched as he filled the hole, firming the tree into the ground.

Jeanette touched the leaves gently and murmured something, but I didn't catch what it was. Then she turned and invited everyone back to the main garden to toast her husband. Head high, she walked sedately, flanked by her daughters.

Mark and I hung back.

'You're a truly decent man,' I said.

'Well, Sebastian wasn't here to offer, and Jeanette and the girls look done in.'

'I'm amazed at how well they're doing in general, but yes, they are exhausted now. The sooner the guests leave the better, I think.'

We joined the others just in time to hear Sebastian call for silence.

'He may not have wanted speeches, but my father can't exactly stop us now. I think it's fitting for me to say a few words as his only son.'

My eyes searched for Jeanette. She was standing stony-faced by the drinks table, gripping a glass of whisky.

I went over.

'I knew he'd do this,' she said. 'I even told Walter when we were talking about his wishes. He laughed and said we'd better let him get on with it. Let him think he was important, the spokesperson for the family. We'd know different, that's what he said.'

I nodded. 'Perceptive man, your Walter.'

She smiled. 'He certainly had the measure of his son.'

Sebastian cleared his throat. 'My relationship with my father was not an easy or a close one, as most of you know. When my sister, Anna, and I were little, he was building a successful company and perhaps had less time for family than we all would have liked. But I do remember the excitement of going out on the boat for the first time. My father called me his First Mate and allowed me to take the helm for a while as we cruised out into the bay. And there were family picnics in the summer, often at the vintage car club rallies where he'd tell me about engines and horsepower and instilled in me an appreciation for a well-designed car.'

I glanced over at Jeanette who was looking surprised. Who

would have thought Sebastian had a kind word to say about his father?

Perhaps I'd been impressed too soon. From there on, the speech became a litany of Walter's business achievements and Sebastian's vision for the future of the company. It became more like an annual report than a eulogy.

When I looked at Jeanette again, she had a tight smile fixed on her face. I guessed she'd stopped listening.

When he finally finished, there was a smattering of applause that died out quickly, as if everyone had remembered they were at a funeral not an award ceremony. Sebastian smiled at those assembled like a kindly benefactor.

'Thank you all for coming,' he said, as if he'd organised the whole thing.

'Uncle Sebastian,' piped up a little voice, 'your trousers are undone.'

A titter spread through the assembly. As Sebastian looked down, he reddened then turned and stalked off, doing up his flies as he went.

Jeanette stepped up, glass in hand. She smiled at Rory and the little boy beamed back at her.

'Come and hold my hand, would you? We have an important job to do now.'

Rory trotted over to her side; his chest puffed up. Jeanette took his hand and smiled down at him before turning again to the guests.

'Rory and I ask you all to please raise your glasses and drink to Walter,' she said and drained her drink down in one.

WALTER

Fucking cheek that Gavin Green had turning up. Good thing Hester Rose got rid of him so quickly. I don't know what he was thinking, coming here. I'd like to take a cricket bat to his arrogant little head. How did he know about my death anyway?

It wasn't a bad turn out. That Mark's a good one. I think he's a bit sweet on Hester Rose. They'd be good together. Nice if it happened, my death bringing two decent people into each other's orbit. You never know when life is going to throw these things at you. Meeting Jeanette at a wedding and marrying her less than a year later – best thing that ever happened to me. A new start. The end of dalliances with women I met through work: the manageresses of shoe shops, lady sales reps. Each hoping to become the new Mrs Armstrong and live in the big house.

Anyway.

I couldn't be everywhere at the same time, but I heard more positive things about myself from friends and colleagues than I ever did when I was alive. And some not so good things. But, hey, you can't please all of the people all of the time, can you?

And Sebastian's speech! If I could have done, I'd have fallen over with shock. I'm glad he remembers some of the good times. All the rest that came later made me forget we used to have fun. The rest of the speech – well, it's just who he is.

I hate to see Anna as she is, trying to be invisible.

My other girls were amazing. Didn't feel the need to hold themselves together but still made everyone feel welcome and included. There were some tears. Jeanette told me I couldn't order people not to cry. She was right, as always.

Dorothy was hanging around, as usual. I thought I saw her shaking her head when Ted Vines said those nice things about me. Might even have heard a tut. What would she know? It's one thing haunting me, but I won't be judged. She always was one to offer an opinion and often based on nothing but hearsay. Not long before she died, she called me a trumped-up shop boy. She'd just found out about Delia, I think. Or was it Rhonda, the little Welsh bombshell? I hurt her. I realise it now. Those affairs meant nothing to me, but they did to her.

I saw Ma hovering around at the edges of the gathering and felt heartened by her presence. I could have been a better son, kept in touch more, made sure she was happy in her old age, yet here she is, keeping an eye on me. What a generous woman.

What about the fat mutt, Milly? Hope she'll be all right. Stupid dog.

TWELVE

As the shadows lengthened the guests started leaving until only close friends and family were left. Jeanette was talking to Brigid and Juliet over by the walled garden. Grace was still flanked by friends. Sebastian, Anna and Jeff were by the drinks table working their way steadily through the half-empty bottles. Louise and Marie were helping Mrs Jenkins gather up plates and glasses, Ellen and Mark taking them to the kitchen. Alan had taken the boys for a walk in the fields. They'd managed to get Milly out of the kitchen to accompany them, but she waddled after them, head hanging and tail between her legs. Not a happy dog.

As I started emptying the dishwasher for the second time and clearing the kitchen, I wondered what Walter would have made of the afternoon. Many people said nice things about him, but I sensed there had been some old tensions between him and a few of the people there who had come out of duty, rather than fondness. Still, it was really a day for Jeanette and the girls to be surrounded by people who cared about them, and as such, had gone well. Even Sebastian had behaved himself reasonably well. And little Rory – the star of the show!

Now there was the reading of the will to get through. I wondered what surprises Walter had in store for everybody.

Mark brought in a tray of glasses and put them on the table, then leant against the edge of the kitchen bench. 'You never stop,' he said.

I smiled. 'You're a fine one to talk.'

He shrugged, held out his arms, and I walked into them. He held me, resting his chin on the top of my head. For a while, our hearts beat together.

Noises in the hall made us pull apart. I picked up the tea towel and started drying plates while he filled the dishwasher with the glasses he'd brought in.

'This is the last of it,' said Ellen, bringing in another tray. 'All the food went, thank God.'

'Quite a bit of it into Milly!' I said.

She laughed.

We heard Grace calling goodbye to her friends and then she joined us. 'I'm knackered,' she said, flopping onto a chair.

'I'll put the kettle on.'

Jeanette arrived as I poured the tea, a smile on her face.

'Walter would have loved today with all those people saying such nice things about him. And I'm so glad Brigid and Juliet could get here – I haven't seen much of them lately.'

'Old friends are a comfort,' said Mark.

Jeanette looked at him, her eyes widening, as if she'd forgotten he was there. She nodded and then tucked the strands of hair that had fallen out of her clip behind her ears.

'I suppose we have to read the will soon, do we?' she asked, her smile replaced by a look of anxiety.

'When you're ready. No rush,' said Mark.

'I'll call the others in,' she said. 'We may as well get it over with.'

She went to the back door and called Sebastian, Anna and Louise.

'I think I'll have a Scotch,' she said as she came back in. 'Anyone else?'

'Where are Alan and the boys?' asked Grace.

'They dropped Milly back a few minutes ago and now Alan's taken them out for a pub dinner. They'll have pie and chips and think all their Christmases have come at once,' said Louise. 'They're not usually allowed that sort of thing.'

Ellen laughed and helped herself to a beer from the fridge.

'Before the others get here, is there anything – explosive – we should prepare ourselves for?' asked Jeanette.

Mark raised his eyebrows slightly, acknowledging the question.

'Walter gave me permission to look at the old will, the one he made some years ago with Mr Hill. It's different, and I think it's fair to say there may be some parties who are unhappy with their lot, yes. But it's all perfectly legal and Walter was adamant this was what he wanted.'

Jeanette took a deep breath and pulled herself up to her full height. 'I have a feeling we're in for a shit fight.'

'Time to divide the spoils?' said Sebastian, rubbing his hands together as he entered the kitchen.

'Don't be crass, Sebastian,' said Anna, slurring her words.

'Where would you like to do this, Jeanette?' asked Mark.

'In the drawing room, I think. It was Walter's favourite room.'

Grace and Ellen sat either side of their mother on the sofa. Sebastian stood by the mantelpiece, every inch the Lord of the Manor, and Anna and Jeff took the armchairs. Louise brought in a dining chair, and I perched on the coffee table. I had suggested staying in the kitchen to finish cleaning up, but Jeanette insisted she wanted me there.

Mark stood by the French doors and pulled an envelope out of his inside pocket.

'Walter was clear he didn't want all the legal mumbo-jumbo read out, so I'll get straight to the point as I'm sure you're all exhausted after today and need to have a quiet evening.' He cleared his throat.

Sebastian leant forward expectantly. Jeanette sat very still; her eyes closed. Ellen and Grace each held one of her hands.

'To Jeanette Vivien Baxter, I leave the house and contents, my shares in the company, and whatever monies remain after the following bequests.'

'What the fuck?' said Sebastian. 'Our mother's house. All the shares? That can't be.'

Mark looked at him calmly. 'I have the deeds to the property and it belonged solely to your father, so he can leave it to whomever he wishes.'

Sebastian turned away from him, threw back his glass of whisky and went to pour himself another.

Anna looked shell-shocked. 'I can't believe he'd do this to us. He always used to tell us the house would be ours one day.'

'That was before he had another family, though, wasn't it?' Sebastian sneered. 'Go on. Let's hear the rest of it.'

Mark looked to Jeanette for permission to continue. She nodded.

'To my daughters, Ellen Blaise Baxter and Grace Margo Baxter, I leave each 20,000 pounds to use as they wish but I hope some of it goes on the travels they've always dreamed of.'

Grace gasped and raised her eyebrows and Ellen started crying, quietly. Jeanette held her close.

'To Sebastian John Armstrong I leave the Porsche, the Morgan and the Alvis. Also, my Rolex watch and the painting of his maternal grandfather that currently hangs at the top of the stairs.'

'What? Is that it? The miserable old git. I'm not going to stand for this.' He took a step towards Mark, curling his hands into fists as if it was the solicitor's fault he wasn't getting what he wanted. 'Anna and I have rights. He can't do this to us.'

'Oh, shut up, Sebastian,' said Louise. 'He can do what he damn well likes. It's his money.'

He rounded on her, a steel-like glint in his eyes. 'That's right, defend your dear father to the end, Louise. You never had to live with the bastard.'

'Only because you two made it impossible for Mum and me to stay here,' she said. There was no rancour, she was stating a fact, but it inflamed Sebastian.

'You and your mother were an embarrassment. Her, a shopgirl from the village and you, her illegitimate daughter. Of course we didn't want you here, living in our house, amongst our mother's things. It was an outrageous idea.'

'I agree,' said Louise, 'although not for the reasons you've stated.'

Anna had gone even paler than usual, her lips tight. Jeff patted the back of her hand, but she shook him off.

The atmosphere had gone from cold to glacial. I looked longingly at the door, wishing I could escape back to the kitchen like Cinderella.

'Now isn't the time,' said Mark. For a moment I thought he'd read my thoughts and was talking to me.

Jeanette smiled. 'Thank you. Perhaps you'd continue?'

'To my daughter Anna Barbara Armstrong, I leave my boat, *Sirius*, the remainder of her mother's jewellery and the painting of her mother currently in the attic.'

'Oh fan-fucking-tastic. You've always liked sailing. I hope you get some pleasure from owning a boat,' said Sebastian.

Anna remained like a statue, not even blinking. Sebastian glowered at Mark as if this had all been his idea.

'Lovely,' said Jeff mildly and was rewarded with a scowl from his wife.

'To my daughter Louise Chloe McLeod,' Mark continued, 'I leave the sum of 20,000 pounds and a further 10,000 pounds to be placed in trust for each of the boys to mature when they are twenty-one.'

Louise gasped, her mouth a perfect O.

'This has to be a fucking joke!' shouted Sebastian, slapping the mantelpiece and turning to glare at everyone. 'The old bastard is acting like a bloody charity for waifs and strays.'

Jeanette stared at him. 'As Louise has already said, Walter has the right to do what he wants with his money. And we all know you've been dipping into the company coffers for years, so you can shut the hell up.'

'Mummy!' Grace gasped.

'Well said.' Ellen patted her mother's thigh.

Sebastian took a deep breath and narrowed his eyes as he addressed Jeanette. 'How dare you accuse me of stealing from my own company, my own father.' His voice was full of menace.

'This is neither the time nor the place for this,' said Mark. 'This is the reading of Walter's will.' He looked around the room, making eye contact with every person. When our eyes met, I felt myself blush. I've always liked a man who can command a room.

'I'm sorry, I shouldn't have said anything,' said Jeanette.

Sebastian puffed himself up as if he was just getting going, but Anna stepped in.

'Shut it, Seb.'

He clenched his jaw and marched out.

Jeanette sighed.

'Good riddance,' said Grace and snuggled into her mother.

'With your permission, I'll continue,' said Mark.

Jeanette nodded.

He looked back to the document he held in his hand. 'To GG, I leave 10,000 pounds.'

Anna looked at Mark, a quizzical look on her face. 'GG?'

Mark looked at the will to check, and then nodded.

'Who's GG?' asked Ellen.

'It doesn't matter, darling. Daddy has – had – a right to leave whatever he wanted to whomever he wanted.' Jeanette dabbed at the tears in her eyes.

That was, of course, true, but I glanced at Grace, who looked as if she'd swallowed something foul-tasting.

'Time for tea,' I said. 'Grace, would you help me, please?'

She catapulted off the sofa and fled the room.

I heard Anna saying something about Walter paying off someone he'd shafted at some point as I followed Grace out of the room.

In the kitchen, we stood facing each other.

'I know what you're thinking, but it could be anyone – a special employee for example, or even a some*thing*,' I said in my best soothing voice.

'Who else would it be – otherwise why use initials rather than his whole name?' She bit her lip. Fists clenched, she banged the table, hard. 'How dare he?'

I watched her for a few moments. All four seasons crossed her face: anger, sorrow, hope, desolation.

'Tell me what you're thinking,' I said eventually.

She looked at me, took a deep breath, and said, 'Daddy must've seen us together somewhere and he's paying him off. He must have told him to break it off with me and he'd make it worth his while.' She sank into a chair and started crying.

I put a hand on her shoulder, but my mind was elsewhere. Could Walter have discovered their relationship? Would he have paid Gavin off if he had? And if so, why not just give him the money – why leave it to him in his will? It made no sense.

Grace lifted her head from her forearms and blew her nose. 'I'll never forgive him,' she said. Then she leapt up and ran out of the house.

I was about to follow her when Mark came in. 'Are you okay?' he asked.

'I'm fine.'

He put an arm around me and said, 'You're a terrible liar.'

Laughing, I punched him lightly on the chest. 'All right. I'm concerned about Grace. She's got it into her head that her father was paying this GG off for some reason.'

Mark nodded. 'You know, of course, I can't divulge anything Walter told me.'

'Yes. I won't pump you for information.'

'One of the things I admire about you, Hester, is your discretion.'

'And I, you,' I said. 'Now, more tea.'

Mark pulled me to him and kissed me. I could have stayed there with him, in that moment, for days. But Anna barged in.

'Where's the– oh! Would you look at that – the hired help and the solicitor. Now there's something to think about.'

'Anna–' I said, but she had already turned on her heel and left.

Mark and I looked at each other. He raised his eyebrows. 'Horse has bolted,' he said, and drew me to him. 'Trouble on the horizon, do you think?'

'With this family, who knows. The will certainly seemed unusual, didn't it?'

'Not really. I've seen worse. One old biddy left everything to a girl who did her shopping for her, leaving the entire family fuming. Another donated her house to the local council to be used as a women's refuge. She'd never been abused herself, never had anything to do with victims of violence, so the family were bemused. They tried to contest the will, but it stood.'

'I can't see Sebastian taking this lying down. You saw him. He's furious. And God knows what mischief Anna might try and make now.'

'We've done nothing wrong.'

I smiled at him. 'I know that, and you know that, but Anna may see it differently – I have no idea how that woman's mind works.'

'I don't think we need to worry about her. Now, where were we?'

'Making tea,' I said and giggled as he looked crestfallen. Lifting my lips to his, we kissed.

'Now,' he said, 'I'll put the kettle on, and you can go and find Grace – I saw her dashing off as I came in.'

'Thanks, Mark.' I gave him a peck on the cheek and followed Grace out into the night.

I found her where I thought she'd be. In the walled garden, sitting on the bench looking at Walter's final resting place. The little Japanese maple giving the garden an oriental feel. She stared at it, jaw tight, arms crossed.

'I don't want to talk,' she said without turning.

I stopped where I was and waited, counting my breaths. I wanted to be in the kitchen with Mark, not having to deal with an angry teenager but here I was, trying to be helpful.

'I called him,' she said. 'He said I was being hysterical and then wouldn't talk to me.'

I kept counting my breaths.

'How on earth could I ever have thought he was the one for me? He's a spineless shit. And to think, I was going to run after him earlier and beg him to reconsider!'

Again, I said nothing.

'I bet he just came today to make sure he got what he thought he deserved. And you know the worst thing? They only thought I was worth ten grand.' She started laughing. 'Ten grand. I would have thought I was worth at least ten times that.'

'Of course you are, and more. But I think you're jumping to conclusions – there may be another explanation.'

'Oh yeah? Like what?'

'Like GG isn't Gavin at all, or your father met him some time and–'

'And what? Neither Daddy nor Mummy have been near the school since Gavin started this year because of Daddy's illness. So how could they have met?'

'I have no idea.' But there was something lurking in the back of my mind. Something Gavin had said earlier that I couldn't quite get hold of.

'What?' asked Grace, watching me closely, eyes narrowed.

I shrugged, looked at the maple tree. 'Nothing,' I said, and wrapped my cardigan more tightly round myself.

'You know something, don't you? Come on – out with it.'

'I don't know anything, Grace. Truly. Come back in, your mother will be worried about you.'

No. I'm staying here. You go. Tell her... tell her what you like.'

Oh, Grace and her dramatics. I took a couple of deep breaths. 'I know you're upset, but this isn't the way to deal with it.'

'Oh fuck off, Hester,' she said, then burst into tears.

I sat beside her. She shuffled along the bench and turned her back to me.

We sat for a few long minutes. Every so often, she sniffed and sighed. When I tried to put a hand on her shoulder, she shrugged it off. Eventually I got up to leave, but she caught my hand.

'Ask Daddy's solicitor – he must know. Please?' She looked up at me out of tear-reddened eyes.

As I approached the house, I heard raised voices and then Anna tottered out of the door and into her car, Jeff on her heels.

'Give me the car keys, Anna,' I heard him say.

'Sod off, Jeffrey.'

She got into the driver's seat, revved the engine and screeched away, leaving Jeff standing in the drive watching after her.

'It's been an upsetting day,' I said.

He turned to look at me. 'It's been an upsetting life.'

I had no energy for him so I kept moving, offering a 'sorry to hear that' as I went. I entered the kitchen.

'There you are, Hester,' said Jeanette. 'We were wondering where you'd gone. Have you seen Grace?'

'She's out with Walter,' I said, and Jeanette nodded.

'Will she be all right do you think? Will any of us be?' She collapsed into a chair, looking like a small lost child. Her eyes beseeched me for something positive to hold on to.

I sat too, picked up a napkin and held it. 'I think of life as a piece of clothing: you start out with strong seams and colourful fabric, then a huge hole appears and you spend the next few months trying to patch or darn it. Eventually it's done, but the stitching is never quite as strong, and the colours are a little faded.'

She smiled. 'Thank you, Hester. I value your honesty. So many people today were telling me I'd be okay and to just keep going. Time heals all, they said. But I know there'll always be a shadow in the background, a stitch or two not quite sitting right reminding me of what I had and lost.' She took my hand and held it tightly.

When everyone else had left or gone to bed, Mark and I sat in the kitchen with cups of tea.

'Penny for them?' said Mark.

I looked up at his smiling face and took a deep breath.

'I know you can't tell me who GG is, but can you tell me who he isn't?'

'I suppose so. He isn't Gilbert Grape.'

I laughed. 'Gilbert Grape?'

'It happens to be one of my favourite films. Have you seen it?'

'Yes, and don't try and change the subject. It is a man, then?'

He nodded. 'Male. Yes.'

'If I say a name, can you shake your head or nod? I mean, it's not as if you'd have actually told me anything.'

'Skating on thin ice, though. Is it really important? Walter used initials in order to keep the man's identity a secret. He doesn't want anyone getting upset.'

'And yet by not naming him he has shrouded this man in mystery and made everyone wonder who he is.'

I paused for a moment. It suddenly seemed ridiculous to be even having the conversation. There must be dozens of people with the initials GG. I let out a sigh.

'It's not Gavin Green then?'

I lifted the pot to refill our teacups when I noticed Mark's face had frozen. He put his cup down slowly.

'Oh my God, it is him, isn't it? Grace was right.' I jumped up feeling agitated.

'Hester, what's the matter?'

I sat again, my mind racing. I suddenly remembered what Gavin said that afternoon that hadn't registered at the time: 'Christ, if I'd known–' If he'd known what? That Walter was Grace's father? Was she right – he *had* seen them together and paid him off after all?

I turned to Mark trying to read the answers in his face.

'I'm sorry, Hester. I really can't say any more. I shouldn't have reacted at all, but I always have been a terrible actor.'

'It's okay, I know you have to keep it all confidential.'

'Thank you. This must go no further.'

I looked down at the teapot that was still in my hands. 'I know. You can count on me.'

Mark left not long after and I locked up and made my way slowly upstairs, wondering what it all meant. The great GG mystery.

WALTER

When I rub my hands together, I have no sensation of touch but it's a satisfying gesture, nonetheless.

I knew my will would cause problems and I was mindful of the fact Jeanette would have to deal with Sebastian and Anna's anger, but the fact is she's stronger than she thinks she is, and neither of them deserved any more than they got. Sebastian has a good salary and as Jeanette said, has been dipping into the company coffers for years, falsifying expense claims and invoices right, left and centre. Too stupid to realise I'd known all along. That's why he rarely got a pay rise. And Anna wants for nothing with Jeff working. She'll get a lot out of the boat if she gets over her fear of enjoying herself.

Perhaps I got it wrong leaving GG some money in the will, but there wasn't time to do it differently. Good thing Sebastian had left before hearing it. Anna might tell him but then again, she's more scared of his anger, so maybe not. I didn't want to make things harder for Jeanette. She handled it well, but Grace seemed put out by it for some reason.

What's that?

Oh Christ! Dorothy's here again. Or rather, still. We are

now having these 'conversations' in which neither of us says anything but we both know exactly what the other is thinking. It's fucking irritating.

She reckons it's my fault Anna's turned out the way she has. I tell her it's her fault for dying. That's when things started going wrong. Until then Sebastian actually spoke to me without a sneer on his face and the aggressive tone in his voice, and Anna sought me out occasionally for help with homework or to watch TV together. Then Dorothy died and it was like a switch had flicked. Anna stopped eating, Sebastian started hating me and it all went downhill from there. I tried to create a new family for them. Marie was prepared to be their mother in spite of the fact she had a baby too.

I like that my girls were surprised I left them something. Unlike the eldest two, Louise wasn't expecting anything, neither were Ellen and Grace. Unspoilt, those three. Jeanette's done a good job with Ellen and Grace, and Marie's been a good mum to Louise.

Interesting thing is, now I'm under a tree in the garden I don't seem to be able to leave the house. If I can stick around though, it'll be interesting to see what they do with the company. Now I'm not in charge, I don't give a flying fuck whether they keep it or sell it. As long as Jeanette has enough to keep her afloat. She owns the bulk of the shares now. She could run the whole show.

Fuck off, Dorothy.

Jesus. She's like a fly around a horse's arse. Won't leave me alone.

THIRTEEN

After breakfast when Jeanette and Ellen had left to do whatever they were doing, Grace, puffy-eyed and yawning, asked if I'd spoken to Mark about the identity of GG.

I closed my eyes for a moment, trying to decide what to say.

'You did, didn't you?' she said, reaching out and taking my arm.

I nodded slowly.

'And?'

'And as I told you, he couldn't tell me anything.' So far I hadn't actually lied to her: he hadn't told me anything as such. I hoped she wouldn't press it. But it was Grace I was dealing with.

'But did he give a hint? I mean, any clue at all?'

I sighed and shrugged. 'Look, Grace, I know it's hard but you're going to have to leave it alone. Your father obviously had a reason for keeping this GG secret and I'm afraid you're going to have to live with it. I'm sorry.'

She sat as still as a stone for a few moments, staring at me. I began to feel uncomfortable under her cold gaze.

'I'll make a deal with you. Gavin won't talk to me, but he

might agree to meet you. Just ask him if he ever had anything to do with Daddy. If he says no, and you believe him, I'll drop it. Promise.'

She took my arm again, looking into my eyes and imploring me to help. I couldn't refuse. And I have to admit I was curious, even though I'd tried to tell myself I wasn't.

I was about to call Gavin on the number Grace had given me when a photo popped up and a text.

Guess where I am?

It was a picture of Justin in the kitchen of my flat.

I felt a smile broaden my face.

When did you get there? How long can you stay?

My phone rang seconds after I'd sent my text.

'Hi, Mum, how's it going?'

'Justin, what a surprise!'

'A good one, I hope,' he said, laughter in his voice.

'The best. How long are you down for? Is Georgia with you?'

'No, she had to stay at home. One of her friends is having some sort of crisis and the girls have gathered to offer support, so I thought I'd come and see you. Not too inconvenient, is it?'

'It's perfect. I'll come right over. Be there in under an hour.'

I found Jeanette in the sitting room, writing letters.

She looked up when I entered, and smiled, waving her pen at the sheets of paper on the desk in front of her.

'I'm just dropping notes to everyone who came to farewell Walter yesterday. I was brought up to always send thank-you letters and even though I'd rather be out gardening, here I am, being a good girl.'

I laughed. 'Habits of a lifetime, eh? Better to get them over and done with, then you can get on with what you want to do. Anything I can do?'

She looked at me and shook her head. 'I just need some time on my own, I think.'

Feeling relieved, I said in that case, I'd go home for the night.

We hadn't talked about how much longer Jeanette wanted me to stick around, but when he employed me, Walter had asked me to help the family for a couple of weeks after his death. He'd actually paid me for two months when I first arrived, perhaps hoping he had a little longer to live than he did, so although strictly speaking my work as a doula was over, I liked this complicated family and was quite happy to stay on for the full eight weeks in whatever capacity they needed. But as I drove home, my thoughts left the Baxters and turned to my son. It was unlike him to turn up unannounced and even more unusual for him to be on his own. My stomach sank as I wondered if he was here to tell me they were having difficulties. He and Georgia always seemed so happy together, even though they were very different.

'Tea's made,' he called as I opened the front door. Then he came into the hall and enveloped me in a tight hug.

It was one of those moments where you don't realise how much you've been missing someone until you see them again, and I had to sniff a couple of times to stop myself from crying.

I pulled away and held him at arm's length.

'Let me look at you,' I said and gazed at his perfect face.

'Pass muster, do I?' he said.

'Oh, it's so good to see you!' I hugged him again. 'How long can you stay?'

'Only tonight, I'm afraid. Got to leave early to get back for a meeting at ten.'

Over tea he filled me in on what was happening at his work (not much) and the holiday he and Georgia had been on in the Shetlands (fantastic – you have to go there).

I listened and watched as he talked, just happy to have him there, brightening up the flat with his presence.

'And I popped in to see Peggy on my way.'

I immediately felt guilty. I hadn't seen her for days.

'She's well?' I asked.

'Very chirpy,' he said. 'Sends her love. And how about you, Mum, still with the same people?'

'Yes. Walter, my client, died a week or so ago and the funeral was yesterday, but the family haven't made any move to get rid of me. I don't think they know what to do. It's a complicated set-up – Walter was married three times and had children with each wife, who all see each other but the eldest two can't stand the others.'

He smiled but the look in his eyes was distant, elsewhere.

'What's the matter, love?' I asked. For some reason my heart was beating fast.

He turned to me and took my hands in his.

'Now I know something's wrong,' I said, trying to make light of his gesture.

'Nothing's wrong, but I do have something to tell you.' He sounded serious.

I pulled my hands away and clasped them in my lap. 'Go on then,' I said. But I wanted to put my hands over my ears and close my eyes. Whatever it was he was going to tell me, I didn't want to hear it. It was a struggle to stay calm, to stop myself from snatching the car keys from the table and running away.

Justin sat very still, as if working out where to start.

I bit down on my lip, waiting.

He looked at me and then away again.

I was aware of the clock ticking time away on the wall behind me. I focused on the tick-tock and the sound of the hands clicking over another minute. I was concentrating so hard on the clock that I hardly noticed when he started talking. I had to force my awareness back to him as I watched his mouth move.

'Georgia has a friend who works for UNICEF.' He stopped again.

I noticed his mouth was still. Tick-tock tick-tock.

'She has something to do with data collection and analysis.'
Tick-tock.

'Her name's Linda – although that doesn't really matter.'
Tick.

I saw him moisten his lips.

Tock.

'Anyway, she was crunching some of the data about the Ebola epidemic in Sierra Leone and she came across a name she recognised.'

I couldn't hear the clock anymore. Sierra Leone had silenced it. Sierra Leone always silenced everything around it. I felt myself nodding but the rest of my body was immobile, weighed down by that country, those memories.

Justin put a hand out again, but mine stayed clasped together in my lap, the knuckles whitening.

'Do you want to hear this, Mum?'

I felt myself nod again. My mouth wouldn't move to form the no I was screaming in my head.

'Right, well, the name she recognised was my middle name, Bah. My father's surname. So she looked at the whole name and it was Jusu Karamoh Bah.' He stopped and looked at me.

I stared back, trying to understand what he was telling me, but my brain wasn't making any link between the words he had said and what they actually meant.

'Mum, my dad died in the epidemic in 2014. He was forty-one and lived in Koida.'

'Koida,' I repeated. That much, at least, I understood. It was a diamond mining town in the east.

He got up and came over to put an arm around me. I leant against him.

'I know this has been a shock for you. I'm sorry. I just thought you'd want to know.'

'Koida,' I said again.

He held me tighter. 'Yes, Koida.'

'Jusu.'

'Yes, Jusu.'

'Ebola.'

I felt him nod. And I felt his tears wetting my hair.

As evening claimed the day, we sat talking quietly. The tears were over, but not for good, and we talked about Jusu and the two other Bahs who were on the same list: Yei Mary Bah aged thirty-nine, his wife; and Sarah Kumba Bah, fourteen, their daughter.

'He named his daughter Sarah,' I said.

'Yes.'

'That was my name.'

'I know.'

'I should have tried harder to find him after I left.'

'It was impossible: the civil war, all those displaced people, the lack of records.'

'I assumed he'd been killed – if not soon after I left, then in the war along with everyone else in the village – but he was in Koido. He survived. He married. Had another child.' I looked up at him. 'You had a sister.'

He nodded. 'Half-sister.'

I sucked a breath in, held it as long as I could and let it out slowly.

'I'm so sorry you didn't know her.'

'It's okay, Mum. We can't change that. But–'

'But what?' My heart skipped.

'Well, since Linda told me all this, I've been doing some research and I think Jusu had two more children, and they're still alive.'

I gasped. The skin felt tight across my cheeks.

'And?'

'They're now twenty and twenty-two, live in Koido still. A brother and a sister.'

I tried to picture them. Tall like Jusu, their father, with kind eyes and a ready smile. Like Justin.

'Do you want to meet them?'

It was Justin's turn to go quiet for a while. I waited.

'I don't know. I think maybe I do. But I don't want to burst into their lives and tell them who I am. What if Jusu never told them about you? And he never knew anything about me – that he had another son. I don't want to intrude on their memories of their father.'

My chest swelled with pride for my sensitive son, and with pain for him too. How often had he stepped away from things he wanted to do in case it hurt someone else's feelings? I'd seen it when he was a child, but had I become blind to it as he grew older. Had he wanted to look for his father all these years but not done so in case I was hurt by it? I shook my head.

'What is it, Mum?'

'I love you, Justin. You're the kindest person I've ever met. If you want to meet them, I'm sure you'll find a way to do it without treading on their memories.'

He smiled. 'Thanks.'

'What for?'

'For giving me permission, I guess. I didn't realise I wanted it until you said it.'

We spent the rest of the evening chatting, mostly about Jusu. Justin wanted to hear everything about him even though he must have heard every story and memory I had of his father a hundred times. He never tired of them. I suppose they stood in place of the real thing.

Before we said goodnight, I apologised again that he hadn't met his father.

'Sometimes I wondered what it would be like to meet him,' he said. 'I used to fantasise he'd turn up at school one day, or here.'

'I never knew that.' I saw Justin as a little boy in my mind's eye, yearning for his dad. Tears gathered.

'Don't cry, Mum. I would imagine these scenarios, but the funny thing is, I didn't actually want them to come true. I was happy with you, and I wouldn't have wanted to share you. Very selfish, I know, but true. And I saw some of my friends with their dads, and most of them didn't get on so well. This way, I could hold on to the fantasy of a perfect father.'

'You're so like him. And he would have been so proud of you.'

We hugged, holding on to each other for a long time and then said goodnight again before going to bed. I lay awake for a long time, wondering what kind of a life Jusu had had, and whether he'd been happy. I imagined he had – he'd been so positive, and people loved him for his kindness and his gentle soul. As I fell asleep my mind drifted to a place I hadn't let it go for years: the fantasy of me and Jusu in the village with a brood of children running around, secure in the knowledge they were loved. We'd all lost out because my parents had sent me away. I was sad Jusu had never met his beautiful son.

I let the images run for a while, but it didn't do to dwell on the past, so I put on the podcast I was following – Death in Ice Valley. From tropical Sierra Leone to the frozen hills of Norway at the push of a button.

I was woken early the next morning by a text from Jeanette.
Grace has gone missing.
I rang immediately.
'Oh, Hester, I don't know what to do. She hasn't been home all night. I've rung some of her friends, but they don't know where she is. I'm thinking of calling the police, but Ellen says it's too soon, she probably stayed with a friend who's number I don't have.' Jeanette sobbed. I heard Ellen trying to calm her down.
'I'll come straight away,' I said.
Justin was in the kitchen drinking coffee. His overnight bag was by the door.
'I'm sorry, love. I've got to go. SOS from Jeanette.'
'No problem. I've got to head off too.'
We looked at each other, and at the same time said, 'Love you.' We laughed.
'Thanks for coming down to tell me in person, it meant a lot.'
Justin nodded and gave me a kiss on the cheek.
'And Jus, whatever you decide about your half-brother and sister, it's okay with me. And if you do decide to get in touch, I hope it goes well.' I gave him another kiss. 'Give my love to Georgia,' I said as a left.

As I drove, I forced my thoughts away from my family back towards the Baxters. I clutched the steering wheel tightly and drove just above the speed limit. My jaw was clenched and when I stopped at some traffic lights, I rolled my head to release the tension in my neck. I didn't want to admit it, but I was angry with Grace and resentful of Jeanette's dependence on me to fix everything. And yet I knew I'd allowed her to become reliant on me. It was as much my fault as hers that she felt she couldn't cope. It was another issue I'd have to address at some stage.

I had a pretty good idea where Grace would be, and drove straight to the school to test my theory, getting there well before the boarders were up for breakfast.

There was no-one around, but I didn't want to arouse any curiosity in case there were some early risers out for a morning walk, so I left my car in the lane and made my way to the boarding houses.

Sure enough, her bike was on the grass where she'd dropped it. I could imagine her flinging it there in her haste to confront Gavin. I knocked on the door and stood back, searching for any sign of life.

I heard feet on the stairs and tried to gauge whether it was an adult tread or a boy's. Standing up tall, I waited for the door to open. Fortunately, it was the man himself.

'Hester, thank God you're here.' He came halfway out of the door, glanced right and left and then pulled me into the hall and closed the door behind us.

'This way.' He led me up some stairs and along a corridor. 'She's in here,' he said and entered a sitting room.

I followed, having not said a word.

Grace was lying on the sofa, fully clothed, with vomit down her front. She was on her back, arms akimbo. Her mouth was open and she was snoring. I could see the mascara smudged on her cheeks.

'What happened?' I asked.

Gavin stood, running a hand through his hair, the other hand tapping against his thigh.

'She arrived here late last night demanding to see me. I had to let her in so she didn't wake the whole school. She threatened to scream if I sent her away. She started talking about the will and some money, but she was practically incoherent – pissed as a fart. I tried to calm her down, but she wouldn't have any of it. I made her a cup of tea. She took a sip, threw up a couple of times and then passed out.'

'Why didn't you call her mother? She's been going frantic.'

'Grace's phone was locked and I don't have access to the school database. I was just about to get her up and march her home when you appeared.'

I looked him up and down. He seemed to be telling the truth and I could well imagine Grace turning up and making a scene.

Pulling my phone out, I called Jeanette and told her the good news but not where I'd found her daughter, nor the state she was in.

'I'll take her home, but you and I need to talk.'

He swallowed hard. 'Yes, of course. And thank you, Hester, you've helped me out of a couple of tight spots now. I owe you.'

'You certainly do. Help me get her up and out to my car and I'll see you later in the week.'

Grace started groaning when I sat her upright, but she was far too hungover to make a big stink. We supported her to the car and strapped her in. She was asleep again before I started the engine, slumped against the door.

I looked in the rear-view mirror to see Gavin standing by the school wall, shoulders sagging and head bowed. Something was troubling that young man and it was more than just having a drunken Grace to deal with.

When he was about six, Justin got lost in a shopping centre. One minute he was there, the next, gone. I raced around, frantic with worry, asking everyone I saw whether they'd seen him. I got the security guard to put a message out on the public address system, had shop assistants hunting for him. I was literally beside myself, or more accurately, outside of myself watching as if from the sidelines as this psychotic-looking woman charged around accosting people, her face stretched in fear and panic.

When he sauntered back to where we'd been he couldn't understand why I lifted him into my arms and burst into tears, promising I'd never take my eyes off him again.

'I'm a big boy, Mummy. I can go to the toilet all by myself,' he said, wriggling to free himself. But I held on. In that moment, I couldn't have let him go; my arms were locked around him and weren't about to unlock themselves.

He'd been gone ten minutes.

Grace had been gone twelve hours.

I understood Jeanette's reaction to her return.

I left them in the hall, Grace murmuring something about her head hurting and needing to go to bed and Jeanette holding her upright and smothering her in kisses.

I went into the kitchen to make myself some breakfast. The newspaper was on the table, a headline declaring Ebola was once again ravaging communities in Africa, this time the Congo. With a sinking heart I found myself thinking about Jusu. What a terrible death he must have had. I'd seen news footage of people dying of Ebola and it was a ghastly way to go. I only hoped he didn't know his wife and daughter had contracted the disease too. And I wondered what his life had been like: what he'd done, what he enjoyed. Perhaps if Justin made contact with his half-siblings, they'd be able to answer my questions.

WALTER

I'm beginning to think if Dorothy hadn't had a heart attack, I might have killed her myself. She's here all the time watching, arms folded, the deep vertical line between her eyebrows that makes her look disapproving and angry. Just like old times.

Except in the old days, I could stay away, indulge in a few diversions. Now we're both stuck here.

It seems we can no longer communicate. I tried to talk to her. There were words in my head and I felt a kind of movement where my mouth is/was/should be but there was no sound. It's frustrating, but makes sense, I suppose – if I could talk, Jeanette and the girls would be able to hear me and although that's an appealing thought from my side of things, it would freak them out. I did think, though, that Dorothy and I might continue to be able to have some sort of thought transfer. I mean, it stands to reason, doesn't it? We're in the same boat, as it were.

I turn my back on her, but she floats into my field of vision again within seconds. This morning, desperate to avoid seeing her, I kept turning until together we made a kind of whirlwind. A vortex of the dead. And yet, although we were hurling ourselves in circles, nothing else moved, we didn't create even the smallest eddy in the air around us. It's demoralising having absolutely no impact on anything around you.

Actually, Dorothy clearly wins on that score – she leaves an impression on me. A very negative one. Eyes taking in everything I do. Always judging, scowling. I'll ignore her from now on. I'm damned if I'll let her have the upper hand.

It was a quiet day in the house. Hester went off somewhere – maybe to meet the solicitor although probably not. She must have a life outside of this house we know nothing about. I don't like it when she's gone though. Things fall apart. Jeanette wrote letters all day, Ellen stayed in her room reading and listening to her ghastly music and Grace went out for a walk, came home briefly and went out again. At least when Hester's here they all talk to each other. She's like a beacon the lost and lonely are drawn to. Not that my girls are lost or lonely. Or maybe they are.

My one regret is that I didn't spend enough time with them. What's the old cliché? No-one ever says on their death bed, 'I wish I'd spent more time at work.' It's true. I suppose I was a bit of a workaholic. Comes from starting off dirt poor and wanting to make something of myself. Never knowing when to stop, when enough is enough. And I kept waiting for Sebastian to step up to the mark, but he never did. Had too much too young, I suppose. Never had anything to aspire to. I wanted to give him the start in life I didn't have, take him on holidays, up to London for shows (well, Dorothy did), not have him start work too young. And what happened? He assumes life is going to be handed to him on a plate. Never developed a work ethic. I started him in the factory to learn the ropes and he did as little as possible. When he moved into the office, he'd swan in when he felt like it, do the minimum amount of work he could get away with and leave again. And he thought I didn't notice. If he hadn't been my son, he'd have been out on his ear long ago. But blood is blood. What he needed was a good kick up the backside and I tried a couple of times, but he always slid back to his lazy, entitled ways.

That's the problem with the youth today, if you ask me. Not enough hardship. They've all got phones and laptops by the time they can piss into a toilet and develop these grandiose ideas about how life is going to be, the money they're going to make without lifting a finger. Then they say – whoever 'they' are – there's a mental health crisis. Put them all in the army for a few years. Or make them work in a factory or down a mine – not that we've got many of them left. Get their hands dirty. Work up a bit of a sweat.

Oh, piss off, Dorothy, you mad old bint! Leave me alone.

FOURTEEN

I hadn't had much sleep and decided to take a cup of tea to my room and rest for an hour or two but while I was waiting for the kettle to boil, Ellen shuffled into the kitchen, hair standing out at all angles.

'Hey, Hester,' she said and sat down opposite me.

'How are you doing, Ellen?' I asked. It was meant as a rhetorical question, but Ellen clearly didn't realise that. She frowned, glanced at me, looked towards the door and started biting the edge of a fingernail. I'd seen her do it before when she was worried about something. She took a deep breath as if she was going to say something, but nothing came out.

'Tea?' I asked as the kettle started whistling.

She nodded. 'Thanks.'

My back was turned to her as I made the drinks, but I heard her shifting in her seat as if gearing herself up for a speech.

I passed her a cup and we sat opposite each other. Still she said nothing, but she fidgeted and her fingernail found its way into her mouth again.

'My son came down to see me yesterday,' I said, thinking

that maybe if we chatted about something else, eventually she'd come out with what was troubling her.

She smiled half-heartedly. 'That's nice.'

'Yes. I hadn't seen him for a few months. He's so busy. Well, I am too, of course. Anyway, it was lovely to see him.'

It was clear she wasn't listening. Whatever she was thinking about was taking up all available headspace.

I finished my tea and got up to put the cup in the dishwasher. She hadn't started hers.

She leapt up, scraping the chair back so fast it almost fell over. 'Will you come for a walk with me? We could take Milly over the fields.'

Milly, miraculously back to normal after gorging herself at the Not Funeral, ran round us in ever larger circles, nose to the ground, tail wagging frantically as if she'd never been outside before. We could all learn a thing or two about joy from dogs.

Ellen walked with her head down too, hands in her pockets.

I breathed in the crisp clean air and felt refreshed by it. The sun was pale in the sky, and it was difficult to believe it was the same one that beat down so ferociously on Sierra Leone. I didn't want to think about that place now and forced my mind away from the heat and harsh light of Africa, concentrating instead on the softness of the English landscape: the gently undulating fields, the great coppery beech trees, the sound of birdsong as the sparrows and thrushes ducked and dived through the air as if just for the thrill of it.

'I can't believe he's gone forever,' said Ellen, lifting her head but not looking at me.

'It takes a while to sink in.'

She fell silent again.

We climbed over a stile and Milly found something smelly

and started rolling in it, legs in the air and her whole body writhing in pleasure.

I fell into step with Ellen. I could almost feel her words straining to be spoken but still she remained silent, looking about her now, as if seeing her surroundings for the first time.

Milly bounded up, stinking of the fox poo she'd covered herself in and looking proud of her new scent.

'Grace is in a bad way,' said Ellen.

I nodded. 'Everyone reacts differently, and some show it more than others.'

She stopped. 'She's being a little bitch. Mum doesn't need her show pony antics. We've all lost Dad, not just her. Honestly, she's a selfish little cow.'

I was surprised at the vehemence in Ellen's voice. She'd been annoyed with her sister immediately after Walter's death when Grace was angry and not talking to anyone, but this was different. Stronger.

It was grief, I thought, chafing at the fault lines in their relationship, finding the cracks and pushing at them until they widened. Grief can make us feel isolated and lonely because we all go about it differently. In the end, we're all just little islands in a sea of loss.

'She's hurting. You go quiet. She gets loud. Jeanette understands.'

Ellen started walking again and I fell into step with her. 'Well I don't. She's always been a drama queen.'

'Then how can you expect her to be different now? It's her way of dealing with life, so surely you can't believe she'd suddenly behave any other way?'

'Don't take her side! It's not okay to get drunk and go off like that. Mum was beside herself. She rang the police, but they didn't take it seriously. They said she'd probably fallen asleep at a friend's house and would be home in the morning, tail between her legs.'

I was surprised. Jeanette had said Ellen talked her out of phoning the police, but she'd called after all. Why had Jeanette lied to me? Maybe she'd just forgotten. Either way, it didn't really matter, it was over.

'Yes, Grace was wrong to do that, I admit. And I'm not trying to take sides, but she'll settle down eventually. Perhaps there's other stuff going on for her too.'

'Oh, there's always other stuff going on in Grace's life. She gets bored if there's no drama.'

'Do you know of anything in particular?'

'No. We haven't really had a chance to talk about anything except Dad since I got home.'

We walked a while in silence. Ellen didn't know about the fling with Gavin, which was probably a good thing.

I wondered if Ellen's anger was more about Walter dying than about Grace's behaviour. Many people are angry after a death, but it can make them feel uncomfortable, guilty even. I thought for a moment, trying to work out how to word my question. In the end, I decided not to dress it up.

'Are you angry with your father for dying?'

Ellen looked at me, surprised. 'No. I'd rather he hadn't, but I don't blame him for dying. I mean, he didn't ask to get cancer, did he? No, I'm not angry at him at all. Not even a little bit.'

'I see.'

She stopped again, looked over the tussocky grass of the field, biting her lip.

I watched Milly sniff around a molehill and waited.

'Perhaps I am. Angry, I mean. Not at him dying though.' She turned to me and I got the impression I was meant to understand something more from her words.

I was too tired for games and guesswork.

'Want to talk about it?' I asked.

She shook her head and moved off a little way, watching Milly.

I waited, dreaming of another cup of tea and a nap. I didn't notice Ellen coming back to stand next to me.

In a voice so low I had to lean in to hear her, she said, 'Did he ever ask you to–' She didn't finish the question. She didn't have to.

I inhaled deeply. *Fucking Walter.* 'Yes. He did.'

'But you said no?'

I nodded.

'Because you don't believe in euthanasia?'

'Because I believe if death can be pain free that's good enough. It's usually pain people are afraid of, not the actual dying.'

Ellen started kicking hard at the grass tussock, her breath coming out in gasps. Then she turned to me, her face twisted into an agony of grief.

'I killed him,' she said and started crying.

I took her hand and we stood until her tears started to subside. 'I gave him extra morphine. When you went to get Mum and Grace that night.'

'I know.'

She stopped mid sob, and turned sharply to look at me. 'Why didn't you say anything?'

'It wasn't my place.'

'How did you know?'

'Because I had to check the amount of morphine he was taking to record it for the palliative care team. I knew how much there was.'

She nodded, looked at the ground. 'I gave him a double dose. He'd asked me a few days before to help him on his way when the time came. When you went out of the room the night he died, he opened his eyes for a moment and looked straight into mine. He didn't say anything, but I knew what he wanted me to do. At least I did then, but now I can't stop thinking about it. Maybe he didn't want that at all. Perhaps he was feeling a bit stronger, would have lasted a few more days. What if he was trying to tell me *not* to give him more morphine?'

She fell to her knees and hugged herself, rocking backwards and forwards. Her eyes were closed, her mouth was open but no sound came out.

I knelt beside her, put an arm around her shoulders.

'Your father wasn't going to rally, I promise you.'

'But it's still murder, isn't it? I mean, he would have died anyway but it was my intention to kill him. I'm a murderer!'

'You could look at it as a brave thing to do, a loving act.'

'But you wouldn't do it.'

'That doesn't necessarily mean I think it's wrong, just that I'm a coward.'

She looked surprised. The tears had, for the moment, ceased.

'Go on,' she said.

I took a deep breath. Thinking about my childhood was still painful. It reminded me of all I'd lost.

'I was brought up in a very religious – some would say fundamentalist – household. My father and his church took a very literal view of the Bible. I don't believe in God anymore but sometimes I still feel afraid and very lonely without the certainty my faith gave me. Instead of examining my beliefs, I tend to bury them. I'm not proud of it, but it's how I get by.'

'So a part of you still believes I'll burn in hell for what I did.'

'No. I don't believe that. I think we all make our own heaven and hell, and we are our own judges. At least, that's what I believe here,' I said, touching my head. 'Unfortunately, I have a tiny but insistent voice I can't entirely silence that says I'm wrong. It's just habit. The first words I remember hearing were my father's, telling me and my siblings we had to be good because God saw everything we did, heard everything we said, knew everything that was in our hearts. There was no getting away from Him. And I learned through experience He was a vengeful God. It stays with you that stuff. It has shaped my life in more ways than you could know. Probably even more than I'm aware of myself.'

'I've never believed in God. Dad said, "Religion is a load of bunkum made up by the rich to subjugate the poor".'

I almost laughed. She'd got his northern accent and the tone of his voice down to a tee. I had to bite the insides of my cheeks before I could respond.

'And he may well be right. So let go of the idea you'll burn in a hell you don't believe exists.'

She smiled briefly. 'Okay.' Then, becoming serious again, said, 'So you don't think I should be punished for what I did?'

'I think you're punishing yourself enough – and that you can stop now. You can't change what you did.'

She paused for a moment. 'I think I'm a bit disappointed. I wanted you to chastise me somehow – pass judgement and tell me I'd done wrong so I could fight against you and justify my actions.'

'Sorry,' I said. 'But despite my inadequate response, I think you'll come to some sort of resolution yourself.'

She shrugged. 'I still don't know how I feel about what I did, what Dad asked me to do. But I'm glad I told you. It's been festering, eating away inside me.'

'You're a courageous young woman, Ellen.'

'I'm not so sure, but thank you. Maybe we can talk more another time. Right now, though, I'm starving. I haven't been able to eat for the past few days I've been feeling so nauseated by what I did.'

'I believe there are some eggs and sausages with your name on at home,' I said, and we turned back towards the house.

I had no doubt Ellen would need to talk more about what she'd done but I also felt she'd be okay. Unfettered by the chains of religious belief, she would come to view her actions as a compassionate act for a father she loved.

Just before we entered the kitchen, she said to me, 'Do you think Mum knows?'

'I'm sure she doesn't.'

'Thank God. You won't tell anyone, will you?'

I squeezed her arm. 'Of course not. It's not my secret to tell.'

'Oh, there you are you two. Have a nice walk?' asked Jeanette as we opened the door. Ellen looked at me as if to make sure I wasn't going to blurt out her secret and then smiled at her mother and gave her a hug.

'Lovely, thanks.'

'I thought I'd go into the office this afternoon – see what's what, talk to the staff, let them know their jobs are secure and all that. Want to come with me, Ell?' Jeanette spoke into Ellen's hair as she was still holding on tight.

Finally, Ellen let go and moved back a little to look at her mother. 'Sure. Are you actually going to work there – I mean, run the company?'

Jeanette laughed. 'Oh, good God no. How could I? I have no idea about business. I'll have to get a manager in. But I need to meet the staff and see the books at least. Anything else would be irresponsible.'

I started making brunch for us all. Jeanette made coffee. The smell of it made me feel quite light-headed and I realised I hadn't eaten anything since the night before. I threw a couple of extra eggs in.

'How's Grace?' Ellen asked.

Jeanette paused, frowned. 'Contrite I think would be the best word to describe her at this moment. I don't know what to say – she's taking Walter's death so hard. I can't find it in me to be angry with her but part of me wants to strangle her.'

Ellen looked at me and raised her eyebrows in a 'see, what was I telling you?' sort of way. I smiled and continued to whisk the eggs.

'Speak of the Devil,' said Ellen as Grace came in and sank into a chair.

'What were you saying about me?' she asked in a disinterested way. She looked, if anything, worse than when I'd picked her up, except she'd changed into fresh clothes. Her eyes were red and swollen, her face blotchy and her beautiful hair appeared to be snarling itself into dreadlocks. 'Never mind,' she continued. 'I don't care. About anything.' She put her head on the table and groaned.

'Why aren't you in bed?' asked Jeanette.

'I can't sleep.'

'Room spinning too much, is it?' said Ellen.

Jeanette shot her a stern look. 'That's enough, Ell.'

'What's wrong? I was only pointing out she's had a skinful.'

'Which we all know and she's suffering for it already without you being unkind.'

'Oh, for fuck's sake!' Ellen marched out, adding as she went, 'I'll be drinking Dad's Scotch – it seems to be the only way to get noticed around here.'

Jeanette watched her go, hands on her hips.

'What have I done to deserve this? All I want is to get on with grieving for my husband and I'm surrounded by pantomime horses all of a sudden.'

There was a noise from the table. It started small and grew louder. Grace's shoulders started heaving and she lifted her head and looked at her mother. Jeanette's eyes widened in surprise and then she also started laughing.

'Pantomime horses! Ouch, my head hurts,' Grace said and clutched it between her hands.

'You're the front half and Ellen's the rear end,' said Jeanette and laughed harder.

None of this behaviour was unusual, but it was exhausting, and I wasn't used to being around bereaved families for so long. There's grief before a death of course, but this was different. Walter was dead, his wife and daughters were falling apart, and I was desperately trying to create a space in which they could grieve and not tear each other to shreds. Working with the dying was easy compared to this.

The house was calmer when Jeanette had left for the office. Ellen didn't end up going with her, but both the girls stayed in their rooms.

I lay down on my bed but couldn't sleep. I kept thinking about Jusu and his family. I'd been so certain he was dead. Bringing up his son in honour of the life he'd lost was, at times, the only way I could carry on. I would remember the warmth of his smile, the intoxication of our love for each other, and grit my teeth and get on with the business of bringing up our beautiful child, struggling to make a life for us in a country that didn't feel like mine and didn't welcome mixed-race kids. I wondered what it would have been like living with Jusu in Koido, raising our children together – there would certainly have been more than one had I stayed. I hadn't known any mixed-race families in Sierra Leone – would we have been accepted there any more than we would have been here? Or would we have had to fight for our place in a community that didn't want to acknowledge us? Would Jusu and I really have stayed together if I hadn't left, or was ours a childhood romance that would have sputtered and died as we grew older? All I could hope, in the end, was that he felt as fulfilled and happy in his life as I was in mine.

There were, of course, no answers to be had, so I'd turned my thoughts to the fledgling relationship I was enjoying with Mark when there was a knock at the front door. No-one else answered so I went down.

My mood plummeted when I saw Sebastian on the step.

'Jeanette isn't here,' I said, assuming he wanted to have a rant about the will.

'I know. I saw her arrive at the office, so I slipped out the back door.' He smiled. Not his usual lascivious leer, but a smile that widened his mouth and left his eyes untouched. 'If she wants to see me, she'll have to make an appointment. I won't have her dropping in and expecting me to make time for her.'

I almost laughed. What an adolescent.

He took a step closer. I remained where I was, standing in the doorway so he couldn't come in.

'Grace and Ellen are in,' I said. 'I'll call them.'

He put a hand out, not quite touching my arm. 'No. I came to see you.'

'Me?'

'I need you to do something for me.'

I walked back into the kitchen, too surprised to say a word. He followed and sat at the table.

I busied myself with wiping the stove, keeping my back to him. I didn't want to give him any encouragement.

'Oh for God's sake, sit down!'

I sat, still holding the cloth in one hand, squeezing it and feeling the water drip onto my lap.

'If you want to talk about the will, you should phone the solicitor,' I said.

'Oh, I've already spoken to that smarmy bastard. There's

nothing I can do about it, as you would know, having no doubt seen the psychiatrist who came to assess my father.' He paused. 'You probably organised it. But I haven't come to talk to you about that – what would be the point?'

I stared at him, squeezing the cloth so tight my hands began to hurt. I took a breath and felt my chest expand against the cool cotton of my shirt.

His eyes never left me. I shifted in my seat.

'You have wormed your way into Jeanette's confidence. She's a weak woman, I know. She needs someone to lean on. It was Father, and now it's you. I've seen how she looks to you to stand up for her, even to speak for her.'

I swallowed hard and hooked my feet around the legs of the chair to stop myself from jumping up and taking a swipe at him. Arrogant prick.

He carried on, no doubt convinced of his right to march in and make judgements and unaware he was causing offence. Or not caring.

'So, there's something you can do for me.' He raised his eyebrows and tilted his head slightly.

I said nothing.

Undeterred, he went on, 'You must counsel Jeanette not to stick her nose into the affairs of the business. She has no skills in the area and until now has shown no interest. Tell her to leave running the company to the grown-ups.' He bared his teeth in the parody of a complicit smile.

I stood up, almost falling over in my haste to get to my feet.

'I think you've severely underestimated Jeanette, and mistaken my support of her for something it isn't. Even if I had any influence on her, I wouldn't exert it on your behalf. Jeanette is a strong, intelligent woman and she will do what she thinks best, and I will do my best to help her in any way I can.'

Sebastian remained sitting, waving a hand in front of his

face as if swatting away an annoying fly. I wanted to wipe the smug smile off his face.

'Oh for God's sake, calm down, woman,' he said.

I remained standing, hands on hips, glaring.

'All you need to do is point out she has no experience in business matters. Surely you can do that.'

I kept glaring at him, jaw clenched.

He stood up slowly. 'I thought you were better than this, Hester. Clearly I was mistaken. When are you leaving, by the way? Weren't you just meant to stay until the old man kicked the bucket? Nothing to keep you here now, is there?'

It was none of his business how long I was there, or that Walter had asked me to stay after his death, probably anticipating scenes like this.

'I'll see you out, Sebastian,' I said.

'No need. I was born here, remember? I know this house better than any of you.'

I waited until I heard the door slam before sinking into a chair and starting to shake. Rarely had I met anyone who could make me so angry. I hoped never to see him again.

WALTER

Brava, Hester Rose! Standing up to Sebastian is no easy feat. He's a bully, there's no doubt about it.

What's that? A disapproving stare from you, Dorothy? How unusual. It's your fault he's the way he is. He always was a mummy's boy, running to you with his pathetic little grievances, his scratched knees, his tales of other boys at school picking on him. And you were a willing, even an encouraging, audience. Didn't you realise that over the years the stories got bigger, more outrageous, less truthful?

Everyone's behaving strangely. Pantomime horses indeed.

I don't like to see them cry, though. I don't want them dwelling on the past, gratifying though it is to know I'm missed. I can't do anything about it, and it pisses me off. When I was alive, I'd tell a joke or make a silly face and the tears would stop. Now they flow like rivers. That's probably the biggest thing Hester Rose and I would disagree on; she thinks people need to express themselves. I think it all gets a bit self-indulgent. Better to get on with life, look forward not back.

I'm a hypocrite, though. What do I spend my time doing when I'm not spying on my family? Raking back over my life. I feel like there's a ledger somewhere, with Good on one side and Bad on the other, and I have to work out which way my life was skewed. I never set out to do anyone harm, that I can say, hand on heart. But people did get hurt, I know, that's life, isn't it? There are just some who are driven, who make their way in the world, pulling certain folk along with them and shaking others off along the way.

I wasn't one to philosophise. Always thought it a waste of time, thinking about things with no definite answer. I'm a black and white man. Right's right, wrong's wrong and ne'er the twain shall meet. But now... perhaps it's having all this time on my hands, I can't seem to stop thinking.

What is truth? Is there a soul, and if so, is that what I am now? There's religion creeping in, and I hold no truck with all that but what else can I call this in-between existence? I still have a sense of being me. I'm certainly not anyone else, anyway. But I have no agency and it's killing me. Bad joke.

Because I don't have a sleeping state in this 'life after life' of mine, I have a lot of time to ponder. If I'd thought about things more when I was alive would my life have been different? If, for example, I'd given any thought to the nature of truth, would I have made different decisions? And is saying nothing the same as lying? Should I have told Dorothy I was having an affair, which would have been truthful, or kept it quiet because I knew it would hurt her? When is it okay to lie, or be prudent with the truth? Does knowing something mean you should say it?

I hate this. I'm beginning to hate being here. I hate thinking all these things. I hate not having answers. And most of all, I hate not knowing why I'm stuck here in limbo.

Give me dead or alive. Black or white.

FIFTEEN

The next day, Jeanette and the girls went out after breakfast. I hadn't told Jeanette about Sebastian's visit, and she hadn't said much about her trip to the office except to reiterate her decision to get a manager in. I wondered if anyone would be able to work with Sebastian, who clearly thought he should be running the show. But it wasn't my concern and any thought of Sebastian, or the business, went out the window when Mark rang and invited me for lunch.

We met down a narrow side street in town at a little pub boasting the best home-made pies in England. I sat watching him as he stood at the bar getting the drinks and ordering the food – a chicken, leek and tarragon pie for me, beef and Guinness for him. He was so different to Jusu physically: taller and broader. But there was something about Mark that reminded me of him. They were both kind and thoughtful, able to empathise and put others first. I knew I was falling for Mark and felt momentarily guilty about Jusu. And then I reminded myself he would never have wanted me to be lonely or unhappy, as I wouldn't have wanted that for him. Maybe Mark was the second chance I hadn't allowed myself until now.

He returned with our wine and sat next to me, his thigh touching mine.

'It's good to see you, Hester,' he said.

'You already said that.' I laughed and added, 'It's good to see you too.'

'What's new in your world?'

I told him about Justin's news.

'That must have been painful for you,' he said.

'It was a shock, certainly. I felt guilty I hadn't known, or done more to find him – for Justin's sake as well as mine. Now I feel sad. I hadn't seen him for twenty-seven years, but he was an important part of my life, and Justin's dad, so it still feels like a part of me just died.'

'Of course it does,' said Mark.

The pies arrived and we ate in silence for a while.

'I don't need to talk about it, by the way,' I said, halfway through my very tasty meal. 'I don't want it ruining our lunch. What's been happening for you?'

'Nothing unusual. My mother had a bit of a turn, but she's rallied, and work is work.'

With the mention of work, the issue of Gavin Green leapt to the forefront of my mind, but I knew I couldn't ask about him.

'Any interesting cases?'

'I enjoy my work otherwise I wouldn't do it, but I imagine what I find interesting and what you would are probably quite different.' He smiled.

'That sounds like you're trying to hide something from me,' I said. 'I'm intrigued.'

When Mark laughed his eyes crinkled up and crow's feet fanned out towards his temples. I love a man who can laugh unselfconsciously.

'I'm a terrible liar,' he said, 'so I couldn't hide anything from you if I tried. And it's the main reason I never became a barrister. Can you imagine me defending someone in court knowing, or even suspecting, my client was in the wrong, and tying myself up in knots not to tell the judge exactly what I thought? I would have had some irate clients!'

'I can imagine,' I said. *But Gavin Green would be interesting, you could tell me why Walter left him money. Stop it, Hester.* But the more I tried to push him out of my head, the more I thought about him, until he was all I could think about.

'Are you all right?' asked Mark, leaning in a little, concern written all over his face.

I shook my head, trying to clear it. 'I'm fine. Sorry.' I took a mouthful of my pie and chewed slowly.

'Actually, Mark,' I said when I'd swallowed, 'I think we have a problem.'

He nodded. 'Mr Green?'

'I'm afraid so. I know I can't ask anything about him, but I can't concentrate on anything else. He's sitting right between us like a big bloody elephant.'

'What shall we do?'

I sighed. I knew what we needed to do. And I knew what I wanted to do. And they didn't match up at all.

'I think we'll have to stop seeing each other until this whole will issue is sorted and I've moved back home. Grace is at me to winkle the information out of you, and I must admit I'm curious too, but it isn't really my business and I know you can't say anything.'

He sat back, wiped his mouth on his napkin then folded it and put it down by his plate.

'I can't say I'm happy, but I do see your point. I'll agree to it on one condition.'

'What's that?' I leant in closer.

'You move home as soon as you can. I don't want to let this get in the way of us seeing each other. I accept your concerns because I admire and respect you, but I also fancy you, so don't keep me waiting too long!'

I smiled. He fancied me! And even though it sounded like teen-speak, I liked it.

'I don't plan to,' I said, taking his hand.

We finished our drinks and walked arm in arm back along the street towards his office. When we kissed goodbye, it didn't feel like a farewell, but I was still sad as I walked to my car. And as I drove to the Baxters' house, I became more and more annoyed.

Damn Grace.

Damn Gavin Green.

And most of all damn Walter for creating this bloody mystery and getting me caught up in it.

As I walked through the front door, a message arrived on my phone.

> Am I still allowed to text you?

I smiled and nodded to myself.

> Yes. That would be nice x

Mark Johnstone. *Yes.*

Another text popped up on my screen. Grace.

> Have you found out anything?

> Not yet.

I was starting to feel tense. Deep breaths. This was my fault. I had, after all, said I'd talk to Gavin and couldn't put it off forever, so I rang him. We arranged to meet up the following evening. He sounded agitated but I wasn't in the mood to soothe him. I had more than enough to think about.

Jeanette was in her gardening clothes, a pair of secateurs in hand, when I entered the kitchen.

'I'm just going to cut some flowers, want to join me?' she said.

I knew it was code for 'I need to talk' so I told her I'd make us a cuppa and come and find her in the garden.

She was on her knees over by the wall weeding and snipping the occasional dahlia, placing it in her trug. The weeds were in a mound on the grass beside her. As I approached, she dropped some into the trug. I knelt down and removed them. She saw what I was doing and sat back on her heels.

'I can't concentrate. Not even on bloody weeding.' She looked to the sky, blinking back tears.

'It's early days,' I said.

The tears didn't materialise. 'I'm trying to be strong.'

'You are strong.'

'I don't feel it. All I want to do is stay in bed and howl.'

'But you don't. Getting out of bed takes strength. Every time you want to collapse in a heap and don't, that's strength.'

'You really think so?'

'I really do.'

'What am I going to do without you, Hester? I know you can't stay here forever but I don't want you to leave. The night you weren't here, and Grace went missing, I wanted to crawl under a rock and not have to cope with any of it. Then you found her, and I felt okay again. Not just because you found her, but because of your... presence. It gave me confidence. I'm so lost without Walter and when I'm not sad I'm terrified of the future, of being alone, of not coping.'

'There's not much you can do about your sadness. You loved

him, so you have to feel the sadness of not having him here anymore. But–'

Jeanette glanced at me. 'But what?'

'Well, I'm not your therapist, but what about when you're terrified? How does it feel?'

'Awful. Physically, I shake. Mentally, I shake. I just shake.'

I smiled at her. 'You know, when I was a seventeen-year-old single mother in a new country where I hardly knew anyone, a very wise woman asked me that question and I gave her more or less the same answer. And she said to me, "The part of you that observes your terror isn't terrified. So, you can stick yourself to that part, or you can stay stuck to your terror".'

Jeanette sat staring intently at one of the dahlias she'd picked, a beautiful deep red bloom.

'You're saying I can choose not to be terrified?'

'What I'm saying is you're already making the choice all the time by getting out of bed, going to your pottery class, being out here in the garden and not under a rock howling. The terror is still there, but you're not clamped to it. And when you realise that, maybe the shaking will stop.'

'Wow.' She wiped her forearm across her face and turned to me. 'Who was this wise woman – I need to meet her.'

'My friend Peggy,' I said. 'She was reading a lot of Eastern philosophy at the time. She's always known the right thing to say. She's the wisest, kindest person I've ever met. I would have fallen apart without her.'

'I think you're one of the wisest people I've ever met. And one of the kindest. The girls think so too.'

I blushed.

Jeanette carried on, 'I know you can't stay here forever, even though I'd love you to, but do you think you could give us another week?'

'Of course,' I said.

Before dinner, Anna turned up. She was in her usual designer gear, but her hair was greasy and falling across her face. There was mascara smudged under her eyes. Her breath smelled of alcohol, but that wasn't unusual.

'I've come to pick up the painting of Mother and the jewellery. I should have phoned first, but I forgot.'

Jeanette was in the drawing room. I took Anna in to see her and found her standing in front of the French doors, clutching one hand in the other, crying.

I was about to back out without disturbing her, but Anna rushed in.

'Jeanette,' she said, her tone soft, conciliatory. She reached out as if she was going to put a hand on her arm but thought better of it and let it drop by her side.

Jeanette looked round at me, in the doorway, then at Anna beside her.

'I'm so sorry,' said Anna.

Jeanette nodded but said nothing and looked away from her again.

Anna did put a hand out to her then, patted her gently on the shoulder and came out of the room.

'I really am sorry,' she said to me, as if reinforcing the point.

'What for?' I asked. *For arriving unannounced? For being so horrible to Jeanette and the girls for so long? For Walter's death?*

'It's all my fault,' she said and started to cry.

'You'd better come into the kitchen,' I said, leading the way.

She sat clasping and unclasping her hands, occasionally pushing her hair out of her eyes. I made tea and took the half-cooked lasagne out of the Aga – no point letting it burn.

'Is there any wine open by any chance?' she asked without looking up.

'No. Sorry.'

She shrugged. 'Probably shouldn't have any more anyway.'

The kitchen clock ticked loudly. I heard Milly snuffling at the door but didn't let her in and eventually she left again.

'Everything's gone to shit.' Anna spoke so quietly I had to ask her to repeat herself to make sure I'd heard properly. 'I said, everything in my life has turned to shit.'

'I'm sorry to hear it,' I said.

'I'm so hungry.'

'What?'

'Does it surprise you? Anorexic Anna admitting she's hungry!'

'It does, actually.'

'I suppose you thought hunger was something that went away after a few years. Well, it doesn't. Ever. Usually it's fine. I'm proud to feel hungry and not give into it. It makes me strong.'

I didn't know what to say. In my book it made her damaged rather than strong.

'I miss him. I didn't think I would, but I do. But the worst thing is this hunger. Since he died, I can't think of anything else but this fucking hunger.'

'And have you eaten?' I asked. I had no idea how to speak to an anorexic about food.

'Fill up the emptiness his death has created with food, you mean, or some such stupid psychobabble? No. I haven't.'

'I see.' I didn't. Having never had anything but a healthy relationship with food I struggled to understand the desire to deny yourself such a basic need.

We lapsed into silence again.

'It is all my fault,' she said eventually. 'I meant it.'

'How so?'

'If I tell you, will you pass it on to Jeanette. I don't think I could say it twice.'

I didn't know what to say but it didn't matter because she took a deep breath, wiped her eyes with a tissue, and began.

'I was nine and Sebastian was eleven when our mother died. We weren't close, Seb and me. I don't suppose many brothers and sisters are at that age. He was mad for model aeroplanes and building his tree house. I had dolls and fairy dress-ups. Anyway, when Mother died, Father wasted no time in bringing Marie and her baby into the house.' She sniffed, blew her nose.

'If he'd left it a year or two, we might have coped, but he moved her in just a few weeks after the funeral. It felt like we were being replaced by a new baby and we were meant to forget our real mother. I thought he didn't want Seb and me around anymore; we were surplus to requirements.' She shrugged, shredded the tissue she'd been using.

'So I decided to become invisible and the best way to do that was to stop eating. It wasn't so clear cut or conscious, of course, but that's what happened, in effect.' She paused again, gazed at the half-cooked lasagne on the countertop.

'Anyway, Father started getting at me to eat. He used to get into these terrible rages in those days. He'd go on about kids in Africa starving and here I was with all the food I could eat, refusing to let it past my lips. I'd say nothing but every time he shouted, it strengthened my resolve. Of course, I used to sneak food up to my room – I knew if I ate nothing at all I'd die and I didn't want to do that – but I wouldn't let a single morsel pass my lips in front of him. It made me feel so powerful.' She stopped talking again.

'So you stopped eating in your grief for your mother and because you were angry with your father about his new family, and never really started again?'

'That was never my intention, but then does anyone ever set out to become an anorexic? But two things happened. My father worked very long hours and when he came home, just wanted to retreat into his study with his new woman and a whisky, ignoring us. He would still get angry with me at mealtimes for not eating though. It was the only time he ever noticed me.'

'You had to keep at it, or he'd stop noticing you?'

'Exactly. I've come to understand there was this tension in me between wanting him to see me and wanting to be invisible. It was weird and obviously completely untenable – I couldn't have it both ways. And then the other thing was that Sebastian saw what was going on. Father had as little time for him as he did for me but that was the way Sebastian liked it. He was a shy boy, very quiet and preferred his own company. Sensitive, I suppose you'd say.'

My face must have shown my surprise, because Anna said, 'Hard to believe now, I know, but he was. Very quiet. Wouldn't say boo to a goose. But he didn't like Father shouting at me, so he started standing up to him, protecting me. And it worked. I think Father was so surprised, he forgot to be angry with me and started getting at Sebastian instead.'

'And you went back to being invisible.'

'Yes, and it was a relief, in a way. Although I do remember hating the arguments between Sebastian and Father. It all escalated. Sebastian went on a campaign to get rid of Marie and Louise, and I think by then Marie was over it anyway; looking after warring, eating-disordered step-children wasn't her idea of married bliss.'

'How old were you when they moved out?'

'About twelve, I think.'

'Did Marie never try to make you eat?'

'Of course. She'd cook things she thought I'd like, and I'd eat a few mouthfuls. Enough to keep her trying but not enough to let her think she'd succeeded. Not that I thought about it so clearly back then. A lot of what I'm telling you is what I've figured out in hindsight – and believe me, I've paid several therapists thousands of pounds to try and work myself out. Anyway, Sebastian and Father got locked into this terrible cycle of anger with each other. And it's my fault. If I'd been normal, Sebastian would be a rather shy, quiet man, not this aggressive, insensitive goose he's become.'

She started crying again.

I waited until the sobs subsided.

'So why are you telling this story now? You want Jeanette to know, but what difference will it make to her?'

She sniffed, blew her nose. 'I'm worried about my brother. He's been angry for so long I don't think he knows how to be anything else. But now the object of his anger is no longer here I don't know what he'll do. I saw him earlier and he seemed sort of sunken, as if he's collapsing in on himself.'

I didn't tell her I'd also seen him recently and it wasn't the impression I'd got.

'You mean you're returning the favour – he looked after you all those years ago, and now you're trying to look after him. But I still don't see where Jeanette comes into this.'

'Just ask her to try to understand. And be kind. He's not in a good way.'

'I can do that, although I obviously can't promise how she'll respond.'

Anna gave a little smile. 'She's a good woman.'

I raised my eyebrows and Anna laughed.

'I mean it, although I can see why you're sceptical. But we all get stuck in certain roles in families, don't we? Sebastian the angry, Walter the controlling patriarch, Anna the pathetic little anorexic, Louise the martyr, Jeanette the good. And then one of them dies and everything changes.'

That was true. There is often a period of flux in families after a death. But this was some revelation. If it was true, I was sorry for Sebastian who, in wanting to protect his little sister, sacrificed his humanity. I wondered if it was too late for him to change back into the man he might have been. And Anna – would she finally try and kick this eating disorder? It was nothing to do with me, but I felt touched by her story.

'I think you need to tell Jeanette yourself. It'll be better coming from you.'

Anna sighed. 'I know. Perhaps I just needed to hear it out loud first to see if it made sense. I will tell her.'

'Will you stay for dinner?' I asked, seeing her looking at the lasagne again.

She shook her head. 'No, thank you. I'll go now and come another time to get those things and talk to Jeanette.' She stood to go. 'Thanks, Hester. You're a good listener.'

I put the lasagne back in the oven and went to my room.

WALTER

Fuck me. You could have knocked me down with a feather when I heard what Anna had to say. Well, actually you couldn't because a feather would go straight through me as I have no substance these days. Anyway. Jesus H. Christ. At first, I thought she was talking absolute shite, and I was shouting, trying to make her hear that she was wrong. I was never angry, just concerned. And Sebastian was never the saintly little boy she painted him out to be.

But then Dorothy swept around to stand in front of me and she was nodding. I almost shooed her away, but I noticed she had a rueful little smile on her face rather than the usual disapproving sneer, and she was reaching out as if to touch me, begging me to listen, to consider Anna's words.

When she'd finished, I drifted into the study to think. What I had intended as concern and encouragement she'd experienced as anger and bullying. And her brother coming to her aid had diverted my attention on to him. Given the person he's become, it's hard to remember a time when he was any different, but Dorothy almost nodded her head off when Anna revealed his motive so perhaps she's right.

But what was I meant to do? Let her starve herself to death without saying a word? Pretend everything was hunky-dory? We were all struggling. I'd lost my wife; they'd lost their mother. Granted, I did have Marie to fall back on – I don't mean that quite how it came out. I mean I could talk to her; she was supportive.

But none of what Anna said changes the facts of the matter, which were that she was starving herself and Sebastian was an angry little shit who would argue black was white and white was red. And they were both vile to Marie and Louise. I can remember Anna trying to tip Louise out of her pram and Sebastian used to pinch her when he thought no-one was looking. And he was either rude to Marie or completely ignored her.

So, who's telling the truth? Me, her or both of us? Neither of us? Would Sebastian have yet another version of events? And Marie? Louise was too young to remember any of it, lucky girl. Perhaps the truth lies somewhere in the middle of all our memories. I don't suppose there's any point in fighting about it. Not that I can fight with no voice and no other way of communicating. I tried picking up a pen the other day and nothing happened – my hand passed right through it.

I'm a ghost who doesn't haunt the living, but is haunted by them.

If there's one good thing that's come out of me dying, it's Hester Rose and Jeanette getting to know each other. She's got such a wise head on her shoulders, that Hester Rose. The thing she said about sticking with the bit of your mind that isn't scared was absolutely champion. I wish I'd come up with something like that.

Anyway, I've been thinking about the nature of love. Thinking about truth is too hard. The girls used to watch *Love Actually* all the time. Load of sentimental codswallop I thought at the time, but I'm not so sure anymore. When I reflect on my life it's the people I remember, the relationships that matter. Not work, not golf, not opening more shops and selling more shoes than my competitors. It's Jeanette and the girls. Marie and Louise. Her boys and their bustling chaotic energy, their sloppy kisses and unquestioning affection. Even Dorothy – yes, you, I know you're here – we were so in love when we married. When Sebastian was born, I felt as though I'd never really known what love was – the kind of love that reaches into the deepest part of your heart and is pulled out of you by a small bawling infant with scrunched up eyes and patchy hair. And then Anna came along, and I fell in love with her in a different way – more protective, softer.

God, just listen to me. It's all this time I have. I never gave any of this a thought while it was happening, and now I believe I may have missed out on the best moments of my life. Rushed over them to get back to work.

Do I regret the way I lived? No. I can honestly say I don't. I was driven to provide for my family, and I did it well. I don't believe I could have done that and been around more, been the hands-on dad some men are.

Dorothy just gave me one of her looks, like she knows I've been lying to myself all these years. Perhaps I have, who knows?

Ma's pitched up again. She just stands in the corner, fingers fretting at the hem of her apron. She was always on the go, couldn't relax. I wonder if she too spends all her time thinking. Maybe that's why she looks so frazzled. She and Dorothy ignore each other. I'm not sure if it's because they never got on or whether they're unaware the other is here.

I wonder if her presence means I'm off soon. It was her who was around before I died, standing at the end of my bed, watching. Is she going to show me how to leave this place?

I'm ready. And I'm not.

Absolutes have gone out the window.

SIXTEEN

'He still won't talk to me,' said Grace, flopping down at the kitchen table the next morning. 'He's such a jerk. I can't think what I ever saw in him. Obviously it wasn't the stiffness of his spine.'

I couldn't help laughing. Poor Grace. So pissed off, so indignant.

'What?' She was ready for a fight.

'Sorry – the spine thing tickled my funny bone.'

'Well, it's true. I'm surprised he can stand up straight.' She giggled.

'I've arranged to see him tonight,' I said.

'I'll come with you. He won't turn me away if you're there too.'

'Definitely not.'

'Please?' Grace batted her eyelashes at me.

'Not a chance.'

She huffed and looked at me from under her eyebrows. 'But you'll tell me everything he says.'

'Perhaps, if it has anything to do with you.'

'God, Hester, you're a dragon!'

'Hear me roar,' I said and laughed. Such a misquote. Grace didn't seem to notice. She had got up and started making herself some breakfast.

'What are you up to today?' I asked.

'Mummy and I are going to town. I'm going back to school tomorrow – I feel up to it now. To be honest, I'm getting a bit bored spending all this time at home. My friends texted a bit at the beginning, but they don't know what to say now so they're staying away.' She stopped, looked at me as if she'd just realised what she'd said. 'Is it awful? Feeling bored, I mean? I'm sad about Daddy, of course I am, but I can't sit around grieving for him all the time.'

'Of course you can't,' I said. 'I think getting back to school is a great idea. Anyway, it's not long until the end of term, is it?'

'Two weeks. Anyway, Mummy and I are going to do some shopping and have lunch somewhere nice today.'

I hoped when Grace saw Gavin at school she didn't get upset and say something she might regret or that would get him into hot water.

Ellen ended up going with them, so I had the day to myself. I went to see Peggy at the nursing home.

She was sitting at a table in the lounge with a few other elderly ladies. She looked shrunken in her clothes, her neck too thin for her collar, her wrists swimming in the cuffs of her blouse. There was a broad streak of grey along her parting. I felt a stab of guilt. I hadn't been looking after her in the last few weeks.

They'd been playing cards, judging by the piles of dried pasta spirals in front of each of them, but now were sitting quietly. The TV was on in the corner, but no-one was watching it.

'Darling girl,' she said when she saw me. 'Have you come to invite me to your engagement party?'

I smiled and shook my head. 'Nothing like that. I came to see how you are.'

'Oh, I'm the same as ever. And it was so nice of Justin to drop in the other day. What a fine son you raised. Not many youngsters come to see us old croaks, I can tell you.' She leant forward and gestured for me to come closer.

'Between you and me, I told these ladies he was my grandson. They've not met him before, you see. Now they're intrigued about where his colour comes from but they're too polite to ask!'

'He practically is your grandson – you've certainly been the closest thing he's ever had to a grandmother.' I kissed her on the cheek, and she caught my hand.

'Bless you, Hester. And bless that son of yours.'

'Did he tell you his news?'

'About Jusu? Yes. Very sad. How did you take it?'

'I was shocked, of course, and sad too. But I'm all right. Justin might meet his half- brother and sister one day. I'd like that for him. After all, you and I are the only family he's got.' I said the last bit more loudly for the benefit of any of the ladies who might be listening in. Peggy squeezed my hand.

'And what about this beau of yours?' she asked. 'It's about time you had a nice man in your life.'

'Nothing more to tell than last time, but it might change in a week or two.'

'You make sure it does,' she said. 'But why a week or two?'

'I've promised Jeanette I'll stay a bit longer.'

'Kind girl,' she said.

I told her about the mystery man in Walter's will, and how I was going to talk to Gavin Green later to try and get some answers.

'But why are you getting involved – it's none of your concern, surely?'

I thought for a moment. Why was I seeing him? Because I liked Grace and wanted to help? Or because I was being nosey? Or because I was enjoying the sleuthing?

'I can't stand an unsolved mystery,' I said finally.

Peggy laughed. 'Well do tell when you find out, won't you? You've got me intrigued now as well.'

I stayed for a couple of hours and when I left, I promised to come and do her hair for her soon. She'd always been so particular about it.

'That would be lovely, Hester. You're very good to me.'

As I was leaving, one of the nursing staff asked to have a word.

'Did she tell you?' he asked.

My heart sank. 'Tell me what?'

He pulled at his earlobe, looking uncomfortable.

'Come on – you've got to tell me now.'

'I shouldn't say anything – confidentiality, you know. But you do work here, so...'

'And I'm her next of kin, so spit it out.'

He took a deep breath. 'Peggy saw the doctor today. The cancer's spread into her bones. And given how frail she is already, she won't last much longer. I'm sorry.'

I couldn't breathe and my knees gave way. I sank into a chair and stared at the wall. 'How long?'

'A few months.'

'I'll be here,' I said. 'She won't be on her own.'

I glanced through the lounge door. There she was, talking to one of the other ladies. She saw me, waved and blew a kiss. I sent one back and headed out to the car.

I sat, head on the steering wheel, wondering what I was going to do without her. A crushing weight lodged itself in my belly and refused to leave.

I have no idea how I drove back to the Baxters' house nor what I did for the rest of the day. My body felt heavy, unresponsive, and in my head I was replaying every moment I'd ever spent with Peggy. From the moment we met as two women, vastly different in age, but both struggling in our own ways, to her ever-present smile, her advice, her laughter. She'd been with me the first day Justin went to school when I thought my heart would break being separated from him for a whole day. She'd been my cheer squad when I did my doula course and graduated. She'd been the one to give me a kick up the backside and a pep talk when I was avoiding things, and the one to pick me up again when I was too exhausted to carry on. She'd been a mother to me when I needed one and a steadfast friend. Now I realised her interest in my love life was, at least in part, her trying to make sure I had someone when she was gone. Always thinking of others. What would I do without her?

I decided I would get through the next week as best I could and then I would put myself at Peggy's disposal for as long as she had left. It was all I could do, but it didn't feel like enough.

I pulled myself together enough to go and see Gavin. Like Grace, I couldn't sit around feeling sad, I had to do something.

He was already at the pub when I arrived, a pint in front of him. He jumped up when he saw me, but I gestured to him to sit and went to get my own drink.

With a glass of wine I sat across the table from him.

'How are you, Hester?' he asked.

'Not great, but we haven't come here to talk about me.'

He ran a hand through his hair. 'No, I suppose not,' he said. 'I know I owe you an explanation, but I don't know where to start.'

He picked up his pint. His hand was shaking. He took a mouthful and swallowed hard.

I crossed my arms and waited for him to gather his thoughts.

'Okay,' he said just when I thought he might never speak. 'Fact of the matter is, I don't know what to do.' He swallowed again, closed his eyes for a moment. 'I want you to know I never meant to hurt Grace. She's wonderful, really lovely.'

'I know.'

'Yes, of course.' He moistened his lips. 'I've handed in my notice by the way. I leave at the end of term. It seemed like the right thing to do in the circumstances.' He looked at me, perhaps wanting my approval.

I gave him none. Suddenly I didn't want to be there, didn't want to hear his story, didn't care how he tried to justify his behaviour.

'Frankly, Grace is beginning to scare me. I don't know what she's told you, but she won't leave me alone. I get texts every few minutes, night and day. She sends pictures of herself naked and turns up at my rooms every chance she can. She's going to get me into a lot of trouble. If all this comes out it won't just be the school I'm leaving, it'll be teaching. I've tried to reason with her, but she won't listen. She says she loves me and won't let me go.'

That was a surprise. Grace had told me she was having no contact with him. Little minx.

'So, you're actually more concerned about your job and your reputation than you are about Grace and her feelings?' I was feeling distinctly chilly towards him, and I'd been lied to by Grace. Right then, I didn't particularly like either of them.

He shook his head. 'No, of course not, but I'd be stupid not to be concerned about my career, wouldn't I?'

'Maybe you should have thought about that before you started sleeping with her.'

'What?' His hands flew to his head, his eyes wide. 'We

haven't... I would never... oh my God, is that what she told you?' He slumped forward, head in his hands. 'This is even worse than I thought.'

'So, you're telling me that she's been stalking you? That you haven't been in a relationship?'

'I swear, there's been no intimacy. When her father was diagnosed, she needed to talk. I listened. And then she started turning up everywhere, at all times of the day and night. I didn't know what to do.'

'When you came to the funeral gathering, you said "I'd never have" then you stopped. What did you mean?'

He frowned, thinking. 'I can't remember exactly, but I probably meant I'd never have taken the job at the school if I'd known it was near where Walter lived. I really didn't want anything to do with him.'

I sat back in my seat, going through everything Grace had told me in my head. She'd convinced me they were having a relationship. Who to believe? Gavin seemed genuinely shocked when I accused him of sleeping with her. I took some deep breaths.

'Will you help me? Talk to her, try and make her see reason?' Gavin looked suddenly younger than his twenty-four years, despite his designer beard and carefully tousled hair.

'I don't know what to believe, what to do, but I really think you owe it to her to sort this out with her, face to face. The more you ignore her or refuse to see her, the harder she'll try. She likes getting her own way, most people do.'

'I have talked to her. She won't listen.'

'What do you expect me to do?'

He sighed, staring into space and chewing his lip, grappling with something in his head. I could see why Grace had fallen for him. With his square jaw and hazel eyes, he was a handsome man.

I waited.

Eventually, Gavin looked at me and then looked around at the crowded pub to make sure we weren't being overheard. He took a deep breath and said, 'It gets even more complicated. What I'm going to tell you must go absolutely no further and you must swear you won't tell anyone.'

I raised my eyebrows, intrigued. 'Fine,' I said, 'I promise.'

He paused again, raked a hand through his hair.

Once again, he checked the space around us. No-one was interested in us. There was a darts match on the other side of the room and all attention was on the players.

Gavin started talking, his speech sounded pressured as if, at last, he was confessing to some sin in his past.

'My mother died last year,' he said in a low voice. 'She'd brought me up on her own mostly – she was married for a time, but he wasn't my father, and it didn't last long.' He looked at his drink as if deciding whether to take a swig but left it where it was. 'She never told me who my father was. She said they'd separated before he knew she was pregnant.'

I gasped and my hand flew to my heart, thinking of Jusu and Justin, another father and son who never knew each other.

'Are you okay?'

'I'm fine,' I said. 'Go on.'

'She left me a letter with her will, telling me the name of my father and a phone number, which turned out to be his office. She'd always promised she'd tell me one day.'

My stomach sank. 'Wa–'

'Ssssh, please.' Gavin glowered at me and glanced around again.

'Walter Armstrong?' I whispered.

He bowed his head. 'Yes.'

'Oh my God. And you decided to get in touch.'

We'd been leaning towards each other and our foreheads almost touched. I sat back a little.

'Yes. We met at the end of last year. In London.'

'You knew he had a family? You knew about Grace?' My mind was racing, going off in ten different directions at once.

'Of course I didn't! Do you honestly think I'd end up teaching in her school if I'd known?'

I stared at him. He looked young and confused, but how do you recognise a psychopath? Don't they get away with what they do because they look the same as everybody else?

I closed my eyes and tried to think.

When I opened them, he was staring at me.

He leant in closer again, speaking in an urgent whisper. 'Please, believe me.' He was talking so fast he almost fell over his words. 'Walter told me nothing about himself. I'd tried to stalk him on social media, but you probably know, he had no online presence. All I knew about him was that he was the Walter Armstrong of Shoebridge Shoes. I swear, that's all I knew.' He gazed up at the ceiling as if looking for divine intervention then looked back at me and carried on.

'We met in a nondescript pub in Soho. He demanded a DNA test. I think he thought I was after his money, but I just wanted to meet the man who was my father. We only met the once. I didn't particularly like him, nor he me. My curiosity had been satisfied, and we agreed not to have any more contact.

'It was by complete chance I ended up working at Grace's school. I didn't know where Walter lived, didn't even know he had a daughter.'

He glanced down at his hands and then lifted his head and held my gaze. 'When I met Grace I had no idea who she was. I swear on my mother's grave I had no idea until Davina Lacey co-opted me into going to his wake or whatever it was. I saw the family portrait out by the table and suddenly two and two made a shit load more than four. Well, you saw me that day – I was a mess. Grace had been hitting on me, making my life hell, and she was my sister.'

'Why didn't you tell her?'

He stared at me like I was a two-headed monster.

'Tell her that her beloved father, who'd just died, had another child – one that she thought she was in love with? She was upset enough already; I didn't want to add to that.' He looked at his glass. 'Although trying to avoid her was probably just as brutal,' he added quietly.

He had a point. Or did he? If he'd told Grace who he was, she would certainly have backed off – if she believed him. I knocked back my wine in one go, pushed my glass towards him and said, 'Another, please.'

He nodded obediently and went to the bar. I needed time to think. Poor Grace. Should I tell her? Jeanette? Had he really not known about Walter's family? Was he trying to worm his way in somehow? He seemed upset about the whole situation, but he was a drama teacher, so presumably he could act.

I watched him at the bar ordering my drink. I bit my lip, trying to decide what to do.

He put the wine down in front of me as I scraped my chair back and got up.

'I have to leave,' I said.

'But... what are you going to do?'

'I'm going to talk to my friend Mark.'

'The Mark who was Walter's solicitor?'

'The very same.'

'Oh. What are you going to tell him?'

He looked so young and vulnerable, standing there in the middle of the pub, hands by his sides.

'I don't know.'

'Please, sit down again. Don't rush off.' He gestured to the chair. 'Please.'

I sank into my seat, put both hands around my wine glass.

'Did you know he was leaving you money in his will?' I couldn't look him in the eye.

'He said something about giving me something to make me stay away but I assured him I didn't need anything, and I certainly never received a penny. I'd forgotten all about it until Mark rang me to tell me.'

'He was probably diagnosed not long after you saw him and it went out of his head until he was remaking his will near the end.'

'Hester, I need you to know I don't want his money. I'm going out of my mind over this.' There was a tear on his cheek.

I nodded. Took a few deep breaths.

'Grace is going back to school tomorrow. I suggest you suddenly become so ill you have to leave before the end of term. And block her on all your social media.'

'Oh God. Yes, you're right.' He paused, swilled the beer around in his glass. 'What are you going to tell her?'

We were interrupted by cheering. The local team had won the darts match. I used the time to make a decision then sat up straight. When the cheering died down, I said, 'I'm going to talk to Grace. I don't know who to believe right now. If you've lied to me, your career is over, I'll have to report you to the Education Board. If you're telling the truth–'

'I am telling the truth, but what if she doesn't admit it?'

'I'll appeal to her better nature. If she really loves you, she won't want you to suffer.' I'd tried that line with her before, but I didn't tell him that.

'And then?'

I took a sip of my wine. 'Either way, you have to promise

never to see her again. And you'll either be in the clear or looking for another career.'

Gavin grabbed my hands.

'Thank you, Hester. Please do your best.'

We left the pub together and I watched him walk back towards the school, hands in pockets, head bowed.

I needed to go and talk to Mark. I wanted to get all I'd heard clear in my mind, and he was the only person I could think of to talk to.

Later, sitting with Mark in his cosy sitting room, he listened. I hadn't told him much, in the end, but it was enough to hear myself telling him that Gavin Green would be leaving town very soon and seeking work elsewhere, not wanting to make himself known to the family. After I finished, he pulled me in closer and held me. I felt the steady beat of his heart. It was all I needed right there and then. Almost.

'Now the GG mystery is solved, there's no great big elephant in the room we have to avoid,' I said.

Mark chuckled. 'That's a relief.'

'So, if you wanted to, you could kiss me now.' I looked up at him.

His face creased into a smile as his eyes met mine. 'I would like that very much.'

A little later, I sent a text to Jeanette telling her not to expect me home until the morning.

WALTER

I'm consumed by thoughts. Twenty-four hours a day, thought after thought after thought.

And not just any old thoughts: regrets. I'm being tormented by what I didn't do and should have done, or did do and shouldn't have.

Dorothy's looking smug.

Ma's standing in the corner, arms folded across her chest, waiting.

It would be nice to get some help here, frankly.

Everyone's out such a lot of the time now, leaving me too much time to think. Today I drifted around the house, looking in all the rooms just to distract myself from myself. Fact is, I'm bored. I never was very good at being on my own. Comes from starting off in a big family probably. Lots of noise and movement all the time.

I was in the bedroom I shared with Jeanette until I got too ill to get upstairs, looking at our bed, her make-up on the dressing table. There were strands of her hair caught in her hairbrush and my heart – or what would have been my heart – constricted. I loved her hair, it's thick and lustrous. When we first met, I would lift handfuls of it and bury my face in it, breathe in the scent, feel the weight of it. She'd laugh and say it was only hair but to me it was magnificent, a miracle of nature. She kept it long our entire married life, even though I knew she wanted to cut it into one of those trendy short styles. My Jeanette.

I've realised there is something I have to do or learn before I can leave. And since I still want to cry just looking at Jeanette's hair and I keep thinking about them all, it must be about family. I mean, I'm not stuck at work, am I?

It's clear Dorothy thinks I fucked up with Sebastian and Anna and perhaps I could have been more patient. But I'm not going to accept all responsibility for their behaviour and how they've turned out. Though I do wish it could have been different. Sebastian is the only son I knew, and it would have been nice to do more with him. I tried taking him out sailing, but he wasn't interested, and it would have been too embarrassing taking him to the golf club, given his attitude. Perhaps I should have persisted. And Anna? I don't know. I've never really known how to get close to her. Her not eating scared me. I watched her disappearing and nothing I did made any difference. Or nothing I knew how to do. She starved her way away from me and never came back.

If Louise had carried on living with us, I would have been different with her. She was less complicated. She liked me. It made it easier to like her back. And it does take two to make a relationship.

Yes, Dorothy, I can feel your gaze. I know I'm using your words; you used to berate me for not trying harder with you and the kids but back then I was building a company.

That sounds like a poor excuse to me now. I was the parent. It was up to me. I know. I KNOW! Okay? I wasn't creative enough or focused enough to come up with a way to be a parent and a businessman. Mea culpa.

But I did okay with Ellen and Grace. I'd made it by then, the business was doing well, and I *wanted* to come home to them at the end of a day in the office. Jeanette, the girls and I would have dinner together, go for a walk in the long summer evenings, watch TV, talk.

I miss talking. I miss sitting with my family, even when we weren't doing much. Being a part of something strong and good, knowing I was loved. And I loved them, oh yes, I loved them.

Is that why I'm still here? Do I have to learn to love Sebastian and Anna in the way I loved the others?

Dorothy's nodding her head like one of those ugly dogs people used to have in the back of their cars, so I must be on the right track.

SEVENTEEN

Anna came back to talk to Jeanette. They were in the study for a long time and came out smiling. They even kissed each other on the cheek when Anna left.

'What do you make of Anna's story?' Jeanette asked me over lunch. 'She said she'd told you.'

'Yes, she did. I can't really comment, though, not knowing the family as well as you do. I suppose it's common for a brother to stick up for his sister, but to let all the anger fester for as long as it has – it's sad.'

'That's what I thought. I'm not sure I believe Sebastian was ever anything but angry, but Anna assured me he was a quiet, shy boy until Dorothy died. I really don't know what to think.'

I got up to put our plates in the dishwasher.

'I promised Anna I'd see him, so I've invited him for dinner. I felt I should, just to check out her story if nothing else. I know the girls will be cross with me and will probably go out, but you'll be here, won't you?' She smiled, eyebrows raised. 'Pretty please?'

'Okay. If only because I'm as curious as you are to hear what he has to say.'

When Grace got home from school, she found me in the laundry folding washing.

'He's gone. But I expect you knew, didn't you?' There was an accusatory note in her voice and when I turned to look at her, she had her hands on her hips.

'Grace, we need to talk. Let's go for a walk.'

'Now I'm worried.' A frown line appeared between her eyebrows.

We set off through the garden and into the fields beyond. Milly ran circles around us, barking occasionally at birds, trees, the wind.

My heart was racing as I tried to find the right words to start.

'So?' said Grace.

I stopped, took her hand, looked into her eyes. She swallowed hard.

'You're frightening me, Hester.'

'What was the nature of your relationship with Gavin, Grace? Did you sleep with him?'

She narrowed her eyes at me but said nothing.

'You told me you were having an affair.'

'Of course we were. What did he say? Did he deny it?'

I sucked in some air.

'He said you were very keen on him, and he explained that nothing could happen between you and asked you to back off.'

Grace's eyes almost popped out of her head.

'Spineless shit.'

'Spineless shit because he wouldn't risk his career for you, or because he did and he's lying now?'

Grace walked off a little way. I waited, holding my breath. Milly chased off a pheasant that was pecking for grubs.

'You believe him over me? I thought we were friends.'

'I don't know who or what to believe. All I know is that you're both upset.'

We stood for a long time in silence, Grace scanning the horizon, fists clenched.

And then I saw her shoulders sag and her head drop.

'He was so kind. He was the only one who cared when Daddy was diagnosed. I told him I loved him, and he told me he liked me but we couldn't be together. I tried to make him change his mind. I love him, I really do.'

I let out a deep breath. I was relieved for him. I was also sad for her, and rather concerned that a teenage crush had got so out of hand. But maybe that was part of her grief; a need to have someone who was interested in her who wasn't going to die any time soon.

'He's blocking my calls and has unfriended me on all his apps.'

'I'm sorry.'

'Mrs Lacey announced that he's ill and has already left the school, but I don't believe a word of it.' She dropped to her knees and started wailing.

I turned away, tired of her histrionics. I was exhausted by the whole situation, but I knew it was my own fault for agreeing to get involved. I made a promise to myself to keep better boundaries in future – to say no sometimes.

'I'm sorry you're upset but as you pointed out before, I can't make everything right. Gavin's done what he felt he had to do.'

Grace sucked in a deep breath and I thought she was going to yell at me, but she exhaled slowly and rocked back onto her bum, head on her knees.

'I've made such a fool of myself.'

'It's not so bad. It's not as if anyone else knew about it. I'm sure Gavin won't tell anyone, and I certainly won't.'

She looked up then, and held a hand out to me. I helped her up.

'I'll never see him again, will I?'

'No. I don't think you will.'

'What am I going to do?' she asked, but she was talking more to herself than to me.

'Just keep breathing in and out. You won't feel this way forever.'

We turned for home, calling Milly to come with us. She trotted out of the next field, panting, tongue lolling out of her mouth.

Grace slid her arm through mine and leant on me.

I held her close and we walked home in silence.

Ellen and Grace did pass up the offer of dinner with Sebastian and went out for pizza, but not before Grace had spent so long in the bathroom that Jeanette wondered if she was single-handedly trying to empty the local reservoir.

I reckoned she was washing off every memory of Gavin and it would take a lot more than a reservoir full of water. I felt like doing the same, only I'd be washing off the lies.

'You know what teenagers are like,' I said. 'And there was all sorts of mud and dirt when we took Milly out.'

'It's called the countryside.' Jeanette laughed.

I nodded. 'I suppose it is,' I said. 'Should be used to it by now.'

Anna and Sebastian arrived together. She presented Jeanette with flowers and gave her a kiss on the cheek. Sebastian just marched into the house and went straight to the drinks cabinet.

'So, what is this? Some sort of royal command

performance?' he asked as he poured himself a Scotch and sat down without offering anything to the rest of us.

'Nothing like that,' said Jeanette. 'I just thought we should have a chat about the future.' Her hand shook slightly as she poured wine for the rest of us.

He turned to me. 'Still here then?' His upper lip curled in a sneer.

'It would appear so,' I said. The idea of him ever having been shy and quiet was unbelievable. There was no reason for him to be so rude, yet he seemed to revel in it.

'I've booked myself some sailing lessons,' said Anna.

'That's marvellous,' said Jeanette. 'When do you start?'

'That's marvellous, when do you start?' mimicked Sebastian. 'Since when did you two become so chummy?'

'Don't be such an ass, Sebastian,' said Anna. 'You really are too much sometimes.'

Jeanette took a large swig of her drink and said nothing.

'When *do* you start?' I asked.

'The weekend after next,' said Anna. 'I'm a bit scared, to be honest. I'm not a great swimmer but they assured me I'd be wearing a life jacket the whole time and have my own instructor, so I should be safe. Who knows, this time next year I may be sailing *Sirius* to France!'

'Oh, how *marvellous*,' said Sebastian, his voice thick with sarcasm.

Anna, Jeanette and I exchanged looks. Sebastian poured himself another drink. We were all silent for a few moments.

'Let's eat,' said Jeanette at last, inviting us into the dining room.

'What's this charade in aid of?' asked Sebastian as we tucked into a delicious fish pie.

Jeanette was about to respond when Anna cut in.

'I thought we should all try to get along since we're still family, even if Father's not here anymore.'

'We're no more family than pigs and dogs are. We've got nothing in common except for the fact we've all lived in this house with that miserable old bastard.'

'Sebastian, please,' said Anna. 'Can't you let go of all this anger?'

He swung round to face her, eyes glinting. Anna shrank away from his gaze. Jeanette and I both leant forward, ready to protect her.

'I'm sorry, Seb,' she said in a conciliatory voice, stroking the tablecloth beside her plate as if to smooth over her words.

'Don't be sorry,' said Jeanette. She turned to Sebastian. 'It's you who should be apologising. Ever since you got here you've been rude and arrogant. Anna wanted us to get together because she's worried about you. She wants us to believe you used to be different before your mother died. I was prepared to give you the benefit of the doubt, for her sake. But I've had enough.' She looked at Anna. 'I'm sorry, but I can't take any more of him. He's had his chance.'

'And I've had enough of this intervention. I'm sorry if you don't like me but this is how I am, and I won't change.' Sebastian stood up and threw down his napkin. 'And yes, I'm angry. My father wasn't a saint, and neither am I, but what you see is what you get with me, at least I'm honest.'

Anna stared at him, wide-eyed.

'Oh, yes, and this mystery GG in the will? Who else would it be but a mistress or a child?'

'I think you should go now, Sebastian,' said Jeanette quietly.

'Don't you want to know the truth? Well, believe what you want but you'll see I'm right. Oh, and while we're at it, I'm selling my shares in the company. I'm not staying to see you run it into the ground. And I suggest you do the same, Anna. Protect your interests while you can.'

Jeanette leapt to her feet. 'Good! It'll be so much easier to manage the business without you there, sabotaging things at every turn and fiddling your expenses. You can empty your desk in the morning and be gone by ten.'

Sebastian looked to Anna for support. She remained seated and said in a calm voice, 'I'll be keeping my shares, Seb. I trust Jeanette to do the right thing. She was married to Father for long enough to learn a thing or two from him and she's got a clear head on her shoulders.'

I felt like cheering. Anna looked alarmed and covered her mouth as if she couldn't believe what had come out of it. Sebastian was standing, jaw clenching and unclenching, not saying a word. I think he'd been bluffing, and he'd been called out on it.

Jeanette looked magnificent. Her cheeks were pink, but she was standing tall, not giving an inch.

'Right,' said Sebastian at last. He took a last long drink of his Scotch, turned on his heel and walked out. In that moment, I realised he was completely stuck in a role of his own making, and I almost felt sorry for him.

After a few minutes of shocked silence, I said, 'Shall we adjourn to the lounge?' There seemed little point in staying at the table since none of us had taken a bite since Sebastian's departure.

Jeanette sank into the sofa, eyes closed.

Anna's bottom lip was quivering. 'I miss my father,' she said. 'But I meant what I said. You'll do what's right, Jeanette.'

I went back into the dining room to clear the table and start the dishes. There was so much I wanted to say about Sebastian and his behaviour, but it wasn't my place. Better to remove myself.

I heard Anna leave about twenty minutes later. Jeanette came into the kitchen.

'What an evening,' she said.

I nodded. 'Are you okay?'

She shrugged.

'You don't seem upset by what Sebastian said – about the mystery GG?'

'There is no mystery. Late last year, Walter told me he'd been contacted by a young man who said he was his son. Walter wanted nothing to do with him, but I said the least he could do was hear the man out.'

'That was understanding of you.'

'I know my husband wasn't a saint, Hester, but I also knew he was honourable. Is that a contradiction? Anyway, he met this GG. I still don't know his real name. A DNA test proved he was who he said he was, but Walter said GG wanted nothing from him, just to meet him and ask if he had any inheritable illnesses, that sort of thing.'

'Wow. I suppose it makes sense to want to know if there's a ticking time bomb in your future.'

'Yes. Anyway, that was it as far as they were both concerned. It was me who suggested he leave him something, for all the years he hadn't been there for him.'

I was stunned. 'You're fantastic, you know that, don't you? First that, and then standing up to Sebastian the way you did. I'm sure he wasn't expecting to leave here tonight without a job.'

She smiled. 'You reckon he didn't mean it about selling his shares?'

'I'd bet my last penny he made it up on the spot. He was just trying to put the frighteners on you. He still thinks the company will sink without him.'

'I won't let it go down. I've already started talking to a head-hunter about the kind of person I want to manage it.'

'Good on you,' I said. 'Although after tonight's performance, I'm wondering why you don't do a business course and run it yourself. You've certainly got the head for it.'

'You think?' She laughed.

'Absolutely. You're a strong, intelligent woman. And you've got guts and passion. You can do whatever you put your mind to.'

She looked thoughtful for a moment. 'You know I might just have a think about it. Thanks.'

'And what about Anna?'

'Oh, she was upset. She's been so ambivalent about Walter, but I think she's just realising she loved him in spite of everything. And she honestly wanted us all to get along. I've told her I won't see her brother again if I can help it, but I'd like to keep in contact with her. We'll probably see each other once in a while.'

'You're very forgiving.'

'She's harmless, unlike her sibling. Plus, we have a long history, even if most of it has been rather negative. I feel sorry for her, I suppose. She's a bit lost. I hope she enjoys the sailing. It might give her a bit of confidence.'

'You have a very big heart.'

'A big breaking heart, right now. I just want some quiet time to grieve for Walter without all these other things getting in the way.'

'So take it. You don't have to do anything else in the immediate future, but at least now you have some ideas of what life might hold for you without him. And I have no doubt you will find your way. You all will.'

As I lay in bed that night, my last in the Baxter house, I thought about the women who lived there, whose lives I'd shared for the last few weeks and would continue to be a part of, as a friend. Jeanette I now had little doubt would end up running the company. Ellen who would go back to university and throw herself into her studies with renewed vigour. And Grace, she'd get into university – maybe even Oxford – and there'd be no looking back.

And I thought about Justin. My beloved son. He'd sent me the draft of an email he was thinking of sending to his half-brother and sister. It was a brief introduction, telling them how his mother had known their father when they were young, and sending condolences for their loss. I hoped it might be the beginning of a relationship between them all. And maybe one day, he and Georgia would give me some grandchildren to dote on.

In my immediate future, I'd be spending all the time I could with Peggy, making sure her last days were as happy and as comfortable as I could make them. And in the evenings, there would be Mark.

I took out my journal and began to write.

WALTER

Oh, my darling. I have never seen you in full flight before. You were, as Hester Rose said, magnificent. Now I know why I haven't been worried about the business. With you at the helm, it can only go from strength to strength.

Anna was brave too, standing up to him. I think she finally came to see he was never the brother she wanted him to be, and maybe never will be. I felt compassion for her and love. But also pride. She is facing her fears and maybe this will be the beginning of her finding a richer, more fulfilling life.

Dorothy faded out completely when Sebastian left, and I haven't seen her since. Maybe she finally realised he's a lost cause. Although, surprisingly, I found myself feeling sorry for him. He can't help himself but nor will he allow others to help him. I was like that when I was younger. Brash, arrogant, believing the world was against me. I see it now. It was you, Jeanette, who helped me see another way to be. I hope he discovers it too, but, sadly, it seems he isn't ready yet.

I feel myself drifting now, no longer anchored to the house, or to you. It's time for me to go, I can feel it. Ma is with me, gently guiding me. She has a smile on her face and she has stopped her ceaseless fretting.

So with a heavy heart, I say goodbye, my love, and offer my deepest, humblest gratitude to you and the girls for making the last twenty-four years of my life the best any man could hope for. The best any man could have.

ALSO BY SARAH BOURNE

Ella's War

Exile

InVisible

The Train

When Lives Collide

ACKNOWLEDGEMENTS

I've had a thing about death and dying for a long time. In my twenties, I volunteered as a bereavement counsellor with CRUSE, and recently I've volunteered as a biography writer for people with life limiting illness. While the people in this book are not based on any of them in particular, I thank everyone I've worked with for the privilege of hearing their stories, and for allowing me into their lives at the most painful of times.

I had invaluable feedback from my Writers Group. Thank you. Your thoughtful comments made the work stronger.

Thanks also to everyone at Bloodhound Books who believed in this book and worked so hard to get it into your hands.

Neil has, as always, been my sounding board, cheer squad and all-round rock. Thank you.

A NOTE FROM THE PUBLISHER

Thank you for reading this book. If you enjoyed it please do consider leaving a review on Amazon to help others find it too.

We hate typos. All of our books have been rigorously edited and proofread, but sometimes mistakes do slip through. If you have spotted a typo, please do let us know and we can get it amended within hours.

info@bloodhoundbooks.com

Printed in Great Britain
by Amazon